The Snow

The Show

T.M. Parris

A Clarke and Fairchild Thriller

The Clarke and Fairchild series of novels

is written in British English

Prologue

STRICTLY CONFIDENTIAL
Transcript 1539
Subjects: Target Yellow (referred to as Malik) and UNKNOWN (referred to as Carlos)
Date recorded: 4/15
Time recorded: 0352 EST
Language: English
Date transcribed: 4/16

CALL OPENED 0348
Yellow: Are you there? [Rustling] Is there someone there?
UNKNOWN: Who is this?
Yellow: Carlos, is that you?
UNKNOWN: It's...how did you get this number?
Yellow: It's Malik here, Malik. [Pause] Malik, you know! We've been messaging.
UNKNOWN: Yes! Yes, of course! It's just that I'm—
Yellow: Did I wake you? What time is it there? [Pause] Where are you?
UNKNOWN: Uh...[Indistinct] Never mind, it's okay. But where did you get this number?
Yellow: Listen, you've got to help me.
UNKNOWN: Help you?
Yellow: Help me! Yes, help me! I'm in such shit, man! You've got to believe me. I said to you, didn't I? I've got to get it back, Carlos. I need the money. All of it, man!
UNKNOWN: Listen—

Yellow:Don't tell me about the exchange, okay? The launch, another delay, just don't. I've run out of time, Carlos. I have so run out of time.

UNKNOWN: Look, it won't be long now. It's all falling into place.

Yellow:Did you hear what I said? I am OUT of TIME! I've been covering for this, moving things around, but he's onto me now, he's onto me, and I've got to produce! I've got to show him the cash, now! Never mind the profit, I can talk him away from that, but the investment, Carlos, what I put in, I need it back or I can't even think about—

UNKNOWN: It's not as simple as that. I told you, didn't I? It gets locked in. But don't worry. You bought the coin. You can see it there, can't you? You can see what it's worth in your account. It's there, isn't it?

Yellow:What good is that? Just numbers on a screen! I need dollars, something we can use! I can't cover for it, not any more. It's too much, way too much.

UNKNOWN: You can use it. There's a site, like I said. You can—

Yellow:Don't bullshit me. You know you can't buy shit on there. Just don't feed me that any more. I've heard enough. Dollars, you hear me? Dollars. Oh, shit.

UNKNOWN: It's coming, my friend. Believe me.

Yellow:Friend? You're calling me friend? Do you know what will happen if I don't return this money? Today, man? Tomorrow? Don't you get it?

UNKNOWN: Just calm down, okay? We're almost there. A little more time, and—

Yellow:He will kill me. He'll kill me! You heard that? [Pause] Carlos, are you still there?

UNKNOWN: Yes, I'm still here. Listen, you just need to tell him it'll be—

Yellow: You have no idea who this is, do you? You think I can go to him and feed him a line? The same story you people fed me? Oh, you had me with all that bullshit about getting in at the start and the world's biggest crypto. But this guy? He's – I'm telling you, I'm telling you like it is, if I can't get this straight I'm a dead man. [Pause] I'm a dead man.

UNKNOWN: It's not a lie, Malik. This coin is way better than dollars. You've seen the values. It's the biggest crypto out there, far bigger than—

Yellow: That's what *she* said! Carlos, man, I heard all that from her! So where is she? Where is she, now? Is she there? Is she there with you? [Pause] I want to speak to her.

UNKNOWN: Malik—

Yellow: Is she there? Put her on! I want to hear her voice! I want to hear her say it! Go on!

UNKNOWN: She's not here. She's not here, okay?

Yellow: So where is she?

UNKNOWN: That doesn't matter. Malik, I promise you, I've been in touch with them all, and it's happening. The launch is happening. The new exchange, it's there, it's already built. I'm telling you it's ready, just like she said. I've seen it. It's there.

Yellow: What do you mean, there? I can withdraw my funds? I can pull the money?

UNKNOWN: Yes! Yes, you can. You can do that, if that's really what you want.

Yellow: What, now?

UNKNOWN: Soon. Real soon. In a few weeks.

Yellow: A few weeks? Are you listening? Are you listening to what I'm saying? Carlos, my friend, my friend. A few weeks? Oh, fuck. Oh, fuck. Oh, my sweet ass.

UNKNOWN: Malik, just give him the bottom line. Tell him what he'll get as soon as the exchange opens. The values are

sky-high already, just like she said. You'll get everything back and way more, many times that. Just tell him to wait. Just wait. [Pause] Malik? Malik?
CALL ENDS 0352

Chapter 1

"Beaten to death," said Walter. "Left by the side of the road. Pushed out of a car, probably. The Tunisian investigation was cursory. Of course we all know who did it and why. Ah! Here we are."

The waiter was bringing beef wellington for him, fish pie for her. The crockery was thick and off-white, the cutlery heavy, the napkins linen, and the furniture in this obscure little eatery he'd brought her to was a dark polished wood. The food smelled good. It was clear what her boss wanted her to ask. Rose took the fish pie but not the bait.

"I don't see what it's got to do with me. Is there a Balkan connection? Sounds more like a North African thing. You're not thinking of pulling me out, Walter? I've only just got started."

It was a year ago that Walter got Rose tangled up in a chase that concluded in Hungary, and six months ago that a reorganisation freed up a post for her in Budapest with oversight of the Balkans, her Croatian experience helping her there also. Finally she was back on a coherent MI6 career path, so it felt, which was why she experienced some trepidation at Walter's sudden summons to London.

Walter ignored her question. "It was crypto, you see. Only it wasn't. Have you heard of it, this New World Coin?"

Rose shrugged, dredging a piece of salmon through creamy white sauce. "Heard something about it. It's not really my game, all this online stuff. The techies must be the people to go to."

"Oh, they are, they are." Walter was making light work of his tender-looking beef. This was exactly the kind of place she'd expect to find Walter late on a Friday evening in Soho.

From the outside it looked like a tired old wine bar, where you could get a warm sherry and some peace and quiet. Walter, of course, knew that the menu was limited but excellent, and the place catered to account executives treating their clients and elderly customers who didn't have to look at the bill before offering their credit card. The sounds of London's West End in the evening barely penetrated its sedate interior. "But the world is changing, Rose. And we must change with it."

She sighed. "I had the feeling we might."

Walter dabbed his lips with his enormous napkin, a typically dainty mannerism. No one looking at this mild-looking man with his threadbare sleeves and outdated cravat would suspect he was one of the most powerful officers – if not the most powerful – within one of the world's leading secret intelligence services. He looked like an uncle treating his niece to a post-theatre treat.

"If you want to steal," he said, "where do you go?" He eyed Rose as he ate.

"What am I stealing?" she asked.

"Money."

"Money?" She paused. "I'd say a bank, but I fear it's a trick question."

"A bank? When did you last go into a bank?"

Rose couldn't remember.

"When you buy something, how do you do it?"

"With a card. Or a payment app, maybe. Or I make a direct payment."

"And where do you go to make this direct payment, or set up your app, or check your balance?"

"Online, one way or another."

"Right. Bank branches these days act as customer service centres and are useful for those businesses that are still cash-based. But most transactions are essentially online."

"Okay. Whatever this is, it still sounds like one for the techies. FININT, not HUMINT. In MI6 we gather intelligence directly from human beings, Walter. From interacting with them, not from accessing their devices. Human, see?"

As ever, he ignored her impatience. "Well, yes and no." He drank a little red. She was on the white. A bottle each: it was going to be a long evening. He carried on.

"Hacking's not easy. A lot of effort is needed to bypass all the encryption, the vulnerability testing, two-factor authentication and so on. The best way these days to get hold of someone's money isn't to steal it at all. It's to persuade them to give it to you."

"Well, then it's not theft."

"Fraud, my dear. Scams. Cons. Some small, some big. This is where the criminal mind is focused now. Instead of battling some complicated algorithm, simply persuade the subject to pay it straight into your account. That was what New World Coin was. That was how this Malik fellow ended up in a ditch in Tunisia."

"He scammed someone?"

"No. He was scammed himself. To the tune of around two million dollars. We picked up some phone taps between him and various characters who were marketing the coin. Sadly, it wasn't his money. He was looking after the interests of Youssef Al-Hashemi, a Tunisian with an interest in feeding Europe's cocaine habit via West Africa and the Mediterranean. A significant portion of the profits thereof have found their way to extremist Islamic groups. Malik decided to be enterprising and take the initiative, drawn in by some extravagant investment promises. They didn't come off, and unsurprisingly Al-Hashemi was unimpressed."

"It doesn't sound like a tragedy. If these fraudsters have diverted millions of bucks away from the hands of terrorists, why should MI6 have a problem with it?"

"Well, in a sense they've done us a favour this time. But the point is, fraud of this nature isn't essentially technical. Of course you need an online front for it all. But at its heart it's one person lying to another. Gaining their trust by pretending to be something they're not." Walter's face lit up with mischief. "And that all sounds like it's very much our bag." He took another sip. "Very human indeed."

Chapter 2

"So, how does this work? Am I allowed to call her your girlfriend now?"

Zack didn't waste much time. It was barely three in the afternoon but he was already settled in at a balcony table above a heaving Bourbon Street bar. Fairchild had had to push past the swelling crowds, packed in behind barriers running right through the French Quarter. When he finally squeezed his way through, Zack was sitting back, a daiquiri in his hand and a section of patterned ironwork reflecting across his mirrored shades.

"So you've found us a nice quiet corner, then." Fairchild sat and lifted a beer bottle in greeting. He had to raise his voice to be heard.

"It's New Orleans. Get into the spirit, Fairchild!"

"And we're here because…?"

"Had to get out of Miami. Side-step the fallout from some epic screw-up."

"Anything I should be aware of?"

"Let's just say that an executive director had a bad day on the horses."

"Horses?"

"Please, let's just leave it there for now. Hell, I love this city." Zack raised his glass. And then moved right in with the *girlfriend* question.

"How about we don't discuss her at all?" Even though they'd been seeing each other for a year now, Fairchild was still uncomfortable talking about Rose. And that word was wholly inadequate for so many reasons. But Zack was persistent.

"How about we do? In a roundabout kind of way, she's the reason I wanted to have this little catch-up."

That didn't sound right. As the closest thing to Fairchild's best friend, Zack had been suspicious of Rose since they'd first met. The ice had thawed recently, but this still sounded odd.

Zack met his narrowed eyes with bland innocence. "Something wrong?"

"Why summon me half way across the world to talk about Rose? You don't even like her. Even in a roundabout kind of a way."

"That's not true." Zack gave a mock sniff. "We didn't get off to a great start but we're on the same page now. Yeah, for sure." The American made a play of considering this statement again, seemed pleased with it, and necked his daiquiri.

Fairchild had to follow up. "Are you in touch with her?"

"Me and Rose? Every now and then. For work. Not recently. I know she's in London, though." He was watching for Fairchild's reaction.

"London? She's in Budapest."

"Budapest until yesterday. Today, this evening – well I guess kind of around now, in fact, being taken out to dinner by Walter Tomlinson himself."

Fairchild shrugged. "We don't report in to each other. Do you know how many times we've seen each other over the past year?" He felt a sudden impatience with the laid-back American. "Look, if you're going to play analyst mind games on me, could you at least take those infernal sunglasses off so I can see your face?"

Zack's eyebrows appeared above the frame and stayed there, but then softened. "Sure. No need to get jumpy." He took them off and folded them on the table between them, revealing a pair of quizzical brown eyes. He was probably right: Fairchild didn't respond well to mentions of Walter Tomlinson.

"Walter is her boss, you know," said Zack. "Kind of normal for him to be briefing her on a job. Best done in person, I think. Don't you?"

Fairchild drank some beer. "Does that mean you wanted to see me about a job?"

"That's right!" Zack said it almost as if he'd forgotten.

"Stop playing around, Zack. If you didn't hear about Rose being in London from Rose, you must have heard about it from Walter. You and he are working together on some transatlantic operation and Rose is involved. If you're thinking of trying to involve me in the same thing, you must have forgotten that Walter and I have history, to put it mildly."

"You mean you have a problem with Walter."

"No, I mean we have a problem with each other."

"Not so, Fairchild. We talked. He's got no issue with you, not anymore. The problem is totally at your end."

Fairchild ignored this. "As for Rose and me working together, that isn't going to happen. It's too difficult. She works for an organisation that's done things I can't forgive."

"I thought that was all in the past." Zack knew every detail of Fairchild's decades-long quest to find out what happened to his parents, which, while successful, or at least concluded, didn't exactly leave Fairchild jumping for joy. He'd decided not to pursue it any further – he had plenty else to live for, now – but MI6 still felt like a dirty word, and maybe it always would.

"That doesn't make us all one big happy family. I'm a freelancer. I work for whoever I choose. Quite often that's you."

"Sure, and I'm working up to asking you to do some more."

"But it involves Rose? And Walter? I don't think so."

Zack looked nonchalant. "I haven't even told you what it is yet."

"No need. The answer's no. You've got plenty of resources to draw on, whichever part of the US intelligence community you're working for now. The subject is closed. Anything else you wanted to talk about?"

"Nope. That was pretty much it."

Zack sucked his straw. A faint sound of music reached them, squeaky trumpets, squealing clarinets, on top of amplified voices and cheers. The balcony drinkers moved over to line up along the railing. Fairchild stood and turned to look down. The street was packed both ways.

Zack appeared next to him, drink in hand. "Parade's coming."

"What parade is this?"

"For the festival."

"What festival?"

"Music. Food. Costumes. Drinking. This is New Orleans. There's always a festival."

A mass of colour and sound filled the end of the street. Dancers strutted in bright yellow suits and trilbies, twirling parasols and blowing whistles. A marching band followed, sunlight glinting on brass tubes, the music matching its brightness. The crowds whooped and jived. The parade filled out behind the band.

"Pretty big event." Zack was nodding along, having to shout now. "I don't think we'll be going anywhere for a while." He turned to Fairchild and grinned.

The timing of their meet was no accident. Fairchild could have left if he'd really wanted to, fought his way out. But it had to be something big for Zack to go to all this trouble. Hell, he'd even taken his shades off. Fairchild hated being played, but it had worked: he was intrigued.

"All right," he shouted. "Just to pass the time, then. What's the job?"

Chapter 3

"Well, you know about crypto currencies, of course," said Walter. "By now there are dozens of them, and a similar number of exchanges where you can buy and sell. Most of them are legitimate, in the sense that they're genuine currencies set up on something called a blockchain."

This rang a bell with Rose: her brother worked in this area. "James raves about that. Says it guarantees that the currency can't be duplicated or messed around with. But people still get hacked."

"Hacked, yes. Their money can be diverted while it's sitting on an exchange, for example. New World Coin was far more fundamental than that. It was aggressively promoted as the next Bitcoin, poised to become the biggest coin with some impressive growth rates. But there was never anything behind it. There was no blockchain."

"No blockchain?"

"None. Just a database that recorded coin purchases so that people could view their so-called holdings online next to some spurious value. In reality they were worth nothing. They also set up a retail site so they could claim that the coin was tradable. But it was full of overpriced New World branded merchandise and other products no one in their right minds would buy. It was all a front."

"Why weren't they called out right from the start?" Rose had to make the effort to concentrate. She was regretting the wine, now almost finished. A dish of Eton Mess, creamy meringue, sat in front of her, too tempting to pass up. Walter was making neat inroads into a Crème Brûlée, its flat caramel layer toasted to perfection.

"It always had its critics," he said, "but New World faced them down. Called them haters, accused them of wanting to defend the establishment and protect their own interests. It developed some of the attributes of a cult. I believe someone even wrote a song about it, and they had some kind of hand signal they'd use when they met, and online in the videos, of course."

"All that for crypto currency?" Rose inserted her spoon into the pudding.

"They made it about far more than that. They described it as a family that people could join. It was going to revolutionise finance. It would give the whole world access to wealth. And they had a point. For the millions in, say, Africa, who don't have bank accounts, getting hold of a currency you could operate simply with a mobile phone was a big step forward. No government regulation, no paperwork needed, anyone could buy. And anyone did. As well as the huge interest across Europe and America, millions of ordinary Africans put money into it as well."

Rose frowned. "How did these people hear about it, if they weren't online?"

"MLM."

Rose gave him a blank look.

"Multi-level marketing, my dear. People with networks. They get to hear about some fantastic product, or quite often they'll be contacted about it, and if it's something they like and can rave about they'll persuade their network to buy in, earning commission in the process. Then those people will do the same thing to their networks the next level down, and so on. In the meantime whoever's at the top creams something off for every transaction further down the line. Everyone is incentivised to go out and find more investors. There's no doubt that some people have got very rich from

New World Coin, but it's not from the coin itself. It's commission from people buying into it further down the pyramid."

Rose took a bit of meringue, soft and sweet, crumbly and light as air all at once. "How," she said when she could speak again, "does someone without a bank account buy the coin in the first place?"

"Cash. They had shops. New World Coin offices in cities and towns. Many sellers gave up their jobs to sell the coin instead. There are stories of farmers taking out loans or even selling land or their homes to buy New World Coin."

"That's mad."

"It was mad. But they were convinced they had to get in at the ground floor, buy early to see their investment soar. And the people doing the persuading were also convinced. Almost all the sellers, even those right at the top, had invested in the coin themselves. Even when the criticism got louder, they had a vested interest in keeping it going. The launch is coming, they kept being told. Just wait. Have faith. It's all coming. So that's what they told everybody else."

Rose focused on whipped cream drizzled with fresh strawberry coulis, knowing Walter would carry on of his own accord. After crunching some more caramel, he did.

"And right at the heart of all this was this woman. Ulia Popovic. Heard of her?"

Rose shook her head.

"Serbian by birth," he continued. "She has a degree in economics and an MBA, and travelled the world promoting this coin. Gave these motivational talks. Loved an audience. And they loved her. She knew all the jargon. It was her coin, her idea, her design, at least that was how it was sold. She was the centrepiece, the queen bee. She got invited to entirely legitimate events as a panel expert on economics and entrepreneurship. She really talked the talk."

"And where is she now?"

"Well, that's the thing, my dear. Everything started to unravel in the end. Investigations were launched. Offices raided. Employees became informants. A key colleague of Popovic was detained in the USA. But the lady herself simply disappeared. There have been a few sightings, the odd rumour. Stuttgart, Bangkok, Istanbul. But basically, nobody knows where she is."

"I don't blame her. But they'll find her, won't they?"

"Not necessarily. She's got millions of other people's money squirrelled away. Possibly billions. That's plenty to stay hidden for as long as you need to."

"It was that big?"

"No one knows for sure. Enough to prompt fraud investigations in numerous countries as well as the USA. It's not the law she should be most afraid of, though. Some of that money belonged to some pretty unsavoury characters. Youssef Al-Hashemi was just one of them. Now the whole thing's in the process of being exposed as a scam, they're going to want their money back. For the sake of saving face as much as anything else. And if they can't get it back, they'll want some other form of satisfaction instead."

"No wonder she's gone missing, then. She's unlikely to reappear any time soon if she's got any sense."

"That's right. And, indeed, that's really the whole point."

She waited for Walter to elaborate on this cryptic comment, but instead he looked around for the waiter, as if there were no more to say.

"Walter, I suppose at some point soon I'm going to find out what all of this has to do with me?"

"Oh, absolutely! Coffee?" Walter signalled to the waiter.

Rose sighed and drained her wine. "I think I'd better."

Chapter 4

"A crypto scam? This isn't your usual game, Zack. Aren't the FBI dealing with it?"

Fairchild's mouth was inches from Zack's ear. He was competing against a street full of drums. The balcony had filled up on either side of them, and all of the other balconies were a mass of flags and flowers and waving arms as far as you could see. Everyone had a drink in their hand, and pretty much everyone was grinning, shouting or grooving to the music.

Zack was watching the parade-side party in the street below. "I'm getting old, Fairchild. I should be down there in the middle of all that."

"Be my guest."

"We aren't finished here."

"Aren't we? I don't see how this merits such a fuss. Or a pan-Atlantic working party. It's law enforcement, not national security."

It was Zack's turn to shout into Fairchild's ear. "Youssef Al-Hashemi. You know who that is." It was a statement, not a question. They had discussed the man before. "We've had an eye on him for months. Got a nice little case building up. We can link his business to the funding of Islamic extremist training and recruitment across North Africa. All we need is to extradite him. Trouble is, he doesn't like to leave home. Normally he doesn't set foot outside his own compound. Ever. We want to encourage him to take a trip some place where the authorities will be amenable to an extradition process."

"Extradition? Process? Why not just send a drone? Blow up his house like you normally do?"

"Fairchild, you know very well we only resort to tactics like that if we have no other option."

Fairchild was unabashed by Zack's disapproving tone: they were both grownups when it came to US security tactics overseas.

Zack continued. "Right now, we do have an option. Al-Hashemi is pretty ticked off that a big chunk of his reserves disappeared into a black hole. His chief accountant has just been scraped off the ground on the side of a highway outside of Tunis. But that didn't get the guy his money back. He's been heard to say that he'd like to meet Popovic in person. Either to persuade her that it's in her interests to return his money, or else to strangle the woman with his bare hands. We know he's capable. And he's motivated. Got a pretty conservative view of how women should behave, which I guess makes him even more fixated on the leading lady."

"Then this leading lady would be well advised to stay hidden."

"Oh, sure. That's exactly what we're counting on." Zack sucked on his daiquiri, his third or fourth, judging from the empties. He was nowhere near drunk. Fairchild knew no one who could hold his drink like Zack, himself included.

"That makes no sense," he said. "If you don't know where she is and you know she's not going to appear, why are you telling me all this?"

"Imagine," said Zack, staring out into the distance as if he were seeing it, "imagine we could decide when and where this woman was going to appear. Imagine it was somewhere not too far from Al-Hashemi's hideout, but on friendly territory. Like Italy, say. Southern Italy. Naples area. He could fly out and back in a few hours. Say he'd heard a rumour Popovic was going to be there for some event or other, that she was trying a comeback, seeing if she could stay under the radar with a new identity. A reliable rumour. More than one rumour."

"But she's not going to."

"No." Zack waited for Fairchild to cotton on. It didn't take long.

"You're going to set a trap for him. Fabricate a rumour, persuade him she'll be there, then pick him up as soon as he lands."

"More or less." Zack waited for him to figure out some more.

"He won't do that just on hearsay. He'll send someone else to check if she's there and that it's really her."

"Which is why she needs to be there."

"You're serious? You're going to impersonate the woman? She's all over the internet. Millions of people know exactly what she looks like."

"What she looked like, Fairchild. Before she went into hiding. People take steps to change their appearance, don't they? She just needs to pass for the woman convincingly enough to lure the guy over for a closer look."

"That's all? That's going to take weeks to prep. Maybe even months. You'll need a big team. A solid base, a lot of surveillance. You won't know when or where the guy will show up, if he does at all. Or what he'll try and do to her, if he doesn't kill her straight away. It's a massive undertaking, Zack. There must be easier ways. Why go to so much trouble?"

Zack nodded slowly as if about to say something wise. "We have our reasons."

"Good. Any chance I might know what they are?"

"Absolutely."

The parade was coming to a close and the crowds spilled out across the street. The balcony thinned out as people went downstairs to party. By the time Zack had finished talking, afternoon had become early evening. They'd returned to the table and Zack had finished off daiquiri number six.

"So, what do you think?" he asked.

Fairchild shook his head as if trying to sort everything into place. "It's crazy."

"Crazy bad, or crazy good?" Zack was watching him.

"Both."

"Okay. Question: who do you think we got in mind to do this impersonation? I mean, it would need to be someone who's been under cover."

"Someone who doesn't mind sitting like a lame duck on the Italian coast waiting for an enraged terrorist to show up and try to strangle her."

"She's got to be able to look after herself. Not scared off easily. Can cope with the unexpected."

"Italian speaker."

"Why? No need. She's visiting, remember."

"Serbian speaker, then."

"Not necessarily. Al-Hashemi doesn't speak Serbian, and I doubt his people do either. A few words would help, but that's feasible if we're talking about someone who already has at least one Slavic language."

"Oh, Christ." Fairchild sometimes wondered how he could be so slow. "No way."

"Really?"

"No way will she agree. She's no fool."

"But she's ambitious." Zack was right about that.

"Even so."

"Well, we'll find out soon enough. Walter's going to be asking her about it."

"When?" Should he speak to her? Try and talk her out of it? Or would that have the opposite effect?

Zack looked at his watch. "Oh, I'd say, right about now."

Chapter 5

"It's insane."

"Really, Rose? Think about it. We know what pushes this man's buttons. We'll make it easy for him."

The coffee was long gone, as were most of the other customers. On the table between them now was a plate of thick chocolate mints. Soho must have been pulsating outside, but Rose could hear nothing. She was totally absorbed in Walter's absurd proposal.

"This woman is wanted by the FBI and a load of other law enforcement agencies. Why would she just pop up somewhere and announce herself? Who would believe that?"

"She'd be using an alias. And she will have altered her appearance. She's been missing for over a year, remember? It's all about the rumours. Getting the word out to the right people, or rather, the wrong people."

"Exactly. How many other criminals has she ripped off? All kinds of unsavoury people are going to be beating a path to her door if they hear the rumours too. You don't steal that much without making some serious enemies."

"That's exactly what we want. It's about making a noise while looking as if you're trying to be quiet. And we'd need sufficient security in place."

"You don't say."

"The FBI is already on board. They'll lend as many bodies as required. They will liaise with the Italian authorities to work out a modus operandi."

"If this was happening for real, wouldn't they simply detain the woman as soon as she landed in the country?"

"She'll have a new identity, Rose. They won't know her alias."

"Thin, Walter. Some shady billionaire businesswoman rocking up? She's going to stick out like a sore thumb, isn't she?"

Walter sat back and picked up a mint. "What's the best way of hiding a needle?"

Rose sighed. Another trick question. "A haystack?"

"A stack of needles. What's the best way of hiding a shell? In a rockpool. What's the best way—"

"Okay, okay, I think I get it. You need a stack of shady billionaires."

"Some subtlety is required. In some ways she needs to stick out like a sore thumb to attract people to the party. But she also needs to evade arrest. We could explain that in a number of ways. We could fabricate some tension between the Italians and the Americans. We could claim incompetence. We could imply some deal has been struck. It's all in our hands. This is a big ensemble piece, remember. We'll all be working together. It only has to be sufficiently credible that Al-Hashemi will be convinced for long enough."

"But what about the timing? You can't have her just sitting about for weeks on end. It's got to be quick, or the cracks will start to appear."

"Indeed. Some event is needed in order to narrow the timeline as much as possible. Some kind of show that's only on for one night. Popovic is widely rumoured to be coming in for the show and leaving again straight away. That's his only opportunity if he wants a face-to-face encounter with her."

Rose gave in and helped herself to another mint. "I'm guessing you have something in mind."

"A vague idea, no more. New World Coin were keen on glitzy events which had some global theme and involved a lot of money being thrown about. They staged a beauty pageant one time, a kind of Miss World."

"Classy."

"It was utterly over-the-top. But it fit with their pretensions of being a global movement, not just a financial product. Also, as you can imagine, a lot of effort has gone into analysing the financial affairs of New World Coin and anyone associated with it. In typical money laundering fashion there are shell companies and trusts and layer upon layer of complexity. It's not unreasonable that amongst all of this one would find an entity indirectly linked to Popovic described as a foundation or charitable trust."

"Some charity."

"Precisely. But it's a hook we can hang something on. This show, whatever it is, will be backed by this foundation and is a fundraiser for some worthy good cause. And our lady can't resist making an appearance. That's the premise. Maybe she's testing the water, seeing how far she can get with a new name. It would need to be a high-profile shindig, very top end."

It was insane. But also intriguing. "Do you have a venue in mind?"

"The Amalfi coast is stuffed with top-of-the-range villas and hotels. It's a stop-off for super-yachts as well. Capri is a good option. You can't get more high-end than that. It's got showbiz connotations, there's a heliport, a lot of promising hotel options, and it's tiny. We could saturate the place."

"Doesn't Fairchild have a hotel on Capri?"

"So I believe." Walter spoke lightly – a little too lightly. A warning bell started sounding deep inside Rose's head, one which should have been ringing for some time, or perhaps it was but she wasn't listening. Rose didn't want to discuss Fairchild with Walter. Over the years they'd had plenty of reasons to talk about the man, but not recently. She hadn't shared how her relationship with Fairchild had developed. But Walter was always a step ahead. In fact, he'd pretty much predicted this outcome years earlier. She moved on.

"So, you need someone to play the starring role. I can ask around in Belgrade. They'll probably have a few ideas. Whoever it is will need a lot of prep."

"Indeed. But she doesn't need to be Serbian. In these international environments it'll be English spoken. Some accent is needed, but another Slavic language would be enough to work on."

He looked entirely serious as he watched her process this and figure out what it meant.

"You're joking. Me? I can't do that."

"Why not?"

"Me, pass for a glamorous Serbian entrepreneur?"

"A glamorous Serbian entrepreneur who's been in hiding. Who has probably changed her appearance. Hair colour, eye colour, take your pick. You're the right age. And the right height. The rest we can work on."

"If that's all you need, there are loads of possibles. All our Russian speakers! Seriously, this isn't my gig, Walter. I've just started something new. I'm only just getting my feet under the desk."

"And that's where you want your feet to be, is it?"

"I'd like a career, if that's what you mean. You've got others who can do this."

"Not with your credentials. You can handle yourself if you need to. Of course we'll have surveillance, security, all that. But there's an element of unpredictability to the whole thing."

"Of course there is."

"I mean, more than we'd usually expect."

"How so?"

"Well..." Walter cleared his throat and talked her through some of the deeper subtleties of his proposal, while the day slipped quietly into the next day, and the restaurant staff waited patiently, at a distance. When he'd finished, Rose blinked a few times, trying to digest it all.

"So you see, my dear, you have the skills," concluded Walter. "You've been in the thick of it. And as for prep, Popovic is online in a hundred places."

"Oh, great. So the whole world knows what she looks like."

"Well, the advantage is that we can study her. Her voice, her mannerisms, the way she holds herself. There's time to get you in shape, get every detail right. And a team to work with you."

"In shape? What does that mean?"

Walter may have reddened slightly. "Popovic is a little...bigger than you."

"Bigger?"

"She has somewhat more in the way of flesh. Of course, she might arguably have lost some weight, but even so..."

"You want me to put on weight?" It was the only part of the scheme so far Rose didn't have a problem with.

Walter looked mildly regretful. "I'm sure we can find ways of making it bearable. This whole venture has a substantial budget attached to it."

Rose's mind had started firing with all the practicalities of this most improbable scheme. "You mentioned Capri, the hotel. Is Fairchild likely to be part of this?" Working with Fairchild: how would that be, now?

"Zack will be handling that approach."

"Zack's involved?"

"Very much so. This is a big operation, Rose. In fact, Zack is likely to take the lead, given the enthusiasm for the operation coming from across the pond. And the resources. So Zack will raise the matter with Fairchild."

"When?" Would she have the chance to talk to Fairchild before making a decision? Or even just work out how she felt about his involvement?

Walter looked at his watch. "Oh, I'd say about now."

Chapter 6

In the street below, the father of all stag parties had just collided with the mother of all hen parties. The shouting and screaming was incomprehensible up on the balcony, and possibly in the street itself. It was still only early evening: things would get ugly later. Zack and Fairchild sat, the party noise too upbeat a backdrop for their conversation. Zack had moved them on to a jug of some house cocktail that involved rum, brandy, whisky, grenadine, and probably one or two other things of potency. Fairchild was starting to feel sluggish. Zack was as bright as a button.

"So here's the thing," he was saying. "She may say yes. You need to factor that in. Walter can be pretty persuasive."

Fairchild didn't answer, instead reviewing all the things Rose had agreed to in the past at Walter's suggestion, and probably shouldn't have done. Fairchild was biased, of course: his animosity to Walter went back a long way.

"And if she does—"

"She won't discuss it with me." Fairchild cut Zack off. "She'll make her own decision. She may not even tell me."

"Right. So once she's in, you're out in the cold. She probably won't share anything. She'll be away for months prepping. You may not even be in contact with her."

"Zack, we've met three times over the past year. That's how we do things."

Zack ignored him. "And then she'll be sitting pretty in some place waiting for this guy to show up."

"If you're expressing doubt about the idea, I concur. A dozen things could go wrong. You'll need a hell of a set-up. A base that's like a fortress. I can't see national law enforcement being too happy."

"They're making the right noises so far. It's a big prize, and all they need to do is stand by and let the FBI do the hard work. That discussion was had with a particular location in mind, though." Zack paused, ostensibly to suck on his straw.

"What location?"

"Capri."

"Capri?"

"Right. It's just off Naples—"

"I know where it is."

"Right. It's tiny. Limited number of entry and exit points. You could close it off in a few minutes if you had to. Pretty exclusive clientele as well."

"Have you been there, Zack? It's packed full of tourists."

"Sure, but only during the day. They leave, don't they? We'll come out at night and play, with the billionaires and the showbiz types." His eyes gleamed. "Hell of a place to stage a massive party for high rollers. What would tempt Popovic more than being the centre of attention at some trendy private event for the uber-rich on Capri? It's got such a ring to it."

Fairchild didn't share Zack's enthusiasm. "I have a hotel on Capri."

"Really?" Zack's eyes were as wide as saucers.

"As if you didn't know."

Zack shrugged. "Okay. I knew. But Capri is the perfect place. As you said, we need a base there. We need to be in complete control, eyes and ears everywhere."

"And security."

"Sure. But it's also got to look good. I mean convincing. To pin down the time we need some event, something showy that everyone will want to be seen at. We need to stage that show, Fairchild. We need to control it. We'll need one hell of a venue, and total access to it, top to bottom. But it's got to draw in a genuine crowd. The real deal, the bosses, the oligarchs off their yachts. Those folk have to be completely convinced. So it's got to be the right place. Somewhere that already has a reputation. A draw in itself."

"And you have my place in mind?"

Zack suddenly came over all non-committal. "Is it top of the range? I mean, I've never been."

Fairchild swallowed some of Zack's murderous cocktail. He'd known Zack long enough to see what he was doing, but even so. Fairchild had a controlling stake in a company with hotel interests the length of Italy, but the Capri property was by far the most exclusive. And also the most expensive to run. And also the most profitable.

"The Hotel Villa Bianca Rosaria has a direct view of the main harbour and its own access to a private beach," he said. "It has cut flowers in every room, terraces with stunning views, top-dollar international chefs and award-winning restaurants, a cliffside function room, a multi-layer pool area, immaculately-tended gardens, and the best management on the island. Probably anywhere in Italy. There's no place with better credentials. But do you seriously think I'd play host to an operation in which my—" He stopped. *Girlfriend* was really a terrible word. "...which makes Rose target practice for some of the world's nastiest operators?"

"I guess you're right. It was just a thought." Zack stretched out, staring up at the sky. "Anyway, there are other places. Yours might be the best but plenty of others would do. Thing is, we're already committed. We're doing this, Fairchild, whether you're in or not. Maybe Rose will turn it down, but I doubt it. Not something this big. So if you're out, we'll go ahead in another hotel and hope for the best. And don't think that you can just show up in the middle of things. You know she won't let you. Anything that even smells like you're trying to protect her, you'll get your marching orders. The only way you can be there is if you're already in right from the start. If you're part of the set-up she can't complain. She'll have to go along with it. And it'll be your place, Fairchild. Your venue, your staff, your event if you want. You can put as many cameras and watchers and plain clothes bodyguards around as you like. As long as it still looks like a hotel and not some kind of spooks' convention. And you'll have a role yourself."

Fairchild looked up at the sky as well. Zack was right, of course. The idea of working with Rose made him nervous: that hadn't always gone well before. But they hadn't necessarily been on the same side, and now they were, or at least he thought they were, about some things, anyway. It could go well – or it could go very badly indeed. The idea of alienating her made him sweat. Were they solid enough for something like this?

"Think about it, Fairchild." Zack had been watching him. "You keep complaining you don't see her very often. How about an interlude together in a top class hotel in one of the most shi-shi venues in the world?"

"Zack, it's my hotel. I can go there whenever I like, and take whoever I like."

Zack was undaunted. "Still, work and pleasure never come together as well as this. We'll pay you, of course, for your time, and whatever rates you're charging for the hotel. As I said, money's no object. So how about it? Are you out, or are you in?"

Chapter 7

Erik was running. Erik was fast. But so were the others. He couldn't break away.

It was dark when they'd set off from the crossroads, where the paved road through town crossed the dirt track into the hills. They'd gathered before dawn like they did every morning, fifty or sixty of them, tall and skinny, shifting from foot to foot, cold in their shorts and vests and woolly hats. They didn't have much to say. They were only there to run. And then they started, the leaders taking them up on the soft ground past tall trees in shadow and clusters of round mud huts. Erik breathed hard and his legs burned. The group was close around him, a big panting animal with hundreds of arms and legs. But as the sky lightened and the moon faded, the pace picked up and the runners spread out. Bicycles and carts appeared on the track, and the mass of bobbing heads dived round them and carried on. Local people stopped and watched them pass, swift like the wind, the only sounds the padding of shoes on dirt and the breathing.

When Erik first came here, the thin air had sapped his energy and made his legs heavy. But he stayed and he ran and he trained. And slowly he got faster and could stay nearer to the front, quicker than most of the hundreds of others training here every day. Erik had come here to make his fortune, to run for his family and for Kenya. This was Iten, the town of champions, the place that formed the best of the Kenyan runners, the fastest in the world.

Erik's village was far from here. His mother and sister farmed their land, and when they had surplus they sold it and sent him money. Erik didn't need much. He lived a simple life here in Iten. He shared a bare room with three other runners in a house with a rusty tin roof. They washed with a bucket outside and sat at night by candlelight. They ate beans and rice and vegetables and ugali, the Kenyan runners' secret, some liked to say. Erik didn't need much else but what he wanted was to be spotted by a manager and get a place in a camp. Then if he trained well the manager could pick him to take abroad to enter races where he could win big prize money. Prize money! Maybe a thousand dollars to start with. That would be enough to pay back his mother and sister. If he kept racing well and winning, he could be like the top runners who win the Boston Marathon and the London Marathon and the other big races across the world, and buy a big field for his family as well as a piece of land here in Iten and a house, and he could dress well and drive a nice car, like the champions did. That was what Erik wanted. That was what kept him running.

He moved easily. He used to run barefoot to school every day – but so did everyone else. He was tall and thin and strong, striding out, racing past the green fields that sloped down into the steep valley – but so was everyone else. Some got discouraged and gave up, saying they would never get picked, there were too many good runners and not enough races. But Erik was a believer. His heart told him that he would make it.

He hadn't been home in a long while. He wanted to focus on his training. After this run he would go back to the house and eat. Then he would sit outside and rest for several hours. Rest was important. Only with many hours of rest would you have enough energy to train properly. Going home took a long time. It made him tired, and he couldn't train. But that was only one reason why he didn't go home. Worrying was bad for you and didn't change anything. So Erik tried to put these things out of his mind and focus on his simple life. Everything would work out all right.

Dennis had told him the same thing last time he was here. "My friend! You're so skinny. Are you eating enough ugali here?"

Dennis was not skinny. He was also from Erik's village but he lived in Nairobi now. Dennis liked to make friends and was very well connected in the city. But he didn't forget about his good friend Erik and came to Iten regularly in his white Mercedes-Benz with leather seats. He always had something to show everyone when they came out and gathered round: the newest products, the latest technology. Good prices, too. A lot of people in Iten knew Dennis now. But he still had time for Erik.

It was Dennis who had told him about the New World Coin and what it meant. That even ordinary Kenyans could invest in crypto currency just like anyone in Europe or America. That if you put your money in early you would see big, big gains. That New World was going to be the world's leading cryptocurrency. Everyone would have it, or everyone would want it, and they'd envy the people who'd got it already!

"The world is changing, Erik. Even people like us have opportunities now with this new technology. The founder, Professor Popovic they call her, she's a big economist. She created it all. They say she's a genius. Look! Watch that!" He'd handed Erik a tablet showing a video of a woman being interviewed on TV with some others. Erik sat in the back of the Mercedes Benz with the air conditioning on and watched her talk about exchanges and merchants and value and how everyone across the world would be a part of things.

"You've met her?" Erik asked.

"Sure! Well – she spoke at a meeting. A big meeting, in Nairobi. Wow! She's the real thing, my friend. But let me tell you. They have these packages, okay? You have to put in a minimum amount. Two fifty, that's all. Two fifty dollars."

Erik had to ask how much two hundred and fifty dollars was in shillings. He was shocked. He had nothing like that, anywhere. But it sounded like such a great opportunity that he went home and got his mother to put something into it from her savings. And when Dennis came back and showed him how much the value had gone up already and what it was worth, he went back to the village and got her to buy up nine more packages, which took all her savings so they had to sell a cow. That was difficult. But with what the coin was worth now, they could buy twenty cows and land to put them on! Erik got excited thinking about the day when the exchange would be launched and he could get all the money and take it to his mother. But the date kept being put off, and Dennis didn't answer his phone and hadn't been to visit for such a long time now. She didn't complain, his mother, but she'd asked a few times now, and things were more difficult with only one cow. And while his mother didn't complain, his sister certainly did. So, really, he could do with getting the money out now. He really could.

Don't take any notice of the haters, Dennis said. Many people from conventional finance and the other cryptos, they want New World Coin to fail, and they spend all their time talking it down. Don't listen to them. And Erik didn't, and he didn't take any notice of the rumours he'd heard about New World Coin investigations and Professor Popovic, and that nobody knew where she was. Erik was a believer. They were going to get their money. He would cash it all in and take it back to the village, and give it to his mother. That would feel so good!

As they hurtled downhill back into Iten, he imagined he was coming up to the finish line of a huge race. He stretched out and thundered forward and overtook some of the really fast people who were training in the camps. It was his best time and when they finally stopped and gathered in the main street, Erik was grinning so hard. It was only a training run and none of the big managers were there to see it. But never mind! He just had to keep training and running, and they would notice him next time. Next time, it would happen.

Chapter 8

You could tell that Valentina Maria started life as a model, eye-catching with her tall willowy elegance as she strode across the piazza. She could still earn a living that way if she chose, appealing to the older market who still wanted to look good. In Milan, everyone wanted to look good, and most people did. Fairchild watched from his table as she approached, hair streaming behind her, a smart green jacket setting off her eyes, a liveliness about her that belied her years, the embodiment of the brand which bore her name, the force of nature that was Valentina Maria.

"Fairchild! Such a long time!" Kisses, a seat, a handbag thrown down (matching her shoes), coffee ordered. "You missed my show again. You rascal! Where do you hide?"

Fairchild apologised emphatically (they were speaking Italian) and complimented her on her label's success. Looking at him closely, she laughed. "You look relaxed, Fairchild. Different. Are you finally in love?"

He looked abashed and suggested that it may be the case. This had been happening a lot. Fairchild set up his network out of desperation and bitterness, and in time it had served its purpose, having dredged up the answers he sought. These days he maintained his personal contacts because he wanted to. He liked coming to Milan – or wherever – and drinking coffee – or whatever – with someone who always knew what was going on, what was being talked about, who was new in town. It was also worth something to people who would pay good money. Well, he had to do something for a living.

They caught up. The gossip, the ups and downs, Valentina's particular take on the politics of Italy, of Milan, of the fashion world. And the economy: "Don't listen to the news. You would think the world was destitute. Plenty of people are making plenty of money. Spending it, too. A little more quietly, but just as much." She somehow managed vivacity and poise in a perfectly balanced and mesmerising way.

"So, tell me," she suddenly demanded. "This proposal of yours. You said I'd have to wait until we met. So now you must tell me everything!"

Fairchild finished his coffee and got to work. "As you said, the high rollers have become a little shy. They need coaxing out of their shell a little. You know my place on Capri."

Her face lit up. "Ah, beautiful!" She'd stayed there a number of times.

"I've had an offer. The owner of a rather large charitable trust wants to hold a fundraising event. One of her representatives approached me. They want to attract an audience of high net worth individuals with an interest in philanthropy."

"Don't we all?" Valentina purred.

"She's envisaging some kind of gala event. A banquet, with entertainment. A show. She wants a fashion theme to it."

Valentina pounced on the word. "She wants a fashion show?"

"She's open to suggestions as to the format. But she wants it to be cutting edge. The top designers. And she's passionate about education. So, young designers, maybe. The most promising students coming up."

"Yes, yes." Valentina was nodding, a hundred ideas germinating.

"An international theme. She thinks global, this lady. It's a global charity. Some competitive element to it as well.

Prizes and so on. It's to raise substantial sums for the foundation."

"I see, I see. Perhaps also to avoid the tax collectors, maybe?" Valentina narrowed her eyes.

Fairchild smiled blandly. "Maybe. But still. The charity will benefit. She wants a big noise, publicity but only in the right circles. For an elite crowd. And the budget's generous."

"Generous?"

"Very generous."

Valentina's face took on a faraway look.

"Within reason," Fairchild added. "Nothing too ostentatious. She's not a Russian oligarch. But getting models from Paris, New York, London, Tokyo and shipping them in, no problem. Same with the designers. In fact, that's the idea."

Valentina was beaming. "You want a catwalk show, yes? You have the space?"

"Remember the ballroom? With the cliff view?"

"Oh yes! Oh – so good! Yes, yes. A banquet, then a show?"

"Indeed. The whole thing needs to be themed. Can you do that? You'd need to go down there. More than once, probably. You'll be paid for your time. You'll be liaising with my staff. Cuisine, décor – they can do almost anything."

"Right." Her imagination was in full flow. "We need to dress the room. We must have a strong theme. But with that view! So many ideas! Leave it to me!" She clapped her hands together like a little girl. Fairchild had to laugh.

Then she gasped suddenly. "But when?"

"June. Date to be confirmed." No more than four or five weeks away.

"Oh, it's too short!" A shadow fell over her face.

"Then you'll have to get to work. Remember, budget's not an issue. If people are booked, throw some money around."

"But names, Fairchild! We must have some big names. For this to be the place to be seen!"

"Exactly, and it's your job to line them up. Bribe them if necessary. Remember, we don't want media or PR. Word of mouth will suffice."

"Really?"

"Really. People will be talking about it. Trust me. You just need to create a wonderful show."

The dazzling smile returned. "You'll be there?"

"Of course. Before that I have to travel." He had a big journey ahead of him. "But come back to me with ideas. We'll stay in touch."

"And will I get to meet this lady? What's her name?"

Fairchild hesitated. "She's shy."

"Shy? How shy? You mean she's not going to be there? She's doing all of this from some island somewhere just to launder money?" The Italian looked disgusted for a moment.

"Now, now." Fairchild was placid. "I haven't asked her about the probity of her affairs. I'm not intending to and I suggest you don't either. I can't tell you her name yet." Mainly because it hadn't yet been decided what her name would be.

Valentina still looked troubled. "Is she for real, Fairchild? It will all happen, won't it? What if I make a big fuss then it ends with nothing? No, no!"

To smooth progress, and the complexion of Milan's most loved fashion guru, he applied the truth lightly. "Yes, she's for real. And this definitely will all happen. And I can absolutely guarantee that she'll be there."

Chapter 9

Saturday dinner at the Clarke household was pizza with DIY toppings. Fiona dressed hers with a modest quantity of artichoke and olives, both of which the children noisily rejected. Henry majored on tuna, sweetcorn and extra cheese while Sophie busied herself arranging slices of pepper in a colourful collage. Rose followed Fiona's lead but with added anchovies. James had everything.

Since they'd got back from Japan Rose had made way more effort to stay in touch with her brother's family, and they chatted easily, Henry ever more grown-up, Sophie reserved but with a quiet confidence. Even Fiona had thawed a little. Japan had been good for them. Even though the circumstances that led them there were bizarre and somewhat dangerous, they'd taken to the place and spent a year in Tokyo before coming back to their Surrey home. Fiona was less nervy. James was more involved. The kids exchanged what sounded like insults in Japanese and ate potato salad with chopsticks. Eventually it was tidying up time, then bath time, then bed time, and Rose was left in the living room with her brother and most of a bottle of red.

"So how's our Mr Fairchild, then?" James stretched and put his feet on the coffee table, taking advantage of Fiona's absence.

"Fine." Rose was as close to James now as they'd been growing up, following a phase when they'd drifted apart. They'd all met Fairchild – and liked him – and James was in the picture as far as how things were between them. "Not exactly around a lot."

"Around where? Neither are you."

"True. I guess we've made our choices. But you know we've only met three times in the past year."

"You've only been on three dates?"

"Perhaps these were a bit more than dates."

"Do tell."

"Well, the first time, we met in India and travelled down to Kerala to spend a week on a boat."

"Lovely."

"The second time was Barbados."

"Also on a boat?"

"A boat was involved, but also a villa. And some islands. And some beaches."

"And the third?"

"Finland."

"Finland?"

"He has a friend with a log cabin. Remote. By a lake."

"More boating?"

"It was winter. The lake was frozen. But there was snow, and Northern Lights, and so on."

"Those are three pretty good dates, Rose. When I asked Fiona out, we went to the cinema in the high street."

"I guess." Rose sat sideways in an armchair and hooked her legs over an arm. "Every time we meet it's like we have to start again somehow. Remind ourselves of all the other times."

"Well, as you say, you made your choices."

She caught his eye. Confidentiality prevented her from telling James anything about her job. He thought she was a diplomat. But she got the impression since the Tokyo thing that he realised there was more to it than that.

"Where is he now?" he asked.

"Italy. I think. But not for long."

"Well, he's welcome here any time."

"Thanks, but he can't be persuaded to come to the UK. Too much history."

James shrugged. "Gives you an excuse to meet in far-flung places."

"I guess."

"So how's Budapest?"

That wasn't really James' question. He was asking her what she was doing here, back in the UK after only a few months in a new role.

"It's fine. But something else has come up. I won't be contactable for a while."

That was the most she'd ever said to James about her work, and the most she could say. He picked up on the meaning, though.

"You're involved in some op? Dangerous, is it? Well you can't tell me, obviously."

Some op? It was worse than she'd feared. "They got to you, didn't they?"

He looked blank.

"After Japan. My colleagues approached you. Got you involved in some kind of follow-up with that hacking group. Tim, was it? The guy you met at the Embassy? I told them to leave you out of all that. You really can't trust anybody."

James looked almost ashamed. "Actually, I went to him."

Rose scrambled upright.

"Well, you were right about it all. Those hackers and everything. What they were doing was dangerous. Evil. An abuse of the technology. So I offered my services. Right thing to do and all that. It's very low-key. But occasionally there's something I can help with on the encryption front. I know the industry, you see, the next big idea. Don't tell Fiona."

"No, of course not." Rose tried to process this. James had just driven a coach and horses through her mental idyll of the Clarke family's innocent existence.

"Anyway, it's no big deal," added James. He certainly looked relaxed enough about outing himself as an MI6 agent, or associate of some kind. "Are you worried about it?"

"Should I be?"

"No, not me! I mean you and this thing that's pulled you away from Hungary after you've only just got there. Is it bothering you?"

She considered. She'd certainly never done this before, called round to see family before going out on an assignment. Maybe she was going soft. Maybe she was more uncomfortable with this one than she thought she was. Her first instinct with Walter had been to say no. But then it generally was with Walter.

"I can't tell you a thing. So let's change the subject."

"Righty-ho."

"So what do you know about New World Coin?"

James hesitated ever so slightly before he reached for the bottle and topped them up. "This is a change of subject, is it?"

"Absolutely."

"Right you are. Well, New World Coin. Bit of a fiasco, that." James was a Bitcoin enthusiast, and, at times, a crypto defender.

"I suppose you knew it was a scam right from the start."

He pursed his lips. "Not quite. But the talk did start pretty soon. Odd, though, that things barely seemed to slow down, even after some serious questions were being asked. It was still being marketed and new people were going in. Even now the site is still live. I suppose people cling on, don't want to admit they've been had. Terrible business." He shuddered.

"Do you have any inside track about it all?"

"Such as?"

"Well – where all the money went, for a start. Where this woman is, who heads it up. Who was really behind it apart from her."

"Nothing very illuminating, I'm afraid. She was Serbian, wasn't she? There was organised crime involved, they say."

"The Serbian mafia?"

"Not just Serbian. But really, the whole scam from top to bottom was organised crime, wasn't it? These days you don't have to go about duffing people up to get your hands on large amounts of money by dubious means. A lot of people must have been involved in the scheme, and a lot of them knew there was nothing behind it. It's crime, and it's organised. Ergo…" He raised his hands.

"But there's a difference between any organised crime and an established criminal gang. Muscle, for a start. How they go about persuading people of their point of view. Or keeping them in line."

"Or going after the money, if it disappears."

"You think Popovic made off with the money?"

"Who knows? It's possible. That would be a very good reason to disappear. It would serve them right as well."

Rose, not for the first time, struggled to follow James' stream of consciousness. "Why would it serve them right?"

"Well, for making her do it in the first place."

"Is that the rumour? That she was made to do it?"

"Not especially. But it's likely."

"Why? The whole thing could have been her idea. They say she's the one who designed the scheme."

"That's how she was presented in public. But it stands to reason that she wasn't the real driver behind it."

"How so?"

James seemed perplexed. "Isn't it obvious?"

"Not to me it isn't."

"Well, she's a woman." He held his palm up as if that were explanation enough.

"So?"

"Women are far less likely to engage in criminal activity than men. When they do, it's often because they're supporting someone else. Or they're coerced."

"You can't make assumptions from that. You can't conclude she's innocent just based on her gender."

"No, but you can talk about statistical likelihood. When you see crime on TV, there are as many women as men involved, but that's just in fiction. You know, to give actresses lots of interesting parts. In real life it isn't like that. The FBI publishes a list of the top one hundred most wanted hackers. Do you know how many of them are female?"

Rose sighed. "No, I don't."

"Guess. Go on."

"Okay then – five."

"None. Zero. Out of a hundred."

"This wasn't a hack, James. It was a scam. A con."

"Okay, well, look at any of the FBI most wanted lists and you'll find way more men than women."

"She's not innocent, James. She must have known what was going on."

"Along with a load of other people. She was fronting it, that's all we know. If anyone does catch sight of her, look very closely at the company she's keeping. That's assuming she's still around anywhere."

"She might be dead, you mean?"

"Maybe. If so, she'll not be the first to be killed over it. A couple of New World Coin promoters were found stuffed into suitcases on the Colombia Ecuador border."

Rose almost choked on her wine. "Jesus."

"Drug cartels use crypto for money laundering, unfortunately. Attracted by the anonymity of it all. I don't suppose that was the only dirty money going into New World Coin."

James was more right than he knew. But then, typically, he started to backtrack.

"Of course, they use all kinds of other things for that as well. Not all crypto is a scam. That's the depressing thing about it all, really. Crypto gets a bad rep. The genuine article is revolutionary and could hugely expand access to finance. More wine?"

"Please." Rose hoped she didn't sound too eager. Somehow James' matter-of-fact Colombian tale shocked her more than the fate of Al-Hashemi's accountant.

"Anyway, be glad you didn't get caught up in it," prattled her brother. "There must be hundreds of thousands of angry investors across the globe. Tens of thousands just here in the UK. Professor Popovic would do well to stay hidden. As soon as she pops up anywhere a load of righteously angry folk are going to be banging on her door. And plenty of not-so-righteous ones as well. Bit of a pity, really, if she was just fronting it. Still, who said the world was fair?" He sipped his wine with a blandly philosophical look.

Rose called Walter as she walked back to the station later. It was a Saturday night, but never mind. He picked up.

"You didn't tell me about Colombia."

"What about Colombia?"

"Two New World Coin promoters, found cut up and packed into suitcases?"

There was a short silence. "Yes, well, we'll need to be on our guard."

"I should say."

"But we did talk about this. You're not having second thoughts, are you, Rose? That wouldn't be like you."

Oh, but he knew how to manipulate. "No. But I am wondering if it's really worth it, this whole show we're putting on. It's a huge amount of trouble. As well as the risk."

Walter spoke quietly but she could make out every word. "It's worth it. We want this fellow, Rose. We need to get him. And this is our best chance. If other flies come buzzing round, we'll just have to slap them away."

As the London train pulled out of the station, Rose realised she hadn't said goodbye to the children. It had never bothered her before.

Chapter 10

Fairchild started in Hong Kong where Dragon Fire Tours was based, his travel agency. Not the agency he used – the agency he owned. While making a nice living for him showing tourists the highlights of Asia, they also sorted out custom itineraries. In their scruffy-looking office in Hong Kong's Western district, Molly took on the whole of Fairchild's extensive tour herself. She knew what he liked and checked in with him minimally. By the time he stepped off the plane at Chek Lap Kok, the next few weeks were pretty much pre-ordained.

In Hong Kong he stayed one night only, at the Hyatt (harbour view), but he made it count. He paid a visit to an unremarkable Central District restaurant and was granted a few minutes with Darcy Tang, the remarkable boss of Hong Kong's most influential mafia clan, while she babysat her two-year-old grandson. It was fair: she owed Fairchild a favour. He also made a late-night appearance in the tiny but lively Lan Kwai Fong scene, where he saw some familiar faces and was introduced to quite a few new ones.

Then onto Beijing. Here he had an apartment which every now and then Walter claimed to own. That complicated story was just a small insight into their pseudo-familial history, Walter thrown into a loco parentis role when Fairchild was an angry boy, a role the older man carried out indifferently. But for the current project, Beijing was key: Fairchild's contacts in business and government there held sway across the globe. Russia may bring bad weather, the spooks in London would say, but it was China that was changing the climate. He shared dim sum with the most internationalised of them, trying out his story in Mandarin. And then to Tokyo.

No hotel here either: instead, the upper floor of a wood-framed house with tatami mats and futons and cats and draughts. He poached himself pink in the public baths and drank far too much beer with his fixer Takao, who knew exactly who he should talk to and took him straight there. The streets of Ginza with their neon signs stacked up, a hostess bar on every floor of every doorway, sent shivers down his spine when he remembered the last time he was here. The piano bar, where Rose had fallen asleep on his shoulder, he avoided; that was before.

From there, via Seoul and Taipei, to Manila. In the midst of a typhoon he'd been propositioned here by the Defence Secretary, but that was some years ago and she was no longer on the scene. Manila was where he'd made the decision to purchase Trade Winds, a chain of exuberantly-themed cocktail bars and restaurants which had gone from strength to strength. Here he caught up with Carmel, who now managed the entire chain, and also kept tabs locally on who and what and where. While there, he tasked her with finding someone with whom he had a mixed past but, he hoped, a better future.

None of this was unusual: it was his life, dropping in on his business interests, cultivating friendships, passing from one unique culture to another, at home in all, yet none. He'd been doing this now for over twenty years. He found Jakarta better, Rangoon worse. He skipped the Gulf and Africa. Skirting Russia he dropped in at Tbilisi (Georgia was another place that put him on edge, though the Russian dogs had been beaten back for now), then Kyiv, then Prague.

Berlin, Brussels, Paris: these icons of western Europe were as familiar as the back of his own hand. Everywhere he went he produced the same story, but he always started it as a question: What do you know about New World Coin? The answer, generally, was quite a lot. A friend, people said, had fallen for that. Lost a load. It was of passing interest, his rumour that the woman was trying a comeback. No one had reason personally to be bothered that the founder of New World Coin, Professor Popovic herself, was all worked up these days about charity, about making a difference, making amends, some might say, with a foundation that was inexplicably rich, and that she was rumoured to be planning an appearance – using another name – at some fundraising fashion event on Capri.

She must be mad, his friend would say once this nugget had sunk in, once the startled gaze had turned into an indifferent eye-roll. They'll have her in cuffs before she's off the plane. Not if they can't prove her identity, Fairchild would point out, as a casual aside. And besides, she's aiming to pass under the radar, make herself known only in the kind of circles that might advance her philanthropic efforts. Is that so? would be the response, accompanied by a sceptical look. Good luck to her, then. It isn't law enforcement she should be most afraid of. Capri you say? June? What was the event again? Well, well.

And then the conversation, naturally, would move on. You're looking good, Fairchild. That matter with your parents, it was resolved, was it not? That explains it. Unless there's something else? You do seem to have a glow about you, a sense of inner peace. None of my business? Since when? Anyway, we don't see you often enough in these parts. How long has it been? Months? No, years! But it's good to catch up. Please, another drink!

And at midnight, or two in the morning, or four, or six, his taxi would drop him back at the hotel, or the apartment, or the house where he'd been offered his friend's friend's cousin's spare room, and always as he lay wondering how much more of this he had and why he'd agreed to it, and how it might end, he'd think about calling London.

Chapter 11

Rose wasn't in London. She was in a country house in Berkshire which had stone walls and lattice windows and uneven floors covered by threadbare carpets, and a large square lawn which ended in a ha-ha and a steep bushy bank that tumbled down to the River Thames. She wasn't taking calls. She was pupating, undergoing a hidden transformation, being secretly reconfigured to emerge later as Ulia Popovic, or rather Ulia Popovic's new persona, who someone had decided would go by the name of Julia Michalaedes.

"It's ludicrous," she complained to Walter on one of his frequent weekend visits. The man seemed to have little going on outside of work. "Her name's Ulia, and her fake ID is Julia? That's error 101. It's barking mad."

"It would be if it were genuine," said Walter as they strolled around the edge of the square of grass. "But she's an amateur, remember? If you're not used to going by a different name, keeping a similar given name is comforting. At least you won't get caught out not responding when someone talks to you. Remember we want it to look like Popovic has gone to some effort to change her identity, but we also want her to be instantly recognisable."

"It's got to be credible, though."

"That's why we can't do it too well. If she surfaced with some pristine legend people would start to ask where it came from, would they not? Who's helping her. And we don't want that. Are they feeding you all right?"

"Very well." They stopped and stared at the aged façade facing them over the lawn. Rose remembered this place from her initial training. It was somewhere in there, amongst the clusters of chimneys and period furniture, that the secrets of the trade first started to be revealed to her and her carefully vetted fellow trainees. She could still feel the excitement at seeing a new world opening up, wished she could live that again. But there were no new recruits here now: the place had been emptied. For this, apparently. For Project Michalaedes, the making of a lie. In order to make the lie good enough, Rose was happy to oblige every meal time with generous full English breakfasts, magnificent buffet board lunches and multiple-course dinners finished off with biscuits and cheese. The food at this place was renowned.

"You look a little rounded out already." Walter stepped back to appraise her.

"Why, thank you." It was disconcerting how easy it was to pile on the pounds.

"How's the voice?"

"Working on it."

"The voice is key. The tone, the idiom. You have to get it ninety percent or it won't be believable."

"I'm working on it, Walter." As well as watching every video of Popovic that could be found online, Rose was listening over and over again to everything the woman had ever said, writing lists of vocabulary and key phrases, making notes of distinctive pronunciations. Popovic had a slightly soft way of saying "ch": instead of *cha*rity, she'd say *sha*rity. Rose walked around mouthing it to herself: *sha*rity, *sha*rity. "You said you'd send a voice coach."

"I will. How are you finding Linda?"

"Thorough." Team Michalaedes included a body consultant, who showed up with a clipboard and appraised Rose's hair, eyes, lips, ears, skin – anything that might show. Linda had observed every detail from every image of Ulia Popovic that the researchers had found. Even Rose's teeth were going to get a polish and some cosmetic adjustments.

Linda had tutted when she ran her fingers through Rose's hair.

"This is a problem."

"What's a problem? The first thing she'll do to change her appearance is dye her hair."

"But the texture's all wrong. Her hair is glossy. Yours is fine."

Linda was right: on all the video clips, Popovic had long, smooth shiny hair with some body to it.

"She'll cut it."

"Maybe. But not all of it. She loves her hair. She'll keep some length. Recolour and straighten, but it needs to be a feature still. Extensions, I think. Well, you don't want a wig, do you?" She'd said that in response to Rose's grimace.

Linda had a problem with Rose's nails as well. "She's not going to turn into a nail-biter overnight. You've seen the clips. Ten long red talons, nicely shaped. She uses a manicurist weekly, probably."

"But now she's on the run."

"Stinking rich on the run. She'll get her nails done. We'll go with a more muted colour and take something off the length. Right – let's look at your feet."

"Do we have to?" Rose valued her feet for their utilitarian value, not as things of beauty.

"I think so, darling. If the lady cares about her nails, she'll be pedicured for sure."

"Can't I just keep them covered up?"

"What with?"

"I don't know – socks?"

"Socks? Socks on Capri? Socks are for sweaty tourists. It'll be thirty degrees in the shade. You think Popovic is the type to go to a gala dinner in socks? You may as well show up in a tracksuit." She pulled a chair over. "Come on, let's see."

Rose took off her shoes and socks and placed her feet on the chair.

"Good Lord." Linda bent in for a closer look, pushing her glasses up her nose. It was precisely at that moment that the door opened and a serious-looking woman – slim, brown hair – walked in and stopped.

"Oh, I'm so sorry, they told me to come straight in."

"Don't worry," said Rose. "It's not what it looks like. Though I'm not really sure what it looks like." Her gaze went back to Linda, who had only glanced up momentarily and was now photographing Rose's toes with her phone. "Who are you, anyway?"

"Close protection," said the woman. "I've been sent from Special Forces." Her voice was calm but she was staring at Linda and her phone.

"Bodyguard?" said Rose.

"Yes." Still staring.

"Hmm." Rose flinched as Linda explored a patch of hard skin with the end of her pen. "No one is going to be looking at the soles of my feet, Linda. I mean there's thorough and there's thorough."

The woman was still watching.

"You know what this game's all about?" Rose asked her.

"Yes." But she was frowning.

"Problem?"

The frown evaporated. "Of course not."

"Not normally the kind of thing you do?"

"I go where I'm told."

"Well, I'm surprised they've sent a woman."

That drew a stare.

"I just don't think the lady would go in for that. I think she'd want to be surrounded by muscle of the very obvious type. Big boys. What do you think, Linda?"

Linda was contemplating Rose's toenails. "Above my pay grade, darling."

"Mine too." There was tension in the woman's face.

"I'll talk to someone," said Rose.

"Like I said, I go where I'm told." She sounded chastened.

"Did they tell you I was a spook?"

Linda's pen stopped moving. There was an awkward silence.

"No, ma'am."

"Ma'am?" Rose smiled and caught Linda's eye. The woman blushed. "Ma'am won't do at all. What's your name? Your first name, I mean."

"Sarah." Her face was still red.

"Well, Sarah, you'll find out more at the briefing. Have they given you a room?"

"Yes."

"Have you unpacked?"

"No."

"Probably wise. You won't be needed for a couple of hours."

After she'd gone, Linda said, "You're wearing 'I'm a spook' t-shirts now? And since when do we invite security guards to briefings?"

"She may as well know. Otherwise the next few weeks are going to seem mighty weird. And we might need to make use of her. This is an unusual op."

"You don't say." Linda glanced again at Rose's toes and shook her head.

Rose did raise it, with Walter, as they strolled back around the other half of the lawn. "Popovic wouldn't have an ordinary-looking slip of a lass for a personal bodyguard. Beef in suits is more her thing. With tattoos."

"We can get a couple of those as well. Have them outside, opening car doors for you, the visible stuff. She can be closer. Go with you to the powder room and so on."

"Well, all right. As long as you know what you're doing."

Walter gave her a sideways look. "Of course I do."

Chapter 12

Erik was out running when the white Mercedes Benz drew into Iten's main street. By the time he returned, Dennis was already surrounded. He was giving something away. When Erik got closer he could see it was samples of vitamins.

"Erik!" Dennis brightened when he saw him. "Take one of these! Will make you run fast. Better than ugali!" Erik took one of the little bottles and they shook hands. There was a tiny hesitation about his Nairobi friend that hadn't been there before. "Come, come. Let's walk." The big man patted his shoulder and they strolled away from the others, all gazing at their new pill bottles.

Dennis asked about Erik's family and the village. Erik gave short answers. "You've been away or something? You don't call me back."

"Busy, my friend, busy. Listen, I've heard some good news. She's coming back."

"Who's coming back?"

"Ulia Popovic, of course! A friend told me, a businessman. Important guy in Nairobi. She's holding some charity event. Raising money for some good thing or I don't know." Dennis didn't sound very interested in charity.

"What does that mean, Dennis? We need our coin, man. I don't know what to say to my mother and Esther."

"You tell them it's coming. This is a good sign. She's back. She had to go into hiding for safety, because of all the haters, but that's dealt with now. It means the launch will happen. The exchange will go live and we can get our money. Why else is she coming back? That must be what it means!"

There was relief in his voice. Dennis had invested too, Erik didn't know how much. More than him, for sure. "So, when?"

"Hey, I don't know when. But this charity thing is in a couple of weeks. It's in Italy. You know where Capri is?" Erik didn't. "It's her show. Her event. She'll be there, flesh and blood. She'll probably make an announcement then, explain all the delays. So! Relax, my friend, focus on your running. It's all okay. The money is coming."

Dennis put his hand on his heart. He'd always looked after Erik. He'd come out all this way to tell Erik this. They stopped and turned to look back at the crowd by the car, everyone comparing their samples and pointing and discussing every feature of the Mercedes, like they always did. The tyres and fenders were coated in red dust.

"You want a Coke?" Dennis pointed at the kiosk.

"Sure."

Dennis wandered over, rolling up the sleeves on his thick white shirt. In the afternoon heat, a line of sweat ran down the middle of his back. Erik was sweaty all over. He'd run a good time, but not good enough. He did stretches until Dennis returned with a thin bottle of Coke, a little bit cold. They stood and drank.

Erik's mind was spinning. Ulia Popovic was back! The woman at the heart of all this. Where had she been? Why was she back now? Dennis was reassuring. But Erik's thoughts went straight back to his village. Esther, in her scorn, had told him how things were now. She didn't think Erik listened to her, but he remembered everything. What she said about Grace, their mother, dragging herself out to work in the fields even on days when she was tired and should rest. How they managed with less for themselves to try and save up more surplus. How much a new shed would help. How little they got from one cow, when they'd been used to two. How Esther had given up hope but Grace had not, and asked often about the money but Esther had nothing to tell her. How Grace still insisted on sending money to Erik, even when they needed it themselves to make repairs on the house, how they went to bed hungry some nights. Grace still had faith, and Erik couldn't break that. He needed the money back to earn that faith, to be the son his mother expected him to be and thought he was. That was his world. That was how much New World Coin mattered to him.

And what of Ulia Popovic? She was so intelligent, so powerful. What did it mean to her, the launch and the exchange and everyone who'd put their faith in her getting their returns? Did she understand how important this was, what it meant in the day-to-day? And suddenly he made a decision, in a flash of lightning, like all the big decisions he'd ever made.

"Dennis," he said, laying his hand on his fat friend's arm. "You always look after me."

Dennis frowned. "Of course. What is it, Erik?"

Erik could feel the sweat on Dennis's arm under his shirt. His lovely tailored shirt, so clean and neat. He looked into the big man's eyes.

"Lend me some money."

Chapter 13

Fairchild reached Capri by jetfoil, boarding late afternoon when the day trippers were returning to Naples. He waited as they flocked past in baseball caps and shorts, sundresses and sandals, with empty water bottles and backpacks heavy with cheap souvenirs. It was hot, even for Naples in June: a heatwave, they were saying. Fairchild waited in the shade in light linen trousers and a short-sleeved shirt, pink. If anywhere was the right place for a pink shirt, it was Capri. He looped a small backpack onto his shoulder and walked straight onto the boat. It was practically empty and he spent the thirty-minute crossing pretending to check his emails.

A businessman. That was his persona. It was an easy role for him to play. His portfolio of concerns had been assembled over the years for intelligence gathering, but not in an obvious way. No disgraced spies touting for work, or sleazy private investigators. His firms were genuine, though at times they did a few extras for him. Hotels, real estate, travel agencies, taxis, cleaners: one could make discreet use of all of them. So being the businessman came naturally. But maybe these days he was playing that part a little too much.

Years ago, the services he provided were a lot more direct. But less and less as time went on, it seemed. He was well into his forties now, could still handle himself, but others were coming up who were barely more than half his age and had the strength and stamina to match. He'd thought about training or mentoring. No one had ever asked him to do anything like that. This wasn't surprising as his skills were home-grown, unlike most espionage freelancers who were previously employed by some state somewhere. Fairchild had always gone it alone and thus didn't enjoy the trust of many within the bona fide intelligence establishment. Certainly not MI6, with the occasional exception of Walter. And not universally stateside either, his main contact there being Zack, and that was usually at arm's length. Pretty unlikely, then, that he'd be asked to come in and train recruits.

Through a window blurry with sea spray, the hunk of vertical rock that was Capri grew rapidly. Did he have something to pass on? Did he mind being out in the cold? He'd always felt pride in being entirely his own master, and maybe some relief, but lately...maybe his experiences could help others. He didn't think he'd have kids. There was only one person he would want to have a child with, and Rose didn't seem interested. Just as well, given the turbulence of his own childhood. No matter: there were plenty of other ways to give back. But it was an idle thought and he put it out of his mind as the craft slowed and turned into the harbour, the wall came alongside, and he stepped onto the quay.

He could have requested a buggy. Someone of his status normally would, he supposed, but he wanted to remind himself of the lay of the land. He'd also been hoping that the air here by late afternoon would be cooler than blistering Naples, but he realised his mistake on the short walk to the main promenade. The paving stones seemed to throb with heat and he was coated with sweat before he even started to climb. He crossed the road: three or four arteries linked Capri town with Ana Capri and the harbours; the rest of the island was permeated by narrow passageways wide enough for a cart or a trailer, or sometimes just flights of steps. Tourists got up to the main square by funicular: Fairchild took a winding route up the side of the hill that was the Naples-facing half of the island.

He took in one or two of the shopping streets, still busy with groups browsing the windows beneath white canopies that matched all the way down the street, each displaying a high-end retail brand. The shops would still be open long after these folk had left, and it would be later that they'd make their living and earn the extortionate rent demanded for a Capri frontage. He passed by a couple of hotel lobbies, not necessarily identifiable as such: they didn't expect drop-in trade. They were all still there just as he remembered them, global recession notwithstanding: Valentina was right. He passed by La Piazzetta and the clocktower and paused to gaze at a window display of sandals that were barely recognisable as such: strings of glittering jewels wrapped around elegant glass display pieces. Rose would have no interest in such items, though next time he saw Rose she was going to be looking very different. He stared, too, at a fan of chiffon scarves: lemon, coral, violet, no price tag in sight. Then he backtracked and took a longer route down the slope to the hotel. Two turns away from the main square was enough to leave the crowds behind, and his own footsteps echoed off the close white walls. He wasn't expecting shadows, but you could never be too careful, and it was a big operation they had planned. If anyone were going to blow it before they even got started, it wouldn't be him.

The Hotel Villa Bianca Rosaria was as shy from the outside as her competitors. She kept her secrets well hidden from the casual gaze. Fairchild claimed that his businesses were there for solid operational reasons, but he couldn't honestly say that about the Villa Bianca Rosaria. The Rosaria was special, and she knew it. Between elegant gateposts in brilliant white, topped with planters of fan-shaped ferns, her wrought iron gates beckoned you towards the sliding glass doors, which moved aside to bestow on you the first scent of her perfumed breath. Shining floor tiles carried you across the lobby, where her view of the blue horizon made you feel as though you were flying. White, pink, purple, delicate and scented, her floral displays fed the senses, and for your refreshment she would offer you a bowl of round white mints, a jug of iced water, a hot towel that smelled of lemons. Despite the heat outside, the world within the threshold of the Rosaria was one of plenty, of perfection, of meeting your every need, not just with comfort but with a bewitching beauty, a care that responded to every sense with an effortless grace. To think of the Rosaria as a bed for the night would be to describe the Titanic as a large canoe. The Rosaria offered no less than a fleeting taste of heaven, invited you to float in a plush cloud, where you could gaze at the beauty of the earth in a state of pure comfort.

Had he really volunteered this place for some sordid con trick? Standing there in the lobby it suddenly felt like an intolerable pollution. He'd often fantasised about bringing Rose here, to her namesake, but hadn't yet spoken of it or found the chance to plan it. Soon they would be here together, but it wouldn't at all be how he'd imagined. He offered up a silent apology to the Villa Bianca Rosaria, and hoped that she would forgive him.

The young man on the front desk was dressed smartly – white shirt, black jacket, satin embroidered waistcoat. His name badge introduced him as Adel.

"Hello, Adel," said Fairchild.

"Good afternoon, Mr Fairchild." They both spoke English, the young staff member with an accent of Asian origin. "Did you have a pleasant journey?"

"Tolerable. You know who I am, then."

"Of course," said Adel smoothly. "It would be embarrassing not to recognise the owner of the hotel, would it not?"

"I suppose it would."

Adel got to work processing his check-in, moving rapidly through the layers of the check-in system.

"Getting the hang of things?" Fairchild asked.

Adel looked up.

"I don't remember you from when I was last here," said Fairchild.

Adel went back to the terminal and started tapping again. "Was that long ago?"

"Longer than I'd have wanted."

"Would you like me to let Nico know you're here?"

"Yes, and bring me a glass of sparkling mineral water."

Fairchild watched while Adel made a couple of quick internal calls. The man was cool, competent and polite. He came back. "Nico's on his way." He held Fairchild's gaze for a moment, then turned to serve someone else.

Fairchild's water appeared, along with a lemon-scented hot towel. He moved away and sat on a sofa. After a few minutes the General Manager walked in.

"Nico." Fairchild shook the Italian man's hand warmly and asked after his health and family, in Italian. Nico had plenty to say: his family was in Rome, which was where he would be had he not been offered twice the going rate to come and work on "this little rock", as he called it.

"I tell you, Fairchild, it's a crazy place. No wonder they won't come. You can't get anywhere in the day when the streets are crammed. Even if you can, nowhere to go. Everything is up or down, nothing flat. No decent beaches. And how can you get anything after the ferries have stopped?" He tutted and smoothed flat his already sleek hair.

"I suppose you cultivate relations with the other hotels, help each other out, maybe?"

Nico shrugged, grumbling. However he did it, the hotel rarely ran out of anything. Fairchild didn't have to tell him how to run a hotel, in Capri or anywhere else on the planet.

"How's the event going?" Fairchild asked. "Is Valentina here?"

Nico rolled his eyes. "That woman is impossible. She changes her mind, she fusses over nothing. The cost! The cost, Fairchild!"

"I said not to worry about that, didn't I?"

Nico shook his head, an expression of disbelief on his face.

"Do you have enough staff now?" Fairchild nodded in Adel's direction.

"No, not enough. People aren't coming. We're in a heatwave. And the pay isn't good enough."

"Then offer more. Go to an agency if you need to. How are the bookings?"

"So-so."

"We're not full?"

"For the gala night? No." That was a concern. Maybe Fairchild needed to spread the word some more. But he couldn't be too obvious about it. "Except for the top floor." Nico looked at him quizzically.

"Don't worry about that. You can be discreet, can't you?"

"Of course. I'm a hotelier." Nico might speculate as to why Fairchild had block-booked the entire top floor, but he'd keep it to himself.

"I'm in the Blue Room?"

"Yes, as you requested." Nico signalled to Adel, but the young man had already got Fairchild's room key card ready.

"And where is Valentina?"

"In the ballroom," sighed Nico.

Fairchild picked up his water and headed that way. Adel looked up briefly as he walked past, then looked away again.

Chapter 14

Fairchild crossed the lobby and went out onto the pool terrace, the view from its cream-cushioned loungers a dramatic one down to the Marina Grande. He carried on through into a walled courtyard garden with flowerbeds full of colour, and in the middle, where two paths crossed, a headless statue of a male torso. Tiny but lovely, this hidden little garden was like the Rosaria's very heart.

He continued through an archway into the ballroom, though really it wasn't a room at all. It was a cavern scooped out of rock, open at the front where a substantial railing separated revellers from the cliff drop below. Straight ahead the deep blue sea and the Amalfi hills rising up on the mainland. This was the party platform, the place where things happened and were seen to happen, Rosaria's smile, her lifeblood, her spirit. With this view as a backdrop vows were made, deals struck, life events celebrated, and people met for the first time. But Fairchild didn't look at the view: there was too much else going on.

An entire army seemed to be carrying in boxes and crates, bulky black gear, cloths of all colours – for the tables? The floor? The walls? Rising up everywhere were piles of glittery frilly material that could be fungal growth from another planet. Gliding through the centre of the room on a trolley, a vanguard of people on all sides of it with their arms raised, was an enormous translucent globe made out of – glass? Crystal? A thousand cut diamonds? Fairchild could have believed it. And the mistress of ceremonies Valentina was in the midst of the shouting throng, doing the most shouting herself.

"Fairchild!" She streamed over, arms outstretched. "This is going to be so sensational. This room! So amazing. And the globe! See where this will go? Up there! Above everyone, slowly spinning and throwing out light!"

"Like a glitterball?"

"Yes! But bigger! And it's the world! A glitter-world!" Her eyes danced.

"You've annoyed Nico," he said.

She swatted a hand. "Nico, he's fine. He makes a big fuss, that's all. Now here," she raised both arms parallel, "the catwalk goes here. Tables there, there, there!" Tables everywhere, then. "And at the top a stage, with spotlights, for speeches. The lectern, here!" She leaped over and mimed a lectern. "And for the auction, the girls line up here, auctioneer with his hammer, everyone can see everyone!" She actually shuddered with excitement.

Fairchild did his best to mirror her mood. She was, after all, doing everything he'd wanted her to do. She'd phoned and messaged him relentlessly as he journeyed, and asked for his approval as her concept developed. He'd been running it past Zack's team, and they'd shaped it a little, but the exact format didn't really matter, as long as it was a big enough event. As long as everyone saw everyone. This was Valentina's baby, then: a show with a global theme, the twenty or more promising young designers selected from various parts of the world, and the signature outfit of each designer would be auctioned off on the night, proceeds to the foundation, of course. "So, it's not a competition," Valentina had said. "But – people will compare the bids, so, of course, it's a competition, kind of."

The show would feature only womenswear. "You do know that most high net worth individuals are men?" Fairchild pointed out.

"Yes, but they dress so dull! They won't buy a daring outfit for themselves! They want to see their wives in it, their daughters, their lovers. They will buy them for others to wear. You don't think?"

He believed her. "And all the designers are bringing their guests?"

"Of course!"

That was all paid for as part of the event. It would boost their occupancy rates at least. All those designers meant a whole lot more people hearing about the event. With that many hangers-on the place was going to look buzzing even before the paying guests. But the paying guests were the whole point, of course. Fairchild would be discussing that later with Zack.

"And the models?" he asked.

Valentina clasped her hands. "Fairchild, it's all come together like a dream! You'll not believe who we've got." She reeled off a list of names, a few of which sounded vaguely familiar. "Some had other commitments, though. We had to offer quite a lot. You said money was no object." She looked coy for a moment.

"No, it's fine. I only hope the bidders realise they're only getting the clothes and not the rest of it."

She mimed stage shock. "Really, I'm sure everyone is completely civilised."

Fairchild wasn't sure about that at all.

Chapter 15

Later that night, refreshed and showered in the spacious luxury of the Blue Room, Fairchild took the steps down towards Capri and settled on the back terrace of a small bar some distance from the main streets, the kind of bar that served the hotel porters, the shop assistants and chambermaids and sous-chefs and ferry workers. Eventually, Zack arrived. He wore green shorts, a Hawaiian shirt that merely emphasised his body width, and a baseball cap.

"You look like you missed the last ferry home," said Fairchild as the American sat. "You could make some effort to blend in. Like spending more than ten dollars on a shirt, say?"

"Why? I'm not invited to your party, am I? I'm not part of the elite. I'm US law enforcement. On vacation if anyone asks."

"You think that's believable? It's not exactly your kind of place."

"Doesn't matter. We want people to think there's something going on, don't we? The place is crawling with FBI. Trying not to stick out, like FBI are so good at. Folk are going to assume it's Popovic they're after, and that's what we want, right?" He broke off to order a Peroni.

"Are you sure it's wise having so many people in on it?"

"It's not only wise, it's essential if we want realism. Besides, we want word to spread, don't we? In all kinds of places. We want the very worst kind of people to hear about this."

"Yes, but we don't want to put them off by overdoing the security."

"Believe me, by FBI standards this isn't overdoing it. And these people have front, don't they? They're not in hiding. They go about life exactly as if they weren't criminals. A lot of them are used to the attention. We've been trying to catch up with them for years. What's the point of being a criminal if you can't spend the proceeds in swanky places like this?"

"And where are all these Federal agents lodging?"

"The budget places. If you can call them that. But all over. The whole island is pretty packed."

"Well, it's high season. Most of these hotels are closed from October to April. They have to make all their money now."

"And how are the bookings going your end?"

"The event? We're not full yet."

"The hotel? The rooms?"

"Not full yet either."

Zack looked thoughtful. "That a problem?"

"Hard to tell. People may need a bit more time. They may be waiting until she actually makes an appearance."

"We don't have more time. We've got about forty-eight hours. Anything more you can do?"

Fairchild shook his head. "I've done as much as I can, credibly. If I make more noise now, people will suspect. This is my network, Zack. These people can't ever know they were drawn into a deception, however well-intentioned."

"And there's no reason why they'd ever know. We planned it that way, remember? No one has actually said that Michalaedes is Popovic. It's only a rumour. It's a rumour that will be forever unsubstantiated, whatever happens here. Plenty of those around."

That appeased Fairchild, but only somewhat. Zack was competent and reliable. But posing on the Amalfi coast was miles away from Zack's normal sphere, which tended to involve camouflage gear and modern weaponry. Fairchild was relying on Zack for just about everything, he was starting to realise. At a time in his life when things were starting to go well for him, he'd just jeopardised it all by putting his livelihood and happiness into the hands of this one man. Speaking of which…

"When is she due to arrive, exactly?"

Zack paused mid-swig to look at him. "You don't know?"

"We haven't spoken for a while. She thought it best to – keep some distance."

"Yeah, I get that. She's undergone a transformation, Fairchild. So I'm told. And she's flying in tomorrow. But expect something unrecognisable."

"That's okay, as long as she transforms back again afterwards. I liked her the way she was." Zack looked nonplussed. Fairchild told himself to try and forget that Zack didn't really like the woman. It wasn't a helpful thought. "Dare I ask about what's really going on in those top floor rooms? I've seen way more equipment than I'd expect."

"We got a whole tech team based up there. You guys are handling that."

"You guys?"

Zack rolled his eyes. "The Brits. GCHQ. It's like a Moscow tourist hotel in the Soviet era. Don't say a word anywhere you don't want recorded on a digital file somewhere."

"That's illegal, Zack."

"So what's new? Anyway the Italians are sweet enough if they can claim a role in the arrest. Anything extra we happen to pick up, that's our business."

"Unlawful bugging isn't going to swing you an extradition."

"It'll help us figure out who's who so we can build evidence. Talking of which – you're going to pass us your guest list?"

"How about a front desk system terminal up there? You can see everything then. Reservations, check-ins, credit cards…"

"Great." Zack necked his beer. But there was something about his manner.

"What?"

"Huh?" He was all innocence.

"What else, Zack?"

"Well, I have a request. Just a small one."

Fairchild doubted that. "Go on."

"You know how we don't really know who might show up, but we kind of hope it'll be some of the bad crowd?"

"Yes."

"And you know how that old friend of yours you put me in touch with a few years back turned out to be really helpful when it comes to tracing the money?"

Fairchild's heart sank. "Zoe?"

"She's not called that any more. But she's the one who's set us up with this charity foundation, so that it looks convincingly disreputable."

"Zoe set up the Michalaedes foundation? You never told me that that before."

"Yeah, well, I'm telling you now. She's good, Fairchild. It was because of her we got Quesada put away in the end. She's helped us with a load of sting operations, especially creative ways of draining the funds of undesirables."

"I'm sure she has." Fairchild hoped he would never be considered undesirable by the US authorities.

"So she's a walking *Who's Who* of dodgy billionaires. Pretty neat for her to be around for something like this."

Fairchild tried to hide his horror. "You want Zoe at the event?"

Zack switched into reassuring mode. "It makes sense. We can gather all kinds of intelligence if this show works out the way we intend. Why not have someone there who can make the connections straight away? You said yourself you're not booked out yet." None of that was the issue, as Zack well knew. He leaned in and adopted a conspiratorial tone. "Look, I know it might be awkward with Rose and all, given you and Zoe were – involved."

"We weren't 'involved' for very long, Zack."

"Exactly! So what does it matter now?"

Too late Fairchild realised he'd walked into a trap.

Zack pursued it. "Look, Rose is the one. She knows that. You know that. Zoe knows that. Hell, even I know it. So you had a passing thing with someone else. Before it got going with Rose. Well before. It happens, to real people. You also saved Zoe's life, didn't you? She won't make things difficult. She's doing great, actually. You'll enjoy catching up. And she's coming on the yacht. No need to find her a room." Zack's grin was way too confident.

"You've already invited her, haven't you?"

Zack shrugged. "Maybe."

"You should have mentioned this earlier."

"Maybe."

"But you didn't want me laying any ground rules. Thinking I actually had some influence on any of this."

"Hey, you've had loads of influence. Don't forget, we could have done this without you."

"Really? And where would your guests have come from? I'm the one who's summoned everyone here. By lying to pretty much everyone I know!" The things Fairchild had started to dislike about this operation were multiplying. Zack's arrogance was definitely one of them.

The man sighed with studied patience. "Don't get het up about some ex. See the bigger picture. It'll be fine. She'll arrive, you and she will get along nicely. And she and she, if they even meet. This must be the easiest gig you've ever had, Fairchild! You're being paid to have a party! That's all! Compared to some of the things you've done, this is child's play. Isn't it?"

Chapter 16

The ferry arrived in Naples at 6.15 a.m. coming overnight from Palermo. Erik had spent the crossing sleeping on the floor in a lounge. Before that, another ten-hour ferry journey took him from Tunis to Palermo. He'd flown to Tunis from Nairobi, and a big chunk of the money he'd borrowed from Dennis was already gone. Erik was tired, unwashed and hungry. But as the boat slowed and entered the harbour he felt a shiver of excitement. Naples! Italy! He'd never been out of Kenya before. Whatever happened here, it would be a big adventure for sure.

The port was full of ferries and signs everywhere. Capri! Capri! Seemed like every boat was going there. It took Erik a while to work out where you went to get a ticket. He had to wait, as three or four people were queuing up at each of the windows. But when he got there and pulled his money out he realised he only had Kenyan shillings. The man at the booth shook his head, looking at Erik's cash as though it was something funny.

"Bureau de change. That way." He pointed up into the city.

"Huh? Where?"

He pointed again. "Change money. Bank. Come back with Euros." He waved Erik out of the way and turned to the next customer.

Erik came out of the port and crossed a cobbled street full of cars. He walked alongside a big square of yellow grass. Behind that was a massive square building with round towers. After that, another busy street with lots of straight roads off it, that all looked the same. No bank anywhere. He asked a guy who was pulling up a shutter. Hopefully people

here spoke a bit of English? This man understood and
pointed this way and that. Erik tried to follow but ended up
going up and down the streets randomly. He asked a couple
of other people and eventually found it. But it was closed, a
big metal shutter over the front and no information
anywhere. Erik waited, and eventually sat down on his string
bag on the pavement. People looked disapproving as they
stepped round him. A lot of mopeds came past. And a lot of
people. Not as many as Nairobi, though. Erik's stomach
rumbled. His athlete's body was expecting some food, a big
plate of ugali. But it had to make do with water from the
bottle he'd refilled on the ferry.

The sun rose in the sky. The street got busier. Eventually
a door behind him opened and a man in uniform came out
to lift the shutter. After a few minutes Erik went inside. The
lady at the desk counted all his notes and wrote a number
down on a piece of paper. She pushed it towards him.

"What's that?"

"Euros. You buy Euros with Kenyan shilling."

He stared at the number. "That's all?"

The woman pointed to a number on a screen beside
them. "Here. We sell, we buy. That's the rate. You want it?"

Erik shrugged. He had no choice.

She gave him one note – one! – and a few coins. On the
way back to the port he passed a cafe smelling of fried food.
He went in, and pointed at some round snacks.

"Rice ball?" said the man. But he shook his head when
Erik produced the note. "Too big. I have no change. Smaller,
smaller!" But he shook his head again at Erik's coins. Not
enough.

There was no other place like that nearby, so Erik ignored
his stomach and walked back to the port. But now it was
packed with people! All the ticket windows had fifteen or

twenty people waiting. Erik joined a queue. While he waited, boats arrived and people shuffled off to get on them, but still it just got more and more busy. Eventually he got to the front of the queue.

"Capri."

"Return today?" the man asked.

"No."

"When you return?"

"I don't know."

The man shrugged. "Single, then." He tapped his keyboard. "Three o'clock."

"What?"

"Three o'clock. No tickets till then. All full."

"Oh." Erik felt lost.

The man tutted. "You want it?"

"Yes, yes!"

The man pointed to the screen, where the price came up. Erik's mouth fell open. There must be some mistake. "One ticket, yes?"

The man held up a finger. "One ticket. One way. No return. There." He pointed at the screen again.

How could it be? The price was more than it cost him to get from Tunis to Naples. It couldn't be right. "Capri, yes? The island? Near to Naples?"

The man rolled his eyes. "Yes, Capri! Capri, all boats go to Capri. All these people. You want?"

"There's nothing cheaper?"

"No. All prices the same. You want a ticket or not?"

It would take almost all Erik's money. He wouldn't even have enough to get back again. But what could he do? He'd come all this way. Popovic would be on Capri. He couldn't just go home now.

"Okay, okay." He handed over the note. He walked away with a one-way ticket, not many Euros and six hours to wait. His stomach won the battle and he went back to the cafe. He spent most of his Euros on two rice balls, and ate them in no time. He filled his water bottle at the cafe and found a bench outside to sit and wait.

All those people at the port, all going to Capri. And the price of the ticket! Wow. This island must be quite some place.

Chapter 17

It was always busy on the front desk, but the day before the show, things got crazy-busy. Adel was on check-in with two others and Nico was still hovering, ready with handshakes and offers of seating and refreshments, desperate to avoid the faux pas of keeping a person of high net worth waiting. High net worth equalled high self-worth, it seemed to Adel. It was sad, maybe even desperate, that a good opinion had to be bought, even one's opinion of oneself.

The first thirty seconds, Nico would say. The impression they get as soon as they step through the threshold, that's the most important moment of their stay. That's when you start weaving your spell. Nico had it all organised, a polisher over the floor every hour, the windows cleaned daily, inside and out. He'd pick withered leaves out of the floral displays and stand outside filling his lungs with the scented air that blew out, giving guests a sense of the rarefied experience they were about to have even before they came inside. What indulgent nonsense it all was.

Adel had only been here a month, but he'd worked hotels before and already knew the front desk system. And besides, they were understaffed. So they took him on, and after a brief but thorough induction he'd made himself useful straight away. He'd become familiar with the inner workings of the place: the concierge and front-of-house staff; housekeeping, the maids, the supplies and laundry; facilities, the pool, gym, spa, fitness rooms and treatment centre; the kitchens, those famous Michelin-starred chefs and their mean tempers, the juniors hanging around all night for 3 a.m. room service; the waiting and bar staff; and events, where all of the above came together chaotically to deliver good times in smooth and elegant style.

But this event, this one that was only a day away now, this was on a different scale. The stock that was being ordered, the gear coming in, the extra staff being purloined from goodness knows where. Still it wasn't enough: they were running low on stock but no one had time to go and fetch more. And the rates! In the hotel trade, you never achieved rack. But Nico had just trebled the rack rate, and still they were selling! The event seated twice as many as the hotel's room capacity, and that was full now too. Many of them would be staying on their yachts, he was told. A lot of people really didn't want to miss this show. So much money for a meal and some schmoozing! It should be criminal.

Not everyone coming in was super-rich, he was discovering as the new arrivals flowed in. By the time they reached the desk he had them pegged. If they were older, dressed conservatively, and barely glanced around as they approached amid a gaggle of deference, they were a paying guest. But some were younger and more diverse in all senses: clothing, jewellery, hair colour, skin colour. "Wow!" they would say as they stepped in, clocking the breath-taking floor-to-ceiling views, the classical sculptures and the soft décor, cooling yet luxurious. These, he quickly realised, were the designers, specially selected and invited here for the freebie of their lives and not really understanding why. They and their retinue were similar to the models, who, in Adel's view, were nothing special to look at but conformed to a certain normality and had no obvious blemishes or distinguishing features: perfect averages from around the world. All these folk had tabs relating to an account set up by Nico; everything would be paid for.

Adel had been working for four hours and was about to go on a break when a punter approached who didn't quite fit. He was young but in a quality silk suit (jacket slung over the shoulder) that shouted old school. A designer shirt, sky blue, and undone at the collar, trainers (branded nonetheless) and fine blond hair that stuck out in clumps as though he'd just rolled out of bed, he raced up to the desk with an excited smile, as though he'd come in to share a private joke with Adel and couldn't wait to tell him.

"You must be knackered behind there!" He slapped down a British passport. "Can't believe this heat! Way hotter than last year. I'm glad I saw your buggy at the harbour or I'd have expired on the steps! It's like a pilgrimage getting here. Every time. All part of the charm, I suppose."

"We do provide a transfer from Naples Airport, sir." Adel keyed in the first three letters of the surname. Zella, Raphael was booked into a suite for five nights at full price. Raphael put his palms on the desk and leaned on them. His shirt was the kind that needed cuff links but one of them was missing.

"I had to stop off on the way. An old friend." A knowing look, as though they shared a secret. He smelled of alcohol. Adel glanced up, looking for the man's entourage. There was none.

Raphael caught his look. "Yes, ah, my luggage, I managed to leave that at the last place. Long story. Involving a woman. It's on the way. Champagne breakfasts really mess your head up, don't they?"

Adel didn't reply. He tapped into more records. The guy's booking wasn't part of the group account and there was no credit card either.

"Problem?" Raphael had noticed his frown.

Adel smiled professionally. "May I take a credit card, please, sir?"

"Ah. Well, here's the thing. That stopover I was talking about. Also managed to leave my wallet, didn't I? It'll be here in a few hours, but – sorry. Is that a real pain? It drives my father nuts when I do stuff like this."

"I'm afraid we need to pre-authorise the card, sir. It's the same for all guests."

"Oh, of course! Totally understandable. It's just that I'm in a bit of a bind here. For the next few hours, anyway. I was really hoping to freshen up, you know?" He perked up. "There's a credit card on the booking, isn't there? Can't you just use that?"

"It doesn't seem to be there, sir. I don't know why, but—"

"Well, I definitely gave one. Must be some problem with the system. It should be on there."

Adel checked again. "I'm sorry, sir. You don't happen to know the number, do you?"

"No, I don't! Do you know how many of the things I've got?" He leaned in and lowered his voice. "Look, I don't want to be crass or anything, but you do recognise the name, don't you? Zella?"

Adel looked blank. "I do apologise—"

"Seriously? You work here and you've never heard of Frank Zella?" He laughed, as if he felt sorry for him. "Look. I don't want to be the one to tell your boss you've never heard of my pa. Let's just sort out the check-in later, okay? It's only a few hours." He tapped his fingers on the desk. Two people were now standing waiting to check in. Nico was nowhere to be seen.

Adel stuck to his guns. "We just need some authorisation for the room before I can check you in."

The end of Raphael's nose was turning pink. "Seriously? Look, I can call him if you want. He'll probably blow a gasket. It might get a bit embarrassing. For you, I mean. Listen, something's obviously gone wrong somewhere. I'll come back down later and we'll sort it all out? My stuff will be here by then. That way I don't have to trouble him. I mean, he's come here every year since whenever but he might decide to go elsewhere if—"

"Problem?" Fairchild had come up behind Raphael and leaned against the desk. The young man turned and took in Fairchild's watch, ring, shirt, jacket, and general air of authority.

"Mr Zella is unable to supply a credit card," Adel said.

"For about the next two hours." Raphael addressed Fairchild directly. "As we speak, it's probably on its way over here in a speedboat. Along with my wallet and all my luggage."

Fairchild raised his eyebrows. "From where?"

"Sorrento. Well – just south of there. She told me the name of the place but I've forgotten. Listen, my father's—"

"Yes. I heard."

"I kind of need to freshen up. I have plans, you know. I'll come down later when my stuff's arrived. If I don't, you can always throw me out, can't you?"

They looked at each other. Raphael had the suggestion of a smile on his face. Fairchild didn't.

"Or I could call my dad," the young man added.

Fairchild glanced at the queue and shook his head almost imperceptibly. "Check him in," he said to Adel.

Adel hesitated.

"I'll square it with Nico," said Fairchild. "Just do it."

"Awfully grateful," said Raphael. Fairchild moved away and crossed the lobby. Raphael watched him and turned back to Adel. "He's the boss?"

Adel handed him his key card and paperwork. "The owner, yes."

Fairchild had paused, in conversation with another guest, a woman. Their voices drifted over.

"He speaks Italian?" asked Raphael.

"He speaks a lot of languages." Adel could only just manage to be civil. There were still two people waiting. "Enjoy your stay."

"Sure!" Raphael seemed embarrassed. "Look, I'm sorry about all that. You were only doing your job. I'll be back down later and we'll get it all straight."

Adel gave a respectful nod. "Of course." He turned to the next in line.

Raphael walked towards the lifts. Adel saw him glance several times at Fairchild as he went past.

Chapter 18

The VIP helicopter landed late afternoon, in time for Capri's after-dark scene, but light enough for all kinds of people to get a good look at them. Rose, her security detail and her luggage filled the copter's leather-seated interior. The flight from Naples took only a few minutes. Descending to the heliport at Ana Capri, she looked down past her newly browned legs and pedicured toes to the rocky coastline below. Dotted with sleek white craft, the deep-blue water glinted with the occasional dinghy or bunch of swimmers. What a life, taking a dip off one's yacht and floating around gazing up at such dramatic beauty. A clifftop viewpoint was crowded with tourists baking in the sun, peering at the bay far below. They looked up as the copter roared overhead, staring enraptured, hands out shielding their faces from the sun, or holding up phones. A glimpse into another life, for them. For the first time, Rose felt some insight into why people did desperate things for money.

The heliport deck radiated heat like a griddle, and the updraught made her light-but-expensive skirt billow up around her hips. She held it down and stepped onto the pad, leaving her bags behind for others to carry, in this case Sarah and one of the butch males who'd been roped in to hang around looking tough. At the edge of the pad an SUV with tinted windows was already waiting. Rose heard Sarah catch up with her.

"This heat is unbe*liev*able!" It was her best Julia Michalaedes voice: deep, vaguely accented, each syllable over-emphasised as if every comment she made were of profound spiritual significance. The pilot and crew were somewhere behind her within hearing distance along with some maintenance staff, though she didn't turn round to check. She was starting to feel Rose receding and Julia coming to the fore.

Sarah looked pink and was blinking in the sun. "Car's over there."

Rose stalked over as if all this were a huge pain in the neck. The door opened automatically and she climbed in, fiddling with her phone looking bored as her crew messed around with her baggage, all designer brands of course. She glanced up as they set off, and tutted. "I'm late for my call."

Sarah looked across blandly. "We'll be there in a few minutes. This whole island is about four miles across."

Julia was unimpressed. There was no call, but it was a reason to be sulking. And to cover how jumpy she felt. There'd be a VIP welcome at the hotel. After weeks of gestation, Michalaedes was about to break out of her pupa and enter the real world. Everyone would be looking, everyone would be curious. At least they would be if Fairchild had done his job. And would Fairchild be there? Hopefully not: it would be easier without. The thought of it made her pulse tick up.

The driver spoke and they made a sharp turn into a driveway between two white pillars. First impression: white walls bright in the sun, purple flowers in pots, decking stretching out of sight, the blue of a pool somewhere behind. They stopped alongside steps. Someone in uniform was opening her door. She used a practised technique to get out of the car, keeping her knees together and her dignity intact. Bloody dresses. She ignored the uniform. A man was hurrying down the steps towards her – black double-breasted jacket, waistcoat, neat hair.

"Ms Michalaedes!" He held out a hand and introduced himself as Nico something-or-other. "General Manager. A very warm welcome to Capri, and to the Hotel Villa Bianca Rosaria!"

She granted him a smile. Did he know? Everyone in this hotel would fall into two camps, those who knew and those who didn't. But she had to put that guessing game aside: she was on display all the time here. A light pressure on the elbow and Nico, General Manager, was guiding her inside through a set of sliding glass doors. As they passed, the air filled with a bewitching scent of roses, cinnamon, bergamot, something else. She allowed Julia some appreciation of the elegance and of the vista, but only to be polite to her guide.

"So beautiful!" Her voice found new depths of sincerity before switching into business mode. "I'm so sorry, I have a call. Can we go straight up? Georg can deal with everything."

"Of course! Allow me." Nico dashed to call the lift.

Rose made sure Julia's voice would carry. "You have my bags? Just the laptop. And that one, yes. I need to change before tonight. It's so hot!"

No one was looking but people heard, she sensed: a group seated near the door, a couple of waiting staff, an unimpressed young Asian on the check-in desk. She clicked her way to the lift, amazed her heels had any traction at all on the shiny floor, and didn't look back to check the others were following.

"A top-floor suite. Views both ways. The terrace looks straight out onto the coast." Nico was just filling a gap as the lift ascended a mere two floors. Normally Rose would walk up two flights of stairs. But not Julia Michalaedes. And not, to be fair, in these shoes.

Nico used his own pass for the door, but Sarah stepped forward. "I'll go in first." She slipped inside and there was a pause of something that felt like a lot more than a minute. Julia checked her watch and tutted again, as if an employed

92

bodyguard's measures to protect her life were an inconvenience.

Sarah reappeared. "All clear."

Rose walked in and got an impression of space, of white and cream and comfort, wooden decking and balcony rails through an open door, beyond that blue sea and sky. On the walls hung paintings of sails in orange, yellow, red. An orchid graced a pot in the middle of a table, beyond which fluttered a lace curtain. She remembered not to be impressed. "Thank you so much, Nico. Oh – sparkling mineral water?" Almost as if he'd asked her if she wanted a drink. Nico nodded and withdrew. The heavy was just finishing depositing all the luggage inside.

"Georg, thanks so much. You'll be right outside, won't you?" Julia waved him away.

Sarah hovered by the door. "That's not Georg. Georg is in the lobby."

"They're both called Georg."

"Since when?"

"Since I said so. Come in and close the door."

With the door closed the sound in the room was deadened. They passed from reception area to master bedroom complete with dressing room and enormous bathroom, back in and into a second smaller bedroom with twin beds and its own, more modest, bathroom. She looked at Sarah and Sarah looked back.

"Why do you think it took me so long to check the place?" Sarah said.

Rose smiled. She was getting to like Sarah's blunt sense of humour. "Unbe*lie*vable!" she intoned, and sank into an armchair. Someone rapped on the door. Sarah checked the spyhole. It was the mineral water.

"You could have just used the minibar." She passed Rose the drink.

"No *ice*, darling, no *ice*. How am I supposed to go hunting around for ice…" Julia faded away as Rose took a long sip. "Help yourself if you want." She pointed to the mini fridge. Rose's ordinary voice sounded odd to her now.

Another rap on the door. But a different door, not the main door to the room. Sarah went over. No spy hole. She looked around. "No key."

"Just try it."

Sarah did, and it opened to reveal Zack, broad but unthreatening in his best holiday gear.

"Hey! Welcome on board. Quite a place, huh? Still, what do you expect?" He landed with some weight on a sofa and stretched his legs out.

"This is Sarah, my close protection," said Rose.

"Oh, hi." Zack waved a hand.

"Zack is in charge of this whole operation on the ground," Rose said to Sarah, who peered through the open door.

"What's in there?"

"A suite just like this one," said Zack. "Only it's full of people. And gear. That's our HQ. We got the whole top floor. Though these two suites make up most of it. And there's the Blue Room. For the boss." He gave her a knowing look.

Rose tried not to blush. "Is he about?"

"Out networking. Glad-handing. The event organiser wants to meet you. Valentina. Fairchild thinks you should go say hello. You may end up with a speaking part in tomorrow's big event."

"That's a good thing?"

"Sure. The more people see you the better. Assuming you're convincing enough, that is."

"Thanks for the vote of confidence. Is my make-up lady here?"

"Linda? Arrived yesterday. We've set up all her gear in a room next door. I had no idea you ladies needed all that equipment."

"It's a complicated thing, looking someone else's best. What's the security like at this event? They'll be checking bags on the way in?"

"Are you nuts? This is a classy joint, not a budget airline."

"Oh, great. So you want me, posing as a fraudster who's ripped off a load of violent and nasty people, to stand up in front of a few hundred of them and make a speech?"

"There'll be a few security challenges."

"You don't say."

"But nothing we can't handle."

"You seem very sure, Zack."

"I don't think these are the kind of folk who'd walk into a gig like this with a gun under their jacket. Besides, they can afford to pay someone else to take you out if they wanted to."

"That's a great comfort."

Zack shrugged. "We just need to plan for all possibilities. You go down there tonight, do the schmooze, the high-level talk, then leave – er – Susan here—"

"Sarah."

"...Sarah, to sort out all the details. We're screening the guest list, anyway."

"The entire list?"

Zack pursed his lips. "Working on it. We're drafting in a little help."

"Great. Any sign of Al-Hashemi?"

Zack glanced at Sarah.

"She's been cleared," said Rose. "Has he taken the bait?"

"One or two possible associates but no one we recognise. They may want to be sure you're here before he commits. He's only hours away, remember. If he's serious we'd expect him to send his operations guy to check you out first. Name of Kamal. We'd know that charmer if he showed up. Nasty piece of work but very influential. Anyway." He stood up. "Oh, don't worry about bugs in here. Nowhere on the top floor is wired. Boss's orders." He winked. "Feel free to relax."

Rose ignored his suggestiveness. "And when do I have to go see this woman?"

"Next hour or so. She's in the ballroom causing havoc, apparently. You know what the event actually is, right?"

"More or less."

There was another knock at the door. Zack dropped his voice. "You expecting anyone?" Rose shook her head.

Sarah peered through the spy hole. "It's a maid."

"Ask her what she wants," said Rose.

Sarah opened the door a crack then closed it again. "Turn down service."

"Clear off, Zack," said Rose.

Zack obligingly disappeared.

"Let her in."

Sarah did. The maid got straight to work. She half-drew the curtains and switched on the table lamp and found a TV channel playing restful running water sounds. In the bedrooms she folded back the bedspreads and turned the corner of the sheet over to make a triangle, removed cushions and plumped up the pillows, sprayed a tiny amount of lavender scent on each one, put slippers on the floor, got dressing gowns out and draped them on the bed ready for use, filled a carafe of water and placed it on each bedside table next to eye patches and ear plugs, then placed a single chocolate on each pillow, and finally retreated. Sarah stood watching. Rose lay back in the armchair and checked her phone. Eventually the maid nodded a quick goodbye.

"Give her a tip, darling." It was Julia talking.

Sarah patted her pockets. "I don't have any money."

"Then ask Georg."

Sarah popped out. It sounded like Georg was amenable to parting with cash. Sarah returned and closed the door.

"Have you never experienced a turn down service before?" asked Rose.

"I'm used to barracks."

"It's an important mark of luxury. I mean, who could expect the wealthy to unfold their own dressing gown of an evening?"

"I never realised there was so much to going to bed. I've just been undressing and getting in."

"That's where you've been going wrong. The best part is the chocolate on the pillow. I'll have mine now, please. You should have one too."

"This is where I'm sleeping?"

"Sure, in the kiddies' room. That's okay, right?"

Sarah gave her an amused look and fetched the pillow chocolates. They turned out to be dark truffles with a creamy filling.

"Mmm. Good. Well…" Rose got up. "Time to freshen up and go see this woman. If I'm not back in an hour, I may have got lost in the bathroom." She pulled her wheely into the master bedroom.

"You want me to do anything?" Sarah looked lost. She often seemed that way when she had nothing specific to do.

Rose put on her Julia voice. "Find me some more of those chocolates, darling."

Chapter 19

Her bodyguard by her side and the two Georgs front and behind, Julia Michalaedes strode through the lobby, a gold satin evening dress turning a few heads on the way. Rose disliked this kind of attention, but Popovic wouldn't mind. She'd like it, though it was dangerous. She'd changed her name, her face, her hair colour, but still there must be tell-tale signs, those people who knew her well. I mean, my God, millions of people knew Ulia Popovic! All those talks, those motivational presentations all over the world, the videos with millions of views, all those people wondering for all this time where she was, angry at her, angry at the marketers, the friends, the relatives who talked up the coin, took her words – her, Popovic! – and turned them into some kind of religion. Or did *she* do that? Did she know it would get so big she'd end up in hiding somewhere? And now here she was, trying to get another bite of the cherry, changing a few things here and there, and coming back for more. Would she love this, or hate it? Or both?

Nothing new about any of this. Plenty of chancers had made themselves scarce when their name became too hot and set up again elsewhere with a new one. But this, it was the scale of it! New World was global, its reach enormous, the sums massive. Would she really think she could get away with it? As Julia walked, feeling the eyes on her, she shuddered a little and narrowed her eyes, almost as though she wanted to stop right there and go back. But instead she took a breath, pulled her shoulders back, lifted her chin and carried on. By her side, the ever-silent, ever-watchful Sarah observed all of this.

Valentina Maria was instantly identifiable from her position of authority in the ballroom. The room was a mess of crates spilling glittering decorations, stacked chairs, bare round wooden tables, power cables, and a half-built lighting scaffold. Above it all hung a giant shimmering globe which at that time was rocking slightly from side to side, causing some alarm below. Valentina stood, arms folded, giving instructions. Tired and harassed, sleeves rolled up, her hair carelessly tied in a pony tail, somehow she still looked like a film star. Would Popovic be envious of that?

As soon as Valentina saw her she smiled and came over. How did she know? Was it clear just from the bling and the bodyguards? Did Fairchild describe her? Or did she see someone who looked a bit like Popovic and go from there? Julia Michalaedes ignored the chaos and glided into the middle of the room. Through the open arches, darkness stretched away under a faint moon, and tiny lights glowed over on the mainland. It was dramatic, but there was no time for that. Valentina came forward with hand outstretched.

"You must be Julia! I can't thank you enough for this. What you're doing is amazing! I only hope it's what you want."

Rose steadied herself for some serious gushing. "Oh, but it will be. Fairchild told me so much about you, I knew you were the right person to do this. And – wow! I mean, amazing!" She gestured with wonder at the frosted globe. "It just says, exactly, what the foundation is all about! Bringing us all together in peace and understanding. And it's all about young people, I mean, for me, anyway," – she pressed her palm to her heart – "because they're the future, and you have to give back, you know, you have to reach out to help those coming up, just like others did to you." Valentina was nodding energetically but couldn't get a word in. "It's the –

I don't know, the life force, with the young, I just find it so inspiring, it fills me with energy and hope and joy, I get so much out of doing this that really, you know, it doesn't feel like charity at all." *Sha*rity.

Valentina looked as though she was going to melt. "Let me talk you through the whole thing." And she did, in fine detail, pointing to the various parts of the room. Sarah started out silent but she got over it and asked a couple of intelligent questions. Julia looked at her fondly.

"She looks after me, this one." Valentina smiled. She didn't seem sure what Julia meant. Maybe she didn't know. Stop it, Rose.

"And you must say a few words." Valentina grabbed Julia's upper arm to emphasise the point. "You absolutely must! Between the show and the bidding. Remind people why they're here. What this is all about. Get them ready to open their wallets! You can do that, can't you?" She turned to Sarah for support. Sarah grimaced.

Julia put her hand on her heart again. "Oh, but…perhaps towards the end, as you say? After the banquet, a quick tour of the room, say hello and then a few words? It wouldn't do any harm, would it?" She turned to Sarah as if asking for permission.

Sarah put on a reluctant face. "It won't be easy." There was a pause. Both women were looking at her. She backed down. "I'm sure we can work something out."

Valentina clapped her hands together. "Oh, that's so good!"

"But I'll need to go through the security arrangements with you." Sarah gazed sternly at her.

Valentina's hands flew up. "Of course, of course! Come back later tonight, tomorrow, we'll sort everything out. Oh, this will be such a night!"

Sarah waited until they'd gone up in the lift and were back in the suite with the door closed and the Georgs outside before saying, "That was very good."

"Very good yourself," said Rose. "Oh, and look at this!" She segued into Julia. "So many, and so romantic!" Housekeeping had left an entire basket of pillow chocolates, so many that they flooded out onto the table in a cascade, and next to them a single red rose.

"I didn't ask for a rose," said Sarah.

"They like their flowers," said Rose, but she wondered if it held a double meaning.

"I think I should check that these chocolates are safe for you to eat. As your close protection officer." Sarah stepped forward, unwrapped one and put it in her mouth. "Absolutely fine," she said eventually.

"Well, that's a relief." Rose popped one too and got another one ready, slipping back into Julia. "Mmmm. So delicious. But so many! What can I do?" She polished off the second one.

"You know, I think you've already put on the required weight for the role. I mean, at this stage you probably don't need to—"

"Shut up." Rose picked up a handful and threw them at her bodyguard. Sarah laughed, for real. For the first time. "Leave me!" Julia ordered. "Leave me, darling!" She picked up the basket and took it into the master bedroom. "Go and talk to Valentina. Make sure I don't get shot. I need to be alone."

She threw another handful out before closing the door. On the other side Sarah was still laughing.

Chapter 20

Erik gazed up at the island of Capri as the ferry approached. It was bigger than he expected. How was he supposed to find one person on that? Well, he'd manage it somehow. Once he'd spoken to Ulia Popovic everything would be fine. Even his lack of cash. After all, he had loads of New World Coin still to spend. He only needed to get hold of it. She'd help, of course she would. She talked on the internet about wanting everyone in the world to have better access to money. Here was her chance to put that into practice. And if she proved unwilling? Then Erik had to persuade her otherwise. Dennis always said you need to give people the reasons. That was Erik's task here. But first he needed to find her.

He changed into his running flats, putting his trainers into his string bag. He ran from the main harbour over the top to the little one at the back. Then he ran up into the north east corner, then back and out again to the south west. Maybe the place wasn't so big. Plenty of hills but he was used to that. He got some pretty weird looks in the middle bit with the clock tower, and all the groups stopped and stared as he ran past, but most of the little alleys were quiet, and he padded along nicely.

But where were all the hotels? It took him ages to recognise them. Most seemed like normal houses and you had to hunt around for a sign or something. And when he went in and asked about Popovic, the staff weren't too helpful. They looked at him strangely and didn't seem to have heard of her, or else didn't want to tell him anything. He would explain that he was a part of the New World Coin family and would be happy to come back later at Ulia

Popovic's convenience, or leave a message, though he couldn't leave a phone number because his phone didn't work abroad. Sometimes he tried doing the New World sign in the air. But that didn't seem to get him anywhere.

He spent hours trailing around. The heat made him tired, so he found a garden with some shade and went to sleep for a while. After that he got up and continued his search. It started getting dark. There were water fountains all around but his body started pining for ugali again. What to do? He only had a few coins. He decided to go back and sleep some more, think again in the morning. Something would show up.

As he jogged along trying to work out the quickest way back to the garden, he noticed a driveway with two white columns. He must have been past it already but it turned back on itself and he hadn't noticed it. He spotted some writing, pretty small, on a bronze plaque by the gate. Villa Bianca Rosaria. What was that? Well, he was passing so he may as well try.

He walked in and felt the cool tiled floor through his thin soles. This was a smart place – lots of people around and a big desk along one wall, and behind that a guy in a uniform who wasn't white, but wasn't black either. The guy watched Erik approach.

"Hey, my friend, is this a hotel?" Erik's voice sounded kind of loud and a few heads turned to look.

The man frowned. His name badge said Adel. "Yes, this is a hotel."

"Only, there's no sign outside that says hotel. It's like that everywhere. What a weird place! How do people know?" He was chattering. Maybe he was more tired than he realised.

Adel looked amused now. "I suppose you're right. Are you looking for a room?"

That made Erik laugh. He held his hands up. "I'd love a room. But I don't have any money, man!"

For some reason that made Adel grin from ear to ear. "That must be a problem."

"Ah, for a while I guess. Listen! I'm looking for Popovic. Ulia Popovic. You know?" Adel's grin vanished but he said nothing. Erik tried the New World air-sign. Adel didn't seem to recognise it. Maybe Erik didn't have it exactly right. He should have practised it in a mirror. "The New World Coin lady. You know New World Coin?"

Adel did a little look around to see if anyone else was listening. Then he came closer and lowered his voice. "What makes you think she's here?"

"Oh, I don't know if she's here in this place or not! But I've tried everywhere else I could see." He tried to keep his tone light. Maybe he was onto something here.

"And what makes you think she's on Capri?"

"My friend Dennis. He heard a rumour. In Nairobi. He has friends in business. He heard she was coming back and said it meant they were launching the coin at last. After all the delays and everything! And – well…" Erik was sharing too much, maybe, but this guy was looking at him very intensely, and not in a bad way. Adel wasn't much older than Erik. In fact, he may even be younger. "I kind of need some of the cash now. For my mother, you know. So she can buy her cow back."

The man's eyes widened. "Your mother sold a cow to buy New World Coin?"

"Yes, but when the value goes up she can buy twenty cows! It's a great investment!" It sounded strange to Erik talking about cows in a place like this. Adel looked thoughtful.

"So she's here, then?" asked Erik.

105

He shook his head. "All I can do is ask around. Where are you staying?"

Erik raised his hands again. "I've got no money, man! But it doesn't matter. I can come back in the morning."

"You're sleeping out somewhere?" It wasn't a sneer, just a simple question.

"Yeah, but it's fine. I found a garden with these low-down arches. Plenty of shade and cover. It's fine."

"I know that place. It's on the other side of the island."

"Sure! Up in that corner." Erik pointed. "It's the best place I found."

"You've been all over the island?" Adel leaned over the desk and saw Erik's shoes.

"I'm a runner. I train every day back home. So I'm running everywhere here. Why not? I'm from Kenya. It's pretty hot. And we have mountains. So it's no big deal."

Adel looked like he was thinking very hard. "Can you carry stuff?"

"What stuff?"

"Boxes, crates, heavy things. Or pull a trolley."

"Sure, I guess so."

"What's your name?"

"Erik."

"Have you had anything to eat, Erik?"

"No, man."

"Do you want something to eat?"

"Sure!"

He raised a finger. "Wait a moment." He went over and talked to someone else, who gave him a bit of paper. He got a business card and a stapler and stapled the paper to the card. He came back and passed it to Erik.

"If you take this to the Mermaid Hotel and bring what they give you, when you get back I'll find you something to eat."

"The Mermaid Hotel?"

"On the other side of the Marina Grande. Did you see the building at the top of the steps with the flags?" Adel described where the place was. Erik had been all around there but didn't see any Mermaid Hotel.

"What's in the boxes?" he asked.

"Bitter lemon."

"Huh?"

"It's a mixer. A drink. We're running low. It's very important." He was smiling a little. "You bring it back straight away, you get a meal. How does that sound?"

Erik's spirits lifted as he ran, and he put on a spurt up the steps to the main square. He knew something would turn up. Did Adel know anything about New World Coin and Ulia Popovic? He didn't say so, but Erik thought he did. Either way, Adel was clearly a man who knew the value of a cow. Round here, that had to count for something.

Chapter 21

It was past midnight, but the Rosaria was in no mood for sleep. Restless and simmering, perhaps she anticipated the upcoming event. Her lounge bar hummed like a live wire. Fairchild settled with a whisky and the *Financial Times* in an armchair with his back to the windows: he'd had enough of staring down cliffs for one day.

Nico stopped by with an update. They were full and the yield was sky-high, though they barely had the staff to meet their clientele's stringent demands. Valentina was causing more havoc in the ballroom. More chairs! More lighting! Where were they supposed to get those at a moment's notice? Complaining aside, things seemed to be going to plan. All they could do now was wait and see if their offer was attractive enough, the rumours sufficiently widely dispersed. Nico departed, grumbling. Fairchild scanned the headlines without much real interest.

"Gilts looking to devalue, you think?"

He looked up. It was the young guy who was checking in the other day. He spoke with a crystal glass British accent. Fairchild had noticed that before – he used to speak like that himself until years of self-imposed exile rubbed the edges off it. The man nodded towards the FT headline.

"I don't have a view on it," said Fairchild.

"You're not exposed there, then?"

"Isn't it a bit rude to ask?"

"I suppose it is," he said cheerily. "Mind if I join you?" He had a glass of what looked like whisky. Fairchild signalled permission. The guy sat, and held out a hand. "We weren't properly introduced before. Raphael Zella. People just call me Raffa."

"John Fairchild," he said, though it was clear Raffa already knew who he was. They shook.

"I was told this was your place." Raffa looked around appreciatively. "Nice piece of real estate."

"I have an interest in the holding company."

"And they run a number of top-range properties up and down the country." Raffa had done some homework. "Nice business to be in."

"Can be risky. In times of economic downturn—"

"Not if you're high enough up the food chain. Those who can afford places like this, they'll be okay whatever's going on further down." Pretty much what Valentina Maria had said.

"Personal experience?"

"I thought it was rude to ask."

That made Fairchild smile.

"I have a portfolio," conceded Raffa. He looked too young to be living off an investment fund. But there was no age bar to these things. Fairchild was actively managing his assets from his early twenties.

"For what purpose?"

Raffa frowned. "Purpose? Never thought about it. So that I can stay in places like this, I guess."

"And get invited to villas just south of Sorrento?"

He grinned. "What can I say? I like this life."

"There's no more to it?"

"Like what?"

"Those shares you trade in. Do you ever think of the people behind them? The bosses, the workers, trying very hard to make something out of nothing?"

Raffa looked thoughtful for a moment, then shrugged. "Money markets are for making money." He knocked back his whisky. It wasn't his first of the evening. His eyes were red and he needed a shave.

"Isn't it your father's money?"

A look of annoyance crossed Raffa's face, then dissipated. "You're entirely self-made, are you?"

"No, I inherited a trust fund. But then I don't brag."

Raffa might have looked slightly chastened but it didn't last. "Maybe I'll develop such sensibilities later in life." There was humour in his eyes.

Fairchild laughed. "Also, I pay my bills when they're due. That credit card showed up, did it?"

"It did indeed. I'll sort it out, don't worry." He looked around. "Seems busy. This show tomorrow is causing quite a stir. Some interesting people expected to come along."

"I'm sure. My table's fully booked, I'm afraid. I'm not sure if there are any—"

"Oh, I've already got tickets." He waved a hand. "A few friends are coming. More young entrepreneurs with no sense of responsibility. They're fun at a party, though. It should be lively. And lucrative, I expect." His eyebrows waggled as though they shared a private joke.

"It's for charity, you know."

"Of course! That's what I meant." Now he was all innocence.

"I look forward to seeing you there." He folded up his newspaper. Raffa took the hint.

"Good to meet you, John. Don't stay up too late. You need your sleep."

Fairchild feigned a stern look as he stood. Raffa sauntered away, giving the front desk a wide berth.

Chapter 22

On his way up to the Blue Room, Fairchild stopped outside the door to the suite. He thought about it for a moment. Then he raised his hand and knocked.

Footsteps. Silence. He gazed into the spy hole. The door opened. It was the bodyguard. She was young as well. He hoped she wasn't going to make jokes about his age. She stood aside.

"Sarah, is it?"

"I'm hoping it's a good thing that you know that."

"You know who I am, then?"

"I certainly do." She closed the door. A woman who looked a little like Rose was sitting on a couch with her feet resting on a stool. She wore baggy clothes but a pair of sandals that were mainly heels lay discarded on the floor next to her, along with a number of sweet wrappers. He stepped forward, fascinated by the shape of her face.

"Get a closer look, darling, maybe shine a torch or something, yes?" Her voice was deep and dark, some implied accent underneath. She'd studied to get that. She patted the sofa next to her but he'd already reached to get a chair. It was always strange to start with, when they met. They didn't see each other often enough for the familiarity to carry over. But this was even stranger.

Sarah was loitering by the door. "I take it you'll be all right?"

She and Rose exchanged some look. They'd been talking about him. "Get your beauty sleep, darling," was the response. Sarah obligingly disappeared.

"She's sleeping in here?" asked Fairchild.

"She won't come out. It's more than her job's worth." At least Rose's voice was back.

"You seem to be getting on all right."

"Do we?" She sounded tired now. Her lips were large and painted a dark red. Dark mascara on the eyes. Even her eyes were a different colour, a light brown. The hair didn't quite match. Maybe that was the point.

"You look—"

"Don't. I feel trussed up like a chicken."

He reached out to touch her lip but she pulled back. "Botox. You wouldn't believe the effort it takes to get me looking like this."

"I preferred the before version." He looked at her body, the way her flesh folded, a cleavage deeper than whatever was there before. Part of him yearned to undress her. Another part didn't want to know what was under there.

She followed his eyes. "I'm fat, Fairchild. Walter made me fat."

"I wouldn't say fat, exactly. You're maybe a little…"

"Big? That's what I mean. And now I can't stop eating." She looked pained. "I don't like this. Not the dressing up. You know what I mean."

Fairchild sat back in the chair. "Me too."

That surprised her. "Really?"

He examined his hands. "Maybe we're getting old. Or I'm getting old, anyway."

She didn't argue with him. When he looked up her eyes were on him, those eyes that had moved him so often, shamed him sometimes. But now they were the wrong colour. He stood up suddenly.

She took an intake of breath. But she got it. "It's too weird, isn't it?"

He reached out and took a strand of her hair between his fingers. Even that felt different.

"It'll soon be over." Now she was comforting him. He thought it would be the other way round. He looked across at the adjoining door. She noticed.

"I locked it. From this side. But yes, the whole team is right on the other side of it. Big day tomorrow." She said it gently. "And I still need to get this makeup off. That'll take at least an hour." She held out her hand. "Help me up, darling." In her deep voice. He did, and found himself standing very close to Julia Michalaedes, charity foundation owner and possible fraudster.

"You even smell different," he said.

"They're very thorough." She was business-like now. "Off you go, then." He made for the door. "Oh, did you send this?" She'd picked up a red rose from the side table.

"Oh, no. That's a thing they do here when they deliver anything to the room. The name of the hotel. Rosaria?" That deflated her. It really was awkward. "Well, until next time, Ms Michalaedes." He gave a small bow as though he were her footman. She waved him away graciously. They seemed to manage things better in character. What did that say about them? He left, resolving to give the matter no further thought.

Chapter 23

Erik materialised as soon as Adel arrived on shift the next morning. Adel didn't ask where he'd slept. He'd returned the previous evening balancing the box of bitter lemon bottles on his shoulder. Adel had given him a bag of leftovers from the kitchen and told him to come back the next day. He would have come back anyway, Adel reasoned, so they may as well make use of him.

The others on the front desk were smirking at this skinny black guy with his worn out shoes and his string bag. Adel ignored them. They were short-staffed and he was problem-solving. Nico didn't need to know exactly how.

He beckoned Erik outside and took him round to where the buggies were parked. A guy was standing by one of them finishing a cigarette.

"I've got you some help," Adel said to him.

"Help how?"

"Loading." He nodded towards the Kenyan.

The driver looked him up and down. "Sure." He wandered round to the driver's side.

"Loading what?" asked Erik.

"Chairs."

"Chairs?"

"They're coming in on the ferry. We need to stack them and get them up the hill. You can ride with him. That okay? There's breakfast waiting when you get back."

Erik shrugged in an easy-going way but then he frowned. "Are these for the event? The show? It's tonight, isn't it? I heard some people talking about it in the lobby. This is the thing she's coming to, isn't it?" There was excitement in his voice.

"No," Adel lied, wondering if he was making a mistake with this guy. "The chairs are for something else. But it's up to you. You can help, or not."

Erik shrugged again. "Whatever." The driver was manoeuvring the buggy out. Erik ducked into the passenger seat, only just getting his lanky figure inside. He banged the roof with his hand, grinning. "Let's go, man, let's go!"

The driver shook his head, smiling. Adel watched them drive off and realised he was grinning too. He shrugged himself as he went back inside.

Mistake? Whatever.

Chapter 24

When Adel got back to the desk, there was a message to call the Blue Room. He went up and knocked on the door. Fairchild let him in. Adel sat without a word.

"Coffee?" said Fairchild. There were breakfast things on the table. Adel shook his head. Fairchild poured one for himself and sat. "So?" he asked.

Adel shrugged. "What?"

"How are things going? Anything to report?"

"Nothing unusual."

Fairchild waited. His grey eyes showed no expression besides a general expectation. This man probably read him better than anyone else who knew him, including family.

"It's not your kind of gig, I suppose," Fairchild said eventually. "But I did explain what all this was for, didn't I?"

"I haven't seen anything that looks like an Islamic State terrorist show up and make threats."

"Were you expecting to? I asked about anything unusual. Out of the ordinary. Not part of the plan."

"The whole set-up is unusual. This whole hotel is a stage! A piece of theatre to make rich people feel important. So what if this guy shows up? Maybe he's got a point."

Fairchild took a sip and considered. He looked so tame sitting there. The first time Adel set eyes on the man was in a jungle in the southern Philippines. It was a harsh place but things were simple then, at least for a time. The world had hard edges. You knew where you were. Now everything was soft.

"You want to be a soldier again?" There he was, reading him like a book.

"I want to do the right thing. Why is it so difficult?"

"You are doing the right thing. We're setting a trap for someone who supplies money to terrorist groups. Like the one you used to serve. Have you changed your mind about that?"

Adel flinched. He knew now that jihad wasn't the answer, or at least the kind of jihad he'd been recruited into. But he was still angry at the world.

"There may be no black and white," said Fairchild, "but there's better and worse. Taking this man and his money out of play will make the world better. Safer."

Adel decided to speak his mind. He had little to lose. "But why do it like this? Why are we all here, posing and playing on this silly little rock of an island? There must be easier ways."

Fairchild looked tired suddenly. "You're right. All I can say is that I didn't devise this whole scheme. I only have a certain influence. I wouldn't have done it like this. But it was going to happen anyway. And it will work. Trust me."

He smiled. So did Adel. Fairchild had made his views known before about people who feel the need to ask for your trust. Adel had made himself useful to Fairchild in various roles. Until now he hadn't felt the need to ask too much about what it was all for. Fairchild had helped him extricate himself from the jihadists and had given him new horizons, further away from home than he'd ever imagined. But lately he'd started to question the man more. He found himself less inclined to follow orders and take things on trust. In that sense he wanted to be less of a soldier, not more.

"What did you make of Raphael?" asked Fairchild.

"Raphael Zella? The English guy?" Adel paused. Fairchild had taken to the guy. Should Adel show some tact to avoid offence? He decided against it. "He's all talk. Making out he's rich to blag his way into places like this."

"So his credit card never materialised?"

"No, and he's putting everything on his room tab. He's racking up a huge bill which he's got no intention of paying. And you're letting him."

Fairchild raised his eyebrows. "You spoke to Nico, then."

"Yes. And he said to leave it alone. He'd never do that normally."

"You think it came from me?"

"Didn't it?"

Fairchild looked amused. "There's a list, isn't there, that the hotels share? A blacklist, people who automatically get turned away at the front desk. Is Raffa on that list?"

Raffa, was it? "No."

"So this is entirely gut feel?"

"No, it's entirely that he hasn't produced a credit card. I don't know why you're cutting him so much slack."

"This isn't business as usual right now. He may have his uses. So do as Nico says and keep overlooking him. It's not as if it's your money anyway."

"Have his uses?"

"Yes. And besides, people get things wrong when they're young, don't they? Take the wrong path? Make poor decisions?"

Was he comparing this Raffa guy with Adel himself? It was hardly the same thing, Adel was going to say – but didn't.

"And who's your friend?" Fairchild asked.

How on earth did he know about that? "Erik?"

"The tall guy who runs everywhere and appears to be sleeping rough."

"He's from Kenya. I got him on some errands, fetching stuff. We're short-staffed."

"But what's he doing here?"

Adel sighed. "He's an investor. He lost money in the scam. He wants to meet the woman."

"And you weren't going to mention that? You're meant to be eyes and ears, Adel. Anything unusual."

"He's harmless. He's just a guy who lost more than he can afford and wants to get it back."

"And how exactly is he intending to do that?"

"He doesn't think New World Coin is a scam. He thinks it's real and when Popovic is back in the limelight it will launch, and he'll be able to cash in."

"Really?"

"Well, those were the rumours, weren't they? He trusted people. I suppose that makes him an idiot."

"If he thinks the launch is imminent, why has he come here to find her? He can sit at home and cash in, if that's all he wants."

Adel had been asking himself that. "I think he's in two places. He's telling himself New World Coin is legitimate but he also suspects that it's not. Or else he doesn't trust the middlemen who sold him the package. He wants to be sure he can get his money out, and he thinks Popovic is going to help. The stakes are pretty high back home."

"For him to come here with nothing, I should say so. Which might make him pretty desperate."

"He won't do anything foolish. He's exactly what he appears to be." And that, in this festering pool of artifice and posturing and flattery, was exactly why Adel liked Erik so much.

"So you're trusting your gut feel?"

"Why not? You do."

"True. But he's practically the only person in the place who hasn't had a background check. That's quite a risk."

"He's fine." Adel knew he was overstating, being defensive. Fed up of doing what he was told.

Fairchild stood. "That's as may be. But as a precaution, keep him away from the event. And Rose. And any business going on with her. And next time, talk to me about your gut feel. We've got an operational briefing now. Want to sit in on it?"

Adel couldn't quite believe what he'd just heard. "What, now?"

"Yes, now. It's next door. Come on, then."

Chapter 25

Fairchild slipped into the meeting just as it was due to start. He'd brought his front desk guy with him, some bright-looking student he'd met in the Philippines, Rose recalled. The young man didn't seem too happy but Fairchild must trust him enough to bring him in here. Though he hadn't cleared it with Zack, who gave the poor guy a long stare as he crossed the room, then turned pointedly to Fairchild.

"I told you about Adel," Fairchild said. "He's being useful to us front of house. And keeping an extra eye on the hotel staff as well."

"I thought Nico was doing that," said the American.

"Nico doesn't know everything. People don't gossip with Nico."

Zack huffed an acceptance. The suite had been reorganised for business. The main meeting table was pushed to one side and covered with computing equipment and monitors serving four workstations, all occupied. Rose wallowed in a low armchair. Sarah sat on a dining chair, hands on her lap. Fairchild and Adel sat side by side on a sofa, since they were the only two seats left. Three technicians continued to work at their screens, but the fourth one, Larry, the team leader, turned his chair around to join them. Rose had worked with him before a number of times, including during her brief stint in Moscow. He knew his stuff and could be relied on to keep his cool.

"Okay." Zack plunged straight in. "So, tonight's the big event. Our girl is going to make an appearance, and then it's all over. No one is going to expect her to spend another two weeks here sunning herself. If anyone has taken the bait – and we think they have – they'll be looking to act straight away, as soon as they've verified identity. Tonight, tomorrow. That's our window."

"Excuse me?" said Rose. "What's this about taking the bait?"

Zack picked up a printed photo and passed it over. "This guy is on the scene. That photo was taken by one of our FBI agents in a cafe just off the main esplanade."

"This is Kamal, isn't it?"

"That's him. In person."

"How long has he been here?"

"That was taken today. Our FBI supposedly undercover agents are photographing everyone with a pulse and sending the mugshots here for us to process."

"That must be keeping you busy."

"Certainly is," said Larry.

"He must be watching the place, though," said Rose.

Fairchild passed the photo to Adel. "You recognise him?"

Adel studied it. "No. I haven't seen him." He passed it on to Sarah.

"Where's he staying?" asked Rose.

"Not here," said Fairchild. "At least not under his real name or any of his known aliases." Adel looked at him. Fairchild nodded towards one of the terminals. "We have access to all guest and stay data. Besides, he wouldn't stay here. Too risky and there's no need."

"His people are keeping the place under surveillance," said Zack. "In a pretty obvious way. At a viewpoint up where the road bends round. You can see who comes in and out from there, the road and the steps. A couple of guys have been up there for about the last eighteen hours. Not the same people. They've swapped in and out." He passed around another two or three images. "Not exactly subtle."

"That's a good thing," said Fairchild. "It suggests they're not afraid. They don't suspect anything."

"If the FBI are as ubiquitous as you say, Kamal's people must have clocked them," said Rose. "Are they really that obvious?"

"Well, put it this way," said Zack. "They look a lot like me. Only with less muscle and a lot less charisma."

"They think the FBI is here for Popovic. It actually gives our play more credibility. Just as you suggested, Zack."

"See, not just a pretty face."

"Okay, so it's worked so far," said Fairchild. "The guy's here, or the right hand man is, anyway. What is he going to do? Is he coming to the show?"

"He's not on the guest list," said Zack. "But they may have put someone in there who can verify you are who you claim to be."

"And then what?" asked Rose. "Is Al-Hashemi going to turn up here? If I'm protected at every moment how is he going to get to me?"

"Does Al-Hashemi need to get near her?" asked Fairchild. "We're looking for him everywhere. As soon as he appears on Italian soil the Feds can move in and apprehend him."

"Sure," said Zack. "And that's what will happen. We got it all squared with the Italian authorities. In theory."

"In theory?" echoed Rose.

Zack rocked back on his chair. He seemed to have possession of the only wheeled office chair in the room. Everyone else was making do with ordinary upright chairs. "It may not go down like that." He swivelled in Rose's direction. She didn't like it.

"How so?" she said.

"If he doesn't fancy coming here himself he may try something else."

"Like what?"

"An extraction."

A short silence. "You think he'll try to grab me and take me somewhere?" asked Rose.

"Did you think of that already?" Fairchild was staring at Zack.

"Didn't you?"

"Now is not the time to get flippant, Zack."

"I'm not being flippant. But it's a possibility, isn't it?"

"What do you mean by somewhere?" It was the first time Sarah had spoken.

"Some safe place nearby," said Zack. "Safe for him, that is. But I don't think he'll try and airlift her all the way to Tunisia. It's too far and there are too many risks. Al-Hashemi hasn't been seen in Tunis for a couple of days. He could be here already, holed up somewhere with a plan to grab Popovic and have her taken to him."

"How? She's protected." Sarah sounded a little miffed.

"We need a few holes in her protection," said Zack. "Let's not lose sight of the objective here. We need to provide Kamal or his goons with an opportunity to get close up with our fraudster so that they lead us to Al-Hashemi. It's the only way we're going to find the guy. We have to give him access to Michalaedes so she can lead us to him."

"Wait," said Sarah. "This is the same guy who thinks she defrauded him out of millions of dollars? The same one who said he wanted to strangle her with his bare hands?"

"We'll be in there before anything happens," said Zack.

"In where? You don't know where he is or even if he's here!"

"Tracers. On her person."

"Where on her person? She's walking around in skimpy dresses. We're in a heatwave."

Rose came in. "Shoes? Handbag? We'll have to be creative to incorporate anything else."

Sarah's jaw was rigid. "I was tasked with protecting you."

"You were assigned to a special mission," said Rose. "If you follow orders, nothing you do here will count against you. Right, Zack?"

"Right," said the American.

Sarah sat back and folded her arms, clearly still unhappy.

"So how do we do this?" Zack asked Rose. "At the moment she's even going to the little girls' room with you."

"I have a vice," said Rose. She picked up her handbag and dug around, milking the dramatic pause. She drew out a pack of cigarettes and held it up. "All the rooms are non-smoking. The entire hotel, effectively."

"So, if you need a smoke you have to sneak outside," said Zack.

"And you don't want anyone seeing you engage in such a nasty habit," said Fairchild.

"She has a room terrace the size of a football pitch." Sarah's mouth was pinched.

Rose put on her Julia voice. "But I can't be going all the way upstairs all the time. Back to the room, back down again, in these shoes? No, no. People are waiting for me. I just need a moment, darling. A back door or something. A fire exit to slip through. That's all."

"If they're waiting, that's all they'll need," said Fairchild.

"And we'll know if they're waiting," said Zack. "We got eyes everywhere. If these guys move from their post, if they come inside, if they go some place else, we'll know. Right?" He looked at Fairchild and Adel.

"Right," Fairchild said. "But let's not forget they might not be the only people after her."

"I haven't forgotten," said Zack. "We've got surveillance right across the island. And Zoe's here. Sailed in last night."

Rose thought she'd misheard. "Zoe? Zoe's here?" No one replied. Fairchild seemed to find other things to look at. "Since when? Why didn't I know?"

"Didn't Fairchild mention it?" Zack was blasé.

"And what exactly is her role in all this?"

"She's coming to the event." At least Fairchild was subdued about it.

"Oh, is she?"

"On Zack's request. I only found out after I got here."

"I said we were getting more help with the screening. She's already spotted some interesting faces," added Zack.

Rose allowed her indignance to fill the room. "Anything else I should know about?"

"I don't think so." Fairchild was not so much subdued as annoyed now, and he was looking at Zack.

"Calm down, guys!" Zack held both hands up. "It was my call and you should both be glad she's here. Let's stay focused and grow up, can we?"

Considerably more frostily, the meeting continued.

Chapter 26

Erik had finished with the chairs ages ago, but there was no sign of Adel. It had taken two journeys and they carried all the stacks into the ballroom. That place was looking amazing! His heart skittered when he stared up at the giant globe and around at all the tables, and at the podium with the speaker's lectern. Adel was lying before, he knew it. *She* would be here. She would be up on that podium later tonight, and Erik was going to make sure he was here to see it.

The buggy driver seemed glad of Erik's company and help, and Erik stayed on to move a few tables around. But then everyone drifted away, got caught up in conversations or hurried off. Erik was left standing around and there was no sign of Adel. He went for a walk round the hotel. Nobody stopped him. Back through the garden, round the pool, down the side to a back entrance that led to the kitchen. But it was noisy in there, lots of people and lots of shouting, so he didn't go in. He carried on round and came out at a small space for loading and unloading at the back. This was where the buggies were parked. But the buggies were gone and there was no sign of the driver either. Erik carried on round. Out of the gate, down the hill, up the hill again and back. He sat on a wall outside for a bit. Two guys were on a bench by a bend in the road above the hotel. The bench faced the other way but they kept looking round. They stared at Erik then exchanged a few words. Arabs, by the look of them. Weird, as they were there before, too, when Erik arrived that morning.

Through the glass doors, he caught sight of Adel behind the desk. At last! He went in, putting on a big smile. "My friend! You've been busy! So much going on here!"

Adel looked distracted. "Sorry, I had to go into a – I had to go someplace for a while." Erik stood expectantly. Adel remembered. "Oh yes! Breakfast. Okay, come with me." He said something to another guy and led Erik out of the hotel and across the road to another house. Erik glanced up. Those two Arabs were still there, watching.

There was no sign on the gate this side. The path stones were broken and the garden overgrown. The paint on the big wooden door was cracked and peeling. Adel swiped his card to open it. Inside was a tiled floor with the varnish worn away, white walls that had gone yellow. Adel led him through to a large room with a buffet table at one end and lots of long tables and plastic chairs. One person was in here, a woman in uniform scrolling through a mobile phone with a disposable cup in front of her. She looked up briefly.

"Staff canteen," said Adel. "Help yourself to anything." All the food was covered by metal lids.

"Hey, thanks so much!"

Adel paused. "Do you have paperwork?"

"Paperwork? Just a passport, man."

"Okay, never mind. Let me show you in here." He opened a door to a small room with four mattresses on the floor. One of them had a person on it, curled up and facing the wall, under a sheet. The outside blind was down and the room was gloomy. An air conditioner gurgled but it was still warm, and smelled of bodies and clothes.

"Temporary accommodation for shift workers," said Adel. "Hot beds. You can sleep here."

"Okay." Erik looked at the lumpy mattresses.

Adel seemed a bit embarrassed. "It's not much. But better than sleeping rough, yes?"

"Sure! This is great."

Adel showed him the bathroom. "Look, I can't give you a key. Just come and find me if you need anything."

"And tonight, my friend? The show?"

Adel pulled a face. "It's difficult. There's security."

"But you'll try?"

"I'll try."

After he'd gone Erik got a plate. There wasn't much left under the metal lids, just scrapings of this and that. Cooked egg, soggy patties of potato or something, beans in a sweet sauce, some greasy salty meat and curly bread. But he piled his plate high and ate it anyway. Adel was being good to him and he'd do his best.

He washed himself in the shower, having found a cupboard of folded sheets and towels, and tidied himself up as best he could. He washed out his t-shirt and draped it over the wall outside in the sun. He put a sheet on a mattress and lay down for a while. The other sleeping body didn't stir. He heard noises and clashing sounds from the canteen, people coming and going through the main door. He slept for a while. When he woke up he was clammy. The air conditioner still gurgled. Outside, his t-shirt was dry. At the buffet the old things had been cleared and there were two big vats of white tubes he thought was pasta, and chopped up vegetables. He filled a plate, ate it, and did the same again. Then he washed and dressed and went back to the hotel.

There must be something he could do. He'd make himself as useful as possible. Just as long as he could be there tonight.

Chapter 27

Zoe, or Ariana as she was these days, came to meet Fairchild at the jetty. Her boat was anchored off the Marina Piccolo, round the back of the island from Naples, on the edge of a mass of craft ranging in size from modest two-berthers to substantial super-yachts complete with bathing areas and helipads. Zoe's was a sailboat – sailing was her joy – but it wasn't the same one on which she'd made her escape that time they'd been together. It was bigger, but not much. She could still skipper single-handed if she chose – it had the best navigation gear and was nicely appointed inside. It was her home now. They sat on deck under a large awning and drank long iced lemon cocktails with the afternoon sun overhead.

"Zack's looking after you, I hope?" said Fairchild.

"Sure. But I'm earning my keep. I've become an expert in low-lifes and their money. Low-lifes living the high life." She gazed up at the sheer cliffs and the villas nosing themselves out of every cranny, impossibly precarious.

She was older, of course, but it was more than that. There'd been something refreshingly girlish about the woman he'd sailed off with that time, years ago now. She'd been the antidote to his own self-loathing, with a simplicity that contrasted with the complexities of his own existence. He'd needed her then – he hadn't forgotten, looking at her now. But he'd wrenched himself away because Rose called him back, though not out of any feelings for him. It wasn't like that then, at least not for her, and he had no hopes that it would be. But then, miraculously, things changed. Those weeks on the ocean with Zoe, miles from anywhere, enjoying the simple pleasures, were merely a memory, but a good one.

She sensed what he was thinking and smiled. "To old times." She held up her glass.

"Old times." They drank.

"How's Noah?" he asked.

Zoe's football-mad brother had been the focus of her life until she had to abandon him in Marseille and run for her life. She grinned. "Studying. And playing. Doing well. We see each other now and again." Her grin faded.

"You seem a little…" What was the word? Tired? Jaded?

He didn't need to supply it. "I shouldn't complain. I've got everything I need, haven't I? But – I dunno."

"You could give it up. Put down roots. Zack would manage."

She looked uncertain. "I suppose."

"Are you worried about your safety? That they'll catch up with you?"

"Maybe." But that wasn't it. Fairchild waited.

Zoe's eyes suddenly filled. "Am I any better than them, Fairchild?"

"Yes. Way better. They were nasty people. You beat them at their own game. That doesn't make you the same as them."

"Doesn't it?"

"No, it doesn't. And you had to get away. They almost killed you, remember?"

"But what am I doing? I'm living the same life as they are! All this money, Fairchild! There's so much waste!"

"You're helping. The work you're doing with Zack, you're nailing some of these people. Aren't you?"

She tilted her head. "It doesn't seem enough. There's too much that's wrong."

He couldn't disagree there. He didn't know what else to say: she'd have to find her own way through this one. At least she could know she was among friends.

"I'm glad you came," he said.

She smiled weakly. "Zack said you had some faces to show me?"

"Yes." He got out the wad of covert FBI photos, gathered from across the island as well as within the hotel. "He wants to know if you've crossed paths with any of these."

She went through them slowly, shaking her head at most. She stopped at one. "That could be the Korean we've been looking at." She gave a potted history of embezzlement, intimidation and evasion of justice. She recognised three or four others, associates of people of interest. At a photo of Raffa, she frowned. "Have I seen him somewhere?"

"British guy."

She shook her head. "No, I'm thinking of someone else." She carried on then handed the stack back. "Nice bunch of people you've assembled here."

"This New World scam seems to have conned quite a lot of unsavoury characters. It's no wonder that Professor Popovic did a vanishing act."

"Will Rose be all right?"

"I hope so. We're preparing for the worst. At least I think we are. Security everywhere. And she can look after herself." He was trying to convince himself. Zoe wasn't fooled. But it wouldn't help anyone to articulate his fears. "You're ready for tonight?" he asked.

"Sure. It sounds unmissable. It'll be interesting seeing who's talking to who. And I'll meet Rose again." They hadn't met since Zoe walked off the job in Monaco.

"She's unrecognisable," said Fairchild. "Doesn't want me near her. Too busy getting into the mindset of an international fraudster with a recently-discovered passion for charity."

"You're using the live account, are you?"

"Indeed. I understand you set up the foundation."

"It's so easy." Zoe encountered thousands of such entities in her money-laundering investigations – and before that, when she was just another Monaco bank employee.

"Well, the auction is real, and it will raise actual money. Quite a lot of money, probably. Once we've recovered the costs of the operation we'll siphon any surplus to reputable existing charities."

"Really?"

"Otherwise we're conning everyone as well, aren't we? Not everyone in the room is there with cynical motives. There are philanthropists around. Youth and education are the themes. Global empowerment. You look unimpressed."

"Should I be impressed? It won't change anything and it's not supposed to."

"You're changing things, Zoe. Zack is certainly happy." Fairchild felt like he was having the same conversation twice in one day. But no one seemed to be on hand to reassure Fairchild that he was doing the right thing.

"It's Ariana now." Her eyes wandered back to the pile of FBI photos. Raffa's image was the one on top. Her brow puckered once more. Fairchild picked up the pile and put it away in his backpack.

"It's hot. You said something about going for a swim?"

She forced a smile. "Let's do it." She stood on the deck and pulled off a skirt, with that simple act transforming herself into something exotic, a swimsuit in yellow and green and a dark athletic body. The sun was behind her as she paused on the platform to turn back to him. The shapes of her body cast memories so sharp they almost made him gasp.

"If you need to change, use the front berth. There's everything in there you'll need." She stepped up to the edge of the deck, raised her arms, tipped, and dropped into the water with barely a splash.

When he followed her down, the water was perfect. He floated on his back, sun in his face, and tried not to think about the evening ahead.

Chapter 28

By early evening the guest areas of the Hotel Villa Bianca Rosaria were buzzing with anticipation. Behind the staff doors, on the other hand, lay utter chaos. There was barely any standing room left in the main bar, where Adel was frantically serving cocktails. Not the ideal job for someone who didn't drink alcohol, but he went where he was told.

Nico came storming into the bar servery just as Adel ran in to stock up on slices of lemon, orange, lime. "Ice! We need ice in there!"

"In the ballroom?"

"Yes, the ballroom!" Nico looked as though he could hit somebody.

Adel looked over to the machines. "How much ice?"

"Lots! She wants a display on each table!"

"A display of ice?"

"Ice floating in water, and then some floating petals, and, I don't know…" Nico ran out of words. "But we need more, and then it will melt, so then we'll need even more later on…"

"The bar's already packed."

"Yes, I know!" Nico opened the three ice machines that stood in a row. Two were half full. The third was empty.

"That one's not working," said Adel. Two out of three ice machines would normally be enough. But not tonight. The machines wouldn't keep pace. They were going to run out. Nico uttered a string of Italian expletives.

"Can we buy some? Get it delivered?" asked Adel.

Nico looked at his watch. "No, it's too late! This silly little island!"

"Borrow some, then? From the other hotels?"

"Ah, we need so much! From the hotels we could get a bag here, a bag there—"

"That could work."

Nico stared. "Who has time to go running up and down for little bags of ice?"

"I'll find someone. Leave it to me. I'll get onto it." Adel turned his back on the flustered General Manager and squeezed his way through the bar, avoiding eye contact with thirsty customers and harassed staff. He managed a speedy but controlled walk through the lobby and over to the staff building, where he'd banished Erik a couple of hours earlier. The guy had been hanging around in the lobby but there was nothing for him to do, and Adel insisted that he return to the staff quarters. Now Erik was sitting on a chair with his feet on another chair staring at the ceiling. When Adel came in he jumped up.

"Want to make yourself useful?" Adel asked.

"Boss, you know I do!" His face exploded into a huge grin.

"We need ice." Adel reeled off a list of the nearest half dozen hotels, between the Rosaria and the Marina Grande. "I'll phone them now to let them know you're coming. One bag, two bags, whatever they can spare. Bring them straight over to the bar. Can you do that?"

Erik's eyes narrowed. "This is urgent, right? Super-important?"

"Yes, it is. We're in a real fix."

"Then I guess I could help." He folded his arms and stared.

Adel sighed. "Okay. Okay. I'll see if I can get you into the event tonight."

"My man! I'm yours! I go now! Watch me!" Erik loped out of the door. He pointed at Adel's chest as he passed him. "But I'll be back later. Don't you forget about Erik, now."

Adel hurried back, thinking hard. He wouldn't forget about Erik. Fairchild wouldn't like it. But he'd have to find a way.

Chapter 29

Erik's spirits were soaring as he ran down the steps towards the Marina. He knew it would all work out, and sure enough it had! Adel wouldn't let him down. He was going to see Ulia Popovic tonight, the woman herself! As he jogged he pictured the expression on his mother's face, their home and land complete with new cows, new barn, all the equipment they needed. She would be so proud of him. Oh, such relief!

The first hotel he reached so quickly Adel was still on the phone to the front desk when he arrived. He had to wait five, maybe ten minutes. It felt like an eternity. He sat in a corner and watched everyone passing back and forth. A couple of guys, friends by the look of them, greeted each other with a handshake. One of them looked familiar. Then a bag of ice arrived. He rested it on his shoulder and ran on to the next hotel. They said sorry, they couldn't help. Erik went on to the next. They had some ready so he hoisted that onto the other shoulder and ran back up the steps. The tourists padding slowly along stopped in their tracks when he powered past them. The ice was wet on his back and he was leaving a trail of drips, but there was plenty left when he got back. At the bar they gave him a trolley and sent him off again.

And so it carried on for the next two or three hours, by which time it was dark and they had a freezer full of ice. Adel handed him something folded up in a bag, and told him to go and shower.

"What's this?" asked Erik.

"A uniform. Put it on and come back in half an hour."

On his way back to the staff building, Erik looked up. Those Arabs were still there. Then it struck him. That was why the guy in the first hotel looked familiar! He was one of them. He was up there the first time he'd noticed them. The other guy was white. But he looked familiar too. Now, where had Erik seen him before?

Chapter 30

She was lit up like the beacon of a lighthouse, the Hotel Villa Bianca Rosaria, visible from out at sea. Okay, other places were as well, but on this stretch of Capri cliff the Rosaria was surely the brightest: throbbing with life, bubbling with a secret, shiny-eyed like a child on their birthday. Fairchild stood on the Blue Room terrace watching the arrivals roll up as though drawn by a siren. The crowds attracted to the Rosaria's gracious bosom came from far and wide, deposited by taxi and buggy, both of which were now queuing to get near the restricted entrance.

The Rosaria was ever-demanding, and expected high standards. Her supplicants knew what she wanted. With the women it was a certain weight of jewellery and height of heel. With the men, the brand of watch and the cut of the jacket. These were the yacht owners and their parties, coming in from the harbours. Another tranche, the paying guests, already had access and were drinking her nectar in their sumptuous rooms. They only needed to perfect their appearance and ensure every detail would meet her exacting criteria, before emerging and making their elegant way downstairs.

Already in a tux, Fairchild stood, hands on balcony rail, and watched. It was all going to plan. And yet, something was wrong. He'd had a prickling feeling down his spine since earlier that evening, but he couldn't place what had set it off. He'd been standing on the esplanade, coming back from Zoe's yacht. He'd seen something, or someone. But what? Who? His subconscious was keeping his conscious out of the loop, and it was making him sweat.

He could give it no more time; he was already late. In the mirror, he checked himself from head to toe. He was overdressed – the invitations said jacket and tie – but he needed to be obvious, to stick out as the owner. He fulfilled the role, he thought: rich, respectable. Was that him in the mirror, or was he playing a role? A difficult question.

In the hallway he stopped to look at the door to the suite of Julia Michalaedes. Two large tattooed gentlemen were positioned outside. They all stared at each other. He thought about knocking. But he didn't, and took the stairs to the lobby.

Here it was heaving with chattering partygoers. He worked through them, greeting those he knew as briefly as possible, and emerged outside on the steps. He'd only been there a few seconds when Zoe arrived. She stepped out of a taxi in something glittering and black. Her hair was sculpted into golden braids arranged as spirals like shells. The whole effect was asymmetric, tall, stylish, utterly eye-catching.

"Wow." He took her arm.

"That's what you'd say if you knew what my stylist cost me." Zoe had already told him she'd arranged for someone to go out to the yacht specifically. She gazed up at the Rosaria's floodlit frontage. "Quite nice."

"I'm glad you think so." They squeezed their way through the packed lobby into the garden, tastefully illuminated to bring out the purple flowers and the statuary.

"This is lovely," Zoe remarked.

That was an improvement. But when they entered the ballroom itself, she stared open-mouthed. Fairchild shared the sentiment. As he'd entirely expected from Valentina Maria, it was completely over the top.

The specially-constructed main stage was dwarfed by a screen the size of the entire wall showing images of young people in beautiful but impoverished parts of the world looking happy and grateful. The catwalk jutted diagonally across the room, spotlit and picked out in white, positioned so that every table could see it. From the tables spiralled tall displays of what looked like oversized Christmas baubles, and some kind of flowery water feature that he didn't recall any mention of before. The arches, through which came a faint clifftop breeze, had been wrapped in white satin. And above it all, the giant frosted globe glowed like the moon and rotated sedately, throwing ever-changing patterns onto every surface.

Zoe managed some appreciative noises. "It's like Michael Jackson is getting married to a Disney princess."

"At Christmas. And we have the best seats." He led her to their table which included Valentina Maria herself and the celebrity – very famous, apparently – she'd lined up to conduct the auction. Valentina seemed relatively calm now, and as the guests filed in she set about introducing Fairchild and Zoe – Ariana – to one designer after another. Fairchild produced squeals of delight by addressing most of them in their native tongue. He was a walking circus show these days, with these language skills he'd worked so hard on, back when he needed them. Now he was just meeting and greeting.

People, more people. Too many people. That was why he couldn't remember – what? That feeling needled him again.

Zoe – Ariana – was impressive herself, switching between English, French and Italian. She bore herself well and had a confidence around these people that was new, though it was laced with sadness.

A phalanx of uniformed staff carrying trays of tiny plates appeared. Dinner was being served. Late, Fairchild noted, though late was a relative term at such events. They took their seats. The banquet was elaborate, with multiple courses high in flavour and presentation. An international theme, of course, dishes inspired from specific areas of Africa and Asia, Europe and the Americas, according to the detailed menu. Fairchild had eaten at household tables, market stalls and backstreet bars in all of those places. Occasionally he recognised a particular taste or influence buried underneath the spices and garnishes. He'd eaten plenty of fine food in his time as well, and appreciated the creativity and artistry that went into it, but this wasn't his passion.

What were things like in the kitchen right now? The challenge of this multitude of back-and-forth with tiny servings, the demand for quality and presentation and timeliness but on a huge scale, was enormous, and these were the kinds of client who'd notice. Nico made brief appearances, usually standing at the doorway gazing around before disappearing again. Adel was bringing drinks from the bar by the tray load. That was a job he wouldn't relish. He was getting more and more dissatisfied, that man. And Fairchild also spotted the gangly Kenyan, dressed in a uniform that was a little too small for him, energetically clearing tables. Fairchild thought he'd made things clear. He'd have to do something about Adel.

Raffa was here, at a table of young guests who didn't look accustomed to this kind of event and were making the most of it. Had Raffa somehow managed to buy the tickets on his hotel room tab? No doubt he was charging their bar bill to his room. Fairchild needed to do something about that as well.

Zoe was also people-spotting. The Korean was here, at a table of other Koreans, looking exactly like a respectable businessman, which on paper was exactly what he was. Zoe leaned to murmur something in Fairchild's ear, nodding in another direction. "That guy over there, he's an associate of

Quesada. He was charged with murder once. Double shooting. The witnesses vanished, though." The guy was daintily cleaning his hands after partaking of the seafood. Could Fairchild judge? He'd killed as well, as often as not outside of any state authority.

Time passed, and still the courses arrived. It got warmer, despite the hour and the semi-openness of the room. Jackets came off, ties slackened, collars undone. It got louder, too: tongues loosened. But people were still glancing around, looks exchanged. Heads turned repeatedly towards the door, and in Valentina's direction, particularly at the single spare seat at their table. It was all underway, and yet the thing everyone was waiting for hadn't yet happened. Valentina was gazing at the door. The show needed to commence. But could she start without the sponsor? She didn't want to. Fairchild checked his watch. It was later than he realised.

His breath caught in his throat. Zoe frowned. "All right?" But it wasn't. In a white-hot flash it had come to him. At the Marina Piccolo, a face in the back of a taxi, a pale face, impeccably made-up, one he thought he'd never see again. It was only for a second before it turned away, but that was long enough. His stupid brain had filed it away, intent on other things. People, too many people. Now it might already be too late.

With a curt nod, he got up and made it out of the door before breaking into a run.

Chapter 31

It was a performance in itself, getting ready for the show. Shaved, sprayed, Botoxed and dressed, and all for hopefully no more than half an hour in front of an audience. In the end they'd gone for a black dress, but this was no run-of-the-mill party number. It was designer (the name memorised in case anyone asked), with a light flowing satin quality in deference to the summer, but some length at the back, since Popovic so clearly favoured the formal dress. It had been specially made for Rose, with a number of fitting sessions which resembled, she imagined, those of a bride-to-be. The experience didn't make her want to run for the altar.

Even after all of that, she had to wait to be late. She'd already made an excuse for the banquet, but needed to be tardy enough for the main event for people to wonder if she were coming at all. It was the longest evening of her life. In the end she lay on a sofa in a darkened room, thinking herself into a migraine – that was her excuse – afraid to move a muscle in case she interfered with Linda's grand designs. Sarah filed in at one point and sat patiently in an armchair.

Linda bustled in. "Here's an idea, darling. Late addition. See what you think. I saw that rose on your bedside table, and thought about something like this. It's very *her*." She produced a puffed-up chiffon red rose. "Right at the breastbone. Or off to one side."

Rose sighed and sat up. "Let's see."

Linda was eyeing her cleavage, the rose in her hand like a grenade. "Actually, not breastbone. You don't have the boobs for it."

"After everything I've eaten? I've stuffed myself silly."

"You've done heroic work, but there's genetics. Anyway, here on the left would look lovely I think. A bit of colour." She pinned it firmly. "I'll get a needle and sew it on." She stepped back. "Nice."

Rose moved to the mirror. She exchanged a look with Sarah. "Not too obvious?"

"It's a thin line. We can ditch it if you like. Or ask for views next door?" Linda hovered.

"Oh, please, no, not another conflab about what I'm supposed to look like. Just do it already."

The accessory secured, Linda withdrew and Rose announced the need for air. The terrace was warmer than the air-conditioned room, though a hint of a breeze from the sea tempered the night's humidity. Rose leaned on the balcony rail and watched shapes forming in white where the sea broke over the rocks below. Sarah joined her. They both stared down.

"This must be the weirdest assignment you've ever had," said Rose.

"It's probably up there."

"What made you join the army in the first place?"

Sarah shifted. The silence stretched out until Rose was about to tell her to forget it, it didn't matter. But then she spoke.

"I was at university. First year. My parents and brother were driving up to visit me in Manchester. Some lorry jack-knifed on the M6. Massive pile-up. The car was crushed. None of them made it."

Rose turned and stared. "None of them?"

Sarah kept looking down. "Yep. My whole family. Gone."

There was a pause while Rose failed to think of a suitable thing to say. Sarah continued.

"I quit uni and joined up. The army is my family now."

"Christ. I'm sorry."

"Sorry you asked, you mean."

"No. Sorry it happened. To lose everyone like that!"

Sarah shifted again. "I'd like to say I'm over it, but…"

More silence. After a while Rose said, "You blame yourself, don't you?"

"It was my fault."

"That's survivor's guilt."

"So I've been told." Another pause. "I don't normally tell people. It turns things weird. I'm all right, by the way. They let me have a gun and everything."

"That's good to know." Rose looked out at the dark sea, thinking about people she'd known and lost. A smiling man in a robe, pointing at the sky. A little girl, curled up next to her on a sofa while guns pounded outside. Was Rose all right? There were times when she hadn't been. The silence stretched on.

"How's the migraine?" said Sarah.

Rose had run out of patience. "Oh, enough already. Let's do it." She straightened.

Afterwards, she couldn't say if she'd seen it or not, the momentary flash of red, but she wouldn't have been quick enough, not without Sarah. A force pushed her from behind. The balcony decking hit her face. From beyond, two chinks of sound, like pottery breaking or someone dropping a glass. Sarah was lying on top of her, breathing heavily. Foolishly, all she could think about was whether her make-up was smudged.

An internal door slammed. A large figure appeared silhouetted in the doorframe.

"Sniper! Get down!" Sarah's words, spoken over Rose's head. The figure dropped. Someone else was in the room behind them.

"Are you hit?" It was Zack.

"No." Sarah was speaking for both of them. Rose felt useless. She should be the one taking control.

"You need to get inside," said Zack.

"They're aiming high," said Sarah. "We'll be okay if we stay low. Can you do it?" She was talking to Rose. She shuffled aside.

Rose could do it, but her dress was caught up under her knees, and she had to pull on the skirt to get herself free. Bloody thing.

"Okay. Run now?" She deferred to Sarah. Zack had retreated inside.

"Go. Keep as low as you can."

Rose ran doubled-up, tripping on the step going back in. Zack grabbed her arm and pulled her further inside. She stumbled head-first into another body, which caught and held her. Her face was up against the stiff shirt of a tuxedo.

Fairchild. He gripped her around the shoulders and said nothing. Neither did she.

Chapter 32

"Open the door, now!"

The two heavies had done as he asked. But when Fairchild got inside, it looked like he was too late. The door to the terrace was open and Zack was crouched beside it. Two bodies lay face down on the terrace. But then one of them got up and stumbled in. Zack caught her and pulled her past him. Then Rose was in his arms.

"They're not hit," Zack was saying. "Sniper had to aim high. One of the bullets caught a window pane next door."

Fairchild could hear the words but all he could focus on was the warmth of Rose's body and how tightly she was holding on to him. Her face was buried somewhere in his chest. Now Sarah was in the room as well. Zack was shepherding them all into the suite next door, away from the windows. The place had suddenly filled up with armed agents milling about.

"Why are they in here?" he said to Zack. "They should be out there looking for the shooter."

"It was a sniper, Fairchild. They could be anywhere."

"No, they couldn't. They had a perch with a view of the terrace. There aren't many places like that. They could be across the road, for God's sake!"

"The laser sight was wide," Sarah said. "Dispersed."

"You know what that means, Fairchild," said Zack. "The shooter was a long way away."

"About as far as you can get." Sarah again.

"And even if we figured out where, they won't be there any more. They'll have packed up and left by now."

"They're still on the island! Get onto the police. Seal off the ports! Make sure they don't get away."

They were standing in the middle of the room. Rose pulled herself away from him and squeezed his hand. "That would mean the end of the op."

"Well, yes! You just escaped being shot. By a hair's breadth." Even without knowing the details, the pallor of Sarah's face told him how close it had been.

"And it probably wouldn't achieve anything anyway. They can ditch the weapon easily enough. We've no idea who we're after." Rose spoke with a forced calm.

"I know who we're after," said Fairchild.

"Oh, you do, do you?" said Zack. "Well, I tell you what, let's all sit down and you can fill us in."

"I'm not sitting down! We need to be after—"

"Sit." Zack's voice was firm. Rose withdrew her hand and sat on a chair. Zack and Sarah also sat.

"Fairchild." Zack pointed at an armchair and waited.

Fairchild sat. "I saw her earlier today, but it only clicked a few minutes ago. I caught a glimpse of her in the back of a taxi."

"Her?" said Zack.

"I used to know her as Comrade Chu. The last time I saw her was in a detention centre in western China. You must remember that incident."

Zack's face showed that he did. Rose's too.

"Chu had access to assassins trained to operate on foreign soil. Snipers. Good ones." And he saw on Rose's face more recollections, people taken out – and almost taken out – by Chu and her snipers.

"Why does the Chinese government want to kill Ulia Popovic?" said Zack.

"She isn't with the government any more. She was discredited after Beijing blamed her for an unauthorised hit.

Chu could be working for anyone now. Plenty of crypto investors in China were caught out by New World Coin."

"Well, on the bright side," said Rose, "We've persuaded someone that I am actually Popovic." Her voice had the tiniest shake.

"Chu's the type who's happy to order the kill first and only check afterwards that she got the right person," said Fairchild. "There could be a whole team of them. They could be in the hotel already. We have to call this off. Sit the event out and leave as soon as we can."

There was a pause. From through the broken window pane came the sound of the party from the ballroom. Loud talking but no music or MC yet. Valentina was still hanging on for Michalaedes.

"We did know that something like this might happen," said Zack.

"We underestimated the danger. That was too close. And we had no idea Chu was here. She was keeping her face out of it, since the two of us know each other. There could be more like her."

"But there's no opportunity now," said Rose.

"Are you mad? Several hundred people are sitting downstairs waiting for you to appear! How many of them have been searched?"

"We talked about this," said Zack. "None of them will do anything as public as that. If they want her dead they'll contract someone to do it, and it won't happen in the middle of some fancy ballroom."

"You can't know that for sure."

"It's a reasonable risk." The tremor in Rose's voice had gone. "And we need to get moving. Could someone fetch Linda? I need a touch-up."

Fairchild felt his jaw drop. "You're going ahead with it?"

"Zack's right. We knew this might happen. We've spent months setting this up and we need to track down this guy. We think they've bought into it. We're so close, Fairchild. We just need to sniff him out, and that's it. Now…" She stood up and turned around. "Is my dress torn?" She said this to Sarah, who didn't move for a second or two, then, as requested, started scanning the sleek material for damage.

"You think this is okay, do you? After surviving that?" Fairchild was being unfair to the woman, but Sarah was unfazed.

"I think it's madness. But I do as I'm told, right?" She looked at Rose.

"Right," said Rose.

Fairchild looked at Zack, but got no support there. "At least aren't we going to put extra security measures in place?"

"The whole point of what happens next is that we create a hole in her security."

"A hole for Al-Hashemi, not anyone else!"

"Like the lady said, we knew all this."

Linda came in and started working on Rose's face with blusher and lipstick. Rose took a breath and let it out slowly. Then, in her best Julia voice: "I'll take care, darling, I promise!"

Fairchild stood. "You know, I could just shut the whole thing down. Turf everyone out of the place and close up."

Rose gave him a magisterial stare while Linda dabbed her chin. "If you do that, darling, I'll never speak to you again."

Chapter 33

One of the Georgs rode in the lift with them. The other went down on foot and was waiting when the lift door opened on the ground floor. Not a word had been said in the lift, and their journey continued wordlessly across the lobby. Julia Michalaedes' black dress, dusted off and miraculously untorn, almost swept along the floor as its owner strode, her watchful bodyguard alongside and the Georgs fore and aft. Despite Zack's relaxed attitude, he'd sent additional bodies out front, and Rose caught a glimpse of one of them loitering on the steps.

The lobby was quiet now, and there was an expectant air, as if the hotel itself were holding its breath. It seemed unnaturally bright inside and the immense windows loomed, huge rectangles of darkness. Who was out there watching and waiting? Rose cast that thought out and carried on. But past the garden and approaching the ballroom itself, she slowed.

On the other side of that door hundreds of people sat waiting for her, though they were pretending not to, ready to absorb every detail of what she said and did, keen to learn if it was really her, really the woman who'd stolen from them. It would be understandable for a little nervousness to show. Popovic would know what a risk this was: she'd know what was at stake. So Julia paused on the threshold, showing a little hesitation and looking around for a familiar face, someone who would welcome her.

She didn't have long to wait. Valentina was coming over already. "Julia! Oh, so pleased!" Her relief was almost palpable.

"I'm so sorry!" intoned Julia Michalaedes. "This migraine, once it starts there's nothing you can do, nothing!" After the air kisses Valentina led her across the room. By her side, Sarah was as straight as a rod, oozing vigilance. The Georgs had fallen back but would be scanning the faces all around, watching for sudden movement. She could feel eyes on her, but no direct stares, just furtive glances as conversations continued. She took a breath and raised her chin. Sarah looked across at her and they caught each other's eye before the bodyguard continued her scan of the room. Her face showed tight professionalism.

A loud pop. Sarah was in front, her hand on Rose's chest, stopping her. The pop was followed by a cheer. A young blond guy was pouring champagne carelessly. His table guests stood to hold out their glasses. Others turned at their whooping and shouting. The blond guy looked up briefly, a playful look on his face. Sarah withdrew her arm. They walked on.

When Valentina reached the table they all stood, as if royalty had arrived. Valentina introduced her to the auctioneer, some quiz show host, apparently. "You know John, of course." And there was Fairchild again, looking urbane, if a little grim. They kissed and his hand touched her waist, but it was nothing; they were actors in a play.

"This is Ariana," he said, and it was Zoe, but older and thinner. Thanks so much for coming, kiss kiss, everyone's watching. That was someone else whose death she'd mourned – until she found out the woman had got away clean after all. They hadn't met since, and now here she was, taller somehow, and glamorous. And sitting next to Fairchild.

"We're starting, we're starting!" enthused Valentina. "Darling, you will stay and say a few words, won't you?"

"Oh, but my head is so bad, I just—"

"Just something, just something quick about the foundation and what it means. It would make so much difference."

The presenter was already up there, tapping the mic. The lights and conversation dropped. Spotlights picked out the catwalk and the stage. Music started, and the introduction to the exhaustively rehearsed event was underway. Julia protested a little more (it would make a sharp exit afterwards more credible) then allowed herself to be led to a VIP seat just as the first designer was being presented. And so she sat politely next to Valentina, Sarah down by her feet staring out at the audience and the Georgs primed and ready. All attention in the room (at least in theory) turned to the show.

Chapter 34

Adel's legs were aching. His whole body was aching. He'd been working for over twelve hours with little in the way of breaks. Tray after tray of drinks he'd brought in, yet their insatiable customers wanted more and more. Finally, a lull as the lights dimmed, the catwalk brightened and all eyes turned that way as the half-naked models started to strut.

It wasn't that long ago that Adel was a jihadist, an active fighting recruit in the Islamic war on the decadence of the west. He'd rejected the murderous fury of the extremists, but he still prayed. He still followed the Koran. He'd been to many places across the world and had seen all kinds of things, keeping his faith but also keeping an open mind about the faiths and beliefs of others, he hoped. But even so, the scene before him struck him as a bizarre spectacle.

Most of the customers who had been clicking their fingers at him and ordering drinks were men. Yet everyone parading on the catwalk was female. How did that work? What did it say about the so-called egalitarian west? And the clothes! You could hardly even call them that. Bits of cloth held up with who knows what, just about covering the essentials, in all kinds of weird colours and shapes. And then the headwear! The footwear! So impractical, and what did it matter anyway what you wore? As for the models, Adel appreciated the attractions of a female body: he was flesh and blood. But so much acreage of skin on display seemed gross. This was supposed to be about fashion and creativity and expression. But those finger-snapping men who were paying for all this, were they looking at the clothes or the bodies?

On and on it went. Adel slipped out, helped the bar staff get things back in order during the lull, checked the ice supply (adequate thanks to Erik), then stopped by the front desk. He wasn't needed there so he wandered back to the ballroom. Finally, things seemed to be coming to a close. Valentina Maria was talking now, introducing someone in the VIP area. If this was Rose, it could be interesting. Adel slipped back inside.

Julia Michalaedes, as introduced, was standing up to a perfunctory applause. How much did you clap someone who'd conned you out of millions and was now playing the philanthropist? A moderate amount, seemed to be the answer. Zack was right. These people cared too much about appearances to show their true feelings in a forum like this. Julia took the mic with an air of nervousness but also eagerness, like this was her natural place despite everything.

"Thank you so much! Thank you so much." Her throaty voice came over the PA system, cracking slightly at first but then settling down. Out of curiosity Adel had gone online to watch some of the Popovic videos. Somehow Rose had managed to capture the mannerism and inflection of Popovic while at the same time looking quite – but not entirely – different. He had to admit she was good.

"So, what do you think of our fabulous designers?" The audience obediently clapped, and a few even cheered, while the tables of hangers-on duly went crazy. "I have to tell you, I'm so overwhelmed." She put a hand on her heart, and did sound almost tearful. "Who can worry about the future when we have young people with such talent and vision? This is what the foundation is all about. Let's not forget that we who are here today, we're the lucky ones."

The room fell silent. Some, Adel thought, might feel that certain people in the room had been luckier than others. Rose continued.

"We're the ones who've had a chance to shape our lives, because other people believed in us. For many across the world it's not like that. Purely because of where they were born, they just don't get the opportunities to rise up, to develop their talents and make the world a better place. That's a tragedy."

A pause, for effect. Rose had really studied those videos. Adel noticed Erik, standing with his back against a wall, eyes wide. His mouth was all but hanging open. For the first time Adel felt a prickling of doubt in his own judgement. Could anyone really be that naïve?

"In this room," Julia was saying, "we have people from every corner of the globe. Just think about it. All the fighting. All the wars. Let's face it – we're different from each other. We have different views and experiences, ideas, opinions. We look different!"

Someone dared to laugh at that but quickly stopped. Julia didn't miss a beat. "But we can get on with each other, can't we? We can celebrate our differences. If we in this room can, so can the world!" She nodded slowly, expecting applause. The audience obliged, though Adel felt she might be overstating the diversity in the room, and a call for world peace was extraordinarily trite. "But nothing comes without hard work. We have such a way to go. And nobody can do it alone. Not me, not you, not anybody. That's why I'm so pleased to see all of you here tonight. And I know that you will dig deep to support the young people who have put on such an amazing show. This is really the start of something big. And you were here right at the beginning!"

That rang a bell. Was Rose actually using the same phrases Popovic used in those workshops and speeches, when she was selling New World Coin? Was she overdoing it? But then all of a sudden she was thanking Valentina and thanking the designers and the models and everyone else under the sun, and handing the mic back and doing a modest kind of a wave, as if the applause now were all too much for her. And then, with a sweep of her long skirt and escorted by that po-faced bodyguard, she walked rapidly out of the room, dispensing smiles and waves as she passed.

Valentina was already making excuses for her – unwell, something about a migraine, dragged herself here, et cetera – and the applause strengthened a little. In the meantime the Italian handed the baton over to the presenter, who launched into an energetic patter. Rose's bodyguard, and the two pieces of muscle, Adel now noticed, still scrutinised the room as their subject approached the exit. But heads gradually turned from Michalaedes back to the stage, where the models were all lined up in their nominated outfits, ready to be sold off. The outfits, of course, not the models, though you could be forgiven for thinking otherwise.

Just before Adel turned to leave, he glanced over to where Erik had been standing – but the man was gone.

"Anything happening out here?" he asked at the check-in desk. No, was the answer. But as he stuck his head outside he noticed a couple of loiterers near the steps. In their bland shirts and their cargo pants, they looked like FBI. He also realised that the two figures at the viewpoint above, the Tunisians who'd been keeping constant watch up there, had disappeared.

Chapter 35

Heading out of the ballroom, Rose made straight for the ladies' powder room in the lobby. Sarah followed her in and the Georgs lined up outside. Anyone needing the facilities would have to go elsewhere for the next few minutes.

Rose turned on a tap. "Well?" Sarah was wearing an earpiece. Rose wasn't.

"The two out at the front have gone. People are in and out of the function room. They can't keep track of everyone."

"Anyone around who looks like Al-Hashemi or Kamal?"

"No sightings."

Rose looked at herself in the mirror. This was it, now. "Well, either they've bought the act or they haven't. Only one way to find out. You need to make yourself visible. People need to see that you're not with me."

Sarah didn't respond.

"Okay?" asked Rose.

"Let me come with you. Whatever they do to you they can do it to me as well."

"No, it's too risky. They may not make a move at all, and this whole thing will have been wasted. We talked about this."

"Do as I'm told?" She was almost sulky.

"You're a soldier, aren't you?"

"I don't much feel like one."

"You saved my life about an hour ago."

"And now I'm letting you make yourself a target again. We've got no idea who's out there."

Rose dried her hands. "Give it ten minutes. No less. Okay?"

Again Sarah said nothing.

Rose left. Instead of heading back up to the lobby, she went the other way, down steps to a fire door that led outside. She felt in her clutch bag for her cigarettes and lighter, resisting the urge to look over her shoulder. What Sarah should be doing behind her was hanging around at the edge of the lobby with the two Georgs, making it very obvious to anyone watching closely that Julia Michalaedes was not, at that moment, with her personal security team. She pushed on the fire door and it opened easily. She stepped out into a close, dark heat, intense after the air conditioned lobby. It was a vehicle access area with just enough space for a small truck or van to manoeuvre all the way round. The noise of the auction carried directly from the cliffside ballroom, with excited shouts from the auctioneer as some bidding war went on. She could smell garbage and grease. A caged area opposite held bins. She lit a cigarette and drew. If she had to keep this up for long she'd develop a habit. Weight gain and carcinogenic activity: Walter had a lot to answer for.

She was prepared for anything, she thought, but the sound of a step made her jump. A figure emerged, tall, gangly, very black: a youngish man. "I hope you don't mind," he said in English with a strong African accent. "I loved your speech." He was wearing a staff uniform. Rose didn't notice him in the ballroom, but there had been hundreds of people.

The guy was smiling tentatively. "I'm Erik." He offered a hand. Rose eyed it. This wasn't what she was expecting.

"You've caught me at a bad time, Erik." She waved the cigarette. "I don't like people to know."

"Oh, I don't care! Listen, can I ask you something?"

"I guess so. But I'm going in a moment. I need to get back inside."

"Oh, sure. Well…" He didn't seem to know where to start. "Look. Is it happening?"

She stared. "Is what happening?"

"The exchange! The launch! Because I tell you, I need my money! It's not for me, you know. If it was just me I could get by maybe. But my mother, my sister…it's a problem. They don't have much and they need it for the farm."

The penny dropped. "You're an investor?" He didn't even ask if she was Popovic. He just dived straight in. That was good, she guessed.

"Yes! Of course. I have the New World Coin. It's worth a lot. A great investment! But all the delays! And now I need it. I need to give it to my mother so she can get her cow back."

"Did you say cow?"

"Yes! Now they only have one for the whole family. It's not enough." He put his hand on his heart just like she had earlier during her speech. "I believed. Like you said. I believed in the coin and that it will make us all rich. I still do! But please, do the launch and give us the exchange because we're just waiting, waiting and we need it now. That's why I came here."

"Came to Capri?"

"Came to Italy. From home. From Kenya."

"You came here from Kenya?" Then what was with the staff uniform? Rose couldn't get her head round it. But this could really derail things. In about six minutes Sarah would come barrelling through that door and the moment would be lost. In the meantime she thought – or imagined – she'd seen something move in the shadows behind him.

"Listen, Erik, how much did you lose?"

"Lose?" his brow crinkled.

"I mean – how much did you invest in the coin?"

"Three thousand."

"Three thousand what?"

"Dollars. US. But it's worth way more than that now! I can see it online, it's ten times that much!"

"Okay, never mind that. Listen. For the full value you must wait for the launch. But to cover your investment, maybe there's something I can do. To compensate you for the delay. But you mustn't tell anyone else, because we can't do this for everyone. We're investing in the coin, you know, the research and development, to give access to everyone. But for you, as you've come all this way, perhaps I can get something out for you."

"He was nodding frenetically. "Okay, okay, okay."

"Give me twenty-four hours and I'll leave something for you at the front desk. You work here, right?"

"Work here, yes!" He laughed, for reasons Rose didn't understand. "I work with Adel. You know Adel? He is my friend."

"Oh, is he? Well, I'll leave it for Adel, then. So, don't worry. Go back to work. I will stay here and finish my cigarette, and I will make sure you're okay. Right?"

"Oh, of course, that's so excellent—"

"Yes, yes." She fumbled in her bag. "I need to make a call now. But don't worry!"

Uttering more thanks he eventually retreated. Rose took the last drag. What was Adel playing at? Three thousand dollars was nothing. They were paying more than that per night just for the suite.

Erik's footsteps had barely faded away when she heard more, coming towards her now. It took all her effort not to spin round straight away but she forced herself to wait, throwing the cigarette down and putting it out with her heel.

They must have been waiting for Erik to leave. If they were anything other than Tunisian, she was in a lot of trouble.

She turned. Two heavies. North African? Maybe. They grabbed each arm.

"Hey, what are you doing?" She was indignant as quietly as possible. One grabbed her clutch bag and threw it down. The contents scattered over the ground. He pinned her arm up behind her back.

"That hurts! Get off me!"

The other did a rough search of her body. She heard a car. A black saloon with tinted glass nosed towards them. One held her by the waist while the other opened the car door. She tried to kick him but in a long skirt she made a poor job of it. They pushed her into the back of the car.

"Let go of her! Leave her alone!" Someone came running up, shouting. Erik! One guy shoved himself next to Rose in the car while the other turned to deal with him. He swung and punched Erik hard in the face. Erik staggered but somehow didn't fall. The puncher landed another one. But Erik was still on his feet. The goon opened the door on the other side and jumped in, shouting at the driver. They set off, but slowly around the narrow access road. Erik sprinted up and got his hand on a door handle. He pulled the door open. The heavy got a foot out and booted him in the chest. Erik landed flat on his back. The car worked its way round the side of the hotel. Erik, on the ground, wasn't moving.

The staff door burst open. Sarah was first out. She looked down and registered the bag and its contents. She sprinted after the car, but they were already out of the gate and speeding down the road. Through the back windscreen Rose saw her standing in the middle of the road staring after them.

Chapter 36

They turned away from the main harbour, up the hill and then towards Ana Capri. The road switched back violently as they climbed. The driver muttered as he tried to speed up but braked sharply at each turn. Rose was sandwiched between the two goons. One of them produced a rectangular black device with a small antenna, not much bigger than a phone.

"Excuse me," he said. At least he was polite. He switched it on and moved it slowly around her person. As he moved down her leg the display lit up.

"Your shoes, please."

"What?"

"Take off your shoes."

Rose hesitated.

"Or I will have to do it."

She leaned down and unbuckled the tiny straps, struggling to feel her way below her dress. Eventually she passed him the jewel-encrusted footwear. He looked disapproving.

"Forgive me." He applied the scanner to her lower and upper body, being impressively thorough. No movement on the display until he waved it across her chiffon rose. Back and forth: each time it passed the rose, it lit up.

"Remove that, please."

"It's sewn on. I can't."

He reached out a hand.

"Okay, okay, I'll do it." She pulled it off, tearing the material. He took it.

On a quiet stretch where the land fell away below, they pulled over. The man got out, took three steps over and dropped the shoes and the flower off the edge of the cliff. A gust of air blew, and the little rose danced briefly before disappearing. The breeze penetrated the car and caught her skirt. It was the first time since arriving in Italy that she felt cold.

They carried on. She recognised the journey after a few minutes. It was the reverse of the one she took when she arrived. They were going to the heliport. The other man in the back made a short phone call. Rose knew enough Arabic to understand "We're on our way" or similar. She reminded herself that Popovic didn't speak Arabic.

As they drew up, a small helicopter was on the pad waiting. The first of the men addressed her. "Any shouts, any struggles, any screams, we will punish you. Do as we say and you won't be harmed."

She complied. They embarked. The copter lifted off and followed the coast down, tracking the string of lights of the coast road. They kept going. A long way. Capri shrunk into a tiny glinting rock in a dark sea, getting smaller by the second until Rose could see it no more.

They slowed and turned towards one of the headlands. She could see little of where they landed. When they got out she could smell cut grass. No one was around. They filed silently across an expanse of lawn. On one side steps led up to a terraced level with a stone wall and a line of trees. Beyond the grass in the other direction was nothing but blackness and distant lights. They passed through an opening in an ornamental hedge, and stepped onto a gravel drive, behind which loomed a substantial house.

They took her inside through a baroque portico. The floor under her feet was cold from the tiles. They entered a wood panelled room that stretched the width of the house. At the other end of it a man stood looking out of an enormous window. She approached, then stopped. Her captors remained on either side of her. He turned. It was Kamal.

"My boss is not a happy man," he said.

Chapter 37

"Adel! My man! You've got to help! Fast, fast!"

Adel was back on check-in and Erik, appearing from nowhere, was jabbering at him over the desk. His eyes were wide and sweat was beading all over his face.

"What is it?"

"They've taken her, man!"

"Who?"

"Popovic! The New World Coin lady!"

Adel instinctively looked around, but nobody was nearby, and on reflection he wasn't sure it mattered anyway. "What do you mean? Who's taken her?"

"I don't know! Some guys in a car. Looked like Arabs. They've been hanging around the hotel for ages."

So Erik had clocked the surveillance. He sure was observant. Some deep suspicion stirred again. "When was this?"

"Just now. Round the back. I went there to talk to her."

"Really? How did you know she was out there?"

A flash of shame in his face turned to defiance. "Hey, I was looking out for a chance to speak to her, you know that. I saw her bodyguards waiting for her and figured she might be round the back somewhere, so I went to check it out."

"You spoke to her, then?"

"Yes, but—"

"What did she say?"

"She said she'd get me my money back. She'd leave it here for me tomorrow."

"Really?" Adel could hardly believe it. Was there any lie they weren't prepared to tell?

"Sure, but as soon as I went off this car drew up and they bundled her in. I tried to stop them but one of them knocked me down."

"Are you okay?" Adel noticed some swelling on Erik's cheek.

"Yes, I'm okay, but what should we do?"

"Was there no one else around?"

"Their bodyguards came out, the woman, but the car had already gone. They got on their radios and went back inside. You think we should tell the police?"

Adel's head was spinning. Erik could unravel this whole thing – and it would be Adel's fault. "If the bodyguards know about it, they'll have phoned the police already."

Erik frowned. "So they'll be looking for her?"

"Of course they will."

He looked around. "But I don't see any police."

"This just happened, right? They're probably on their way. Look, I'll go up to the room if you want. Ask them if there's anything we can do. I'll see what I can find out."

That seemed to pacify him. Adel told him to wait over in the staff room. He went up and knocked on the door of the second suite, the one where the meeting took place earlier. Nothing happened. He went to knock again but it opened. Fairchild was standing there. He looked grim. He ushered Adel in. They were all there just as before, except Rose of course. Sarah, the bodyguard, looked pale and was chewing her lip. Zack sat back, arms folded. "Got something to report?"

"Someone saw her being taken."

"This Kenyan friend of yours by any chance?" Fairchild, second-guessing him as usual.

"What Kenyan friend?" asked Zack.

"He's just a guy doing some casual work," Adel said.

"A New World Coin investor. Who came here to meet the woman," said Fairchild.

"And why did I know nothing about this?" asked Zack.

"I thought Adel was handling it," Fairchild replied.

"I am." Adel finally managed to get into the conversation.

Zack beckoned. "Come on, then. Out with it."

"He wanted to speak to the woman."

"Yeah, like everyone else in the place!"

"Let him tell it, Zack." Both men were jumpy.

Adel continued. "He noticed the bodyguards hanging around and went round the back to find her. They talked."

"Just talked?" asked Zack.

"Yes, just talked. He was walking away when a car came round. He tried to intervene but they knocked him down, he said."

Zack turned to Sarah. "This sound like the guy you saw?"

"Yes, that must be him." Sarah spoke quietly. "He was in a bit of a panic. I told him we were on it and we all went back inside."

Zack turned back to Adel. "And then?"

"Then he came to me on the front desk talking about calling the police. I said her people would be dealing with it, and that I'd come up here to make sure of it."

"Yeah, well, we're dealing with it. He'll be okay with that? Isn't going to scream the place down?"

"He wants to know why the police aren't swarming everywhere."

"Tell him it's a low key response. Nothing visible or public. She wouldn't want to spoil her event and undermine confidence, all that stuff. But it's in hand. Okay?"

"Okay," said Adel.

"Any more problems with him, let me know," added Zack. "Come straight to me." He didn't look at Fairchild when he said this.

"Should I tell Nico?" That was what he'd normally have done first.

"I've put Nico in the picture," said Fairchild, his voice flinty.

There was a pause. They were waiting for him to leave. So much for being part of the team. But he could blame no one but himself this time. He got up to go to the door. On the floor he noticed a black clutch bag, which he recognised. What had they said at the briefing? The handbag, the shoes. He slowed, about to turn and ask about it.

"Get back to work, Adel." Fairchild was curt. The man's eyes, watching him, were grey and cold as steel.

Adel went out and closed the door. He paused on the other side, listening, but could hear nothing.

In the staff room he gave Erik what reassurance he could and sent him back to help in the kitchen. There seemed no harm in it now. Adel returned to the front desk. The party was still going on, but the show was over, he supposed. So far, it had worked. Unless the people grabbing Rose had been nothing to do with Al-Hashemi at all. And – that bag still on his mind – assuming that everyone upstairs knew exactly where Rose was.

Chapter 38

Fairchild waited for Adel to be well away from the other side of the door before he really let rip. "Are you telling me, Zack, that precisely fifteen minutes after she was spirited out of the hotel, you have no idea where she is?"

"They must have used a scanner on her. We didn't expect that. They think she's a fraudster, not an informant. Or a spook. None of us thought they were going to be that thorough."

"Great. And to get back to the point here, you have no idea where she is?"

"The tracers jumped off a cliff on the road to Ana Capri."

"All of them?" That was Sarah, calm and precise.

"All except the one in her bag, which didn't even make it out of the hotel!" Fairchild couldn't manage to be calm or precise.

"But we know where she was going," said Zack. "They went to the heliport and put her on a copter."

"Great! So she's off the island."

"She's off the island. It was headed to the mainland."

"And we know that because...?"

"Because they submitted a flight plan. Which you have to do. And our people are over there right now getting their hands on it."

"And of course they'll stick to this flight plan."

"We're also talking to the hire company. They can tell us where the flight was heading."

"If they'll talk."

Zack took a breath. "Look, it worked, didn't it? This is what we wanted!"

"No, this is not what we wanted, Zack! First, we don't even know if it was Al-Hashemi's lot that have taken her."

Zack looked at Sarah. "You saw them, didn't you?"

She shook her head. "I saw the back of the car. That's it."

"Well, those two goons out the front have disappeared," said Zack.

"Christ, Zack, this isn't supposed to be some guessing game. We were meant to be with her right from the start! How do we move in on the guy now? We're playing catch-up already!"

Zack was keeping his voice calm, but his face was red. "We'll catch up. We'll find them, Fairchild."

Fairchild stood. He pointed down at Zack. "When you do, I want to be there. I'm not going to sit here doing nothing. You tell me as soon as you hear."

Zack stared him down. Fairchild held his gaze. They'd spend the best part of two decades working together in all kinds of situations, sometimes successful, sometimes not. But this was different.

"Well, you'd better get ready, then," the American said. "Unless you want to drop out of a bird in your best tux. And if there's anything else you haven't told me, feel free. Like any more of those random investors hanging around the place. There's more than one way this thing can get messed up."

Fairchild turned and left. He wished he could slam the door but the bloody things all had slow closers. He made up for it with the speed of his departure.

Glancing back, he saw Sarah looking after him, sitting bolt upright, her hands in her lap, eyes round, face pale.

Chapter 39

"You kidnapped me!" Rose made Julia sound indignant and scared at the same time, not something she found difficult.

Kamal didn't seem moved. "My boss would like his debts settled."

"I don't know who your boss is or what he could want with me. If he wanted to talk he could have come to the hotel if he knew I was there."

"Too many cops hanging around."

"I didn't see any."

"The type of cop most people don't see. Why do you think there were so many, huh?"

"How do you expect me to know that?" She raised her chin in defiance.

Kamal stepped forward. "They were there for you. You know that."

"Why would the cops want me? I'm just a—"

"Stop. Stop." He held his hand up. His voice echoed in the sparse room. "Don't try to play me. I know who you really are. You're Ulia Popovic. The one in all those videos. The brains behind the New World Coin. You're the person who scammed thousands of people out of millions of dollars. Billions, even. Don't try to deny it."

Rose allowed her expression to change. She stood taller, prouder. "What if I am?" She sent her voice even deeper. This was the essence of Popovic, the real Popovic, of whom Michalaedes was just a shadow, a persona inside a persona.

Kamal acknowledged this with a slight nod of his head. "My boss invested two million dollars in your worthless coin. Or, I should say, one of his accountants did. They were showing some initiative, maybe. Anyway, they won't be doing it again."

He waited for a response. His English was excellent – educated in an anglophone country, maybe. He was tall and had a bony elegance to him. His hands were large, with long fingers. Nothing was spare. He gave off an aura of power, like a big cat in the wild. He could move very quickly if he needed to.

"It's not worthless. The valuations are all online. As soon as the exchange is launched you can—" Her face stung and she staggered sideways. Her cheek throbbed. She put a hand to her mouth. No blood. Not this time.

Kamal was flexing his fingers. "Please. The whole thing is a Ponzi scheme. You know it. I know it. Mr Al-Hashemi knows it." It was the first time he'd said the name. "Your stupid numbers mean nothing. He doesn't expect the online value." He sneered. "There isn't enough money in the world for you to pay out all of that." His face turned impassive again. "All he wants is to get out what he put in. Plus something else for the trouble he's had to take to retrieve it. An extra million. That's very reasonable, I think you'd agree."

"Three million?"

"They said you were the clever one. Three million, and you can expect to live."

"It's not as easy as you think. The money isn't just sitting in one place – *but*" – she got the word out before Kamal had a chance to move – "it's something we can talk about when we meet."

Kamal's brows rose in a parody of surprise. "You think you're going to meet him? Why? He sent me to do this. Have I not made myself clear?"

She took a breath. "Perhaps it's me who hasn't made myself clear. I don't have the money."

This time she had no *but* to offer. The slap came on the same side again, powerful enough to send her to one knee, turning her throbbing cheek into a solid burn. At least it was only Kamal being physical: her two escorts from Capri were standing way back with their arms folded.

"Of course you have the money." His voice was unchanged, as if the slap hadn't happened. "The money goes in, everything stops, you disappear. Do you think I'm an idiot? Do you think Mr Al-Hashemi is an idiot?"

She climbed to her feet. She brushed her skirt down and wiped her hands. "That doesn't mean *I* have the money." She pointed at her own chest, and was reminded of the torn material on the left side and the chiffon rose that was no longer there.

"Don't make me laugh." Kamal showed no sign of being close to laughter.

"Who do you think is really behind New World Coin?" She raised her chin again. "You think it was just me doing everything? It was a whole group of them. More than one group. I was fronting it, doing all the clever talking. When it started taking off, more came in. They put money in to spread the word, do more advertising, find more promoters. It got bigger and bigger. When they started drawing down the money there wasn't as much as they imagined. They wanted more and more but they were draining it dry. Then they fell out, accused each other of taking more than their share. Little boys, squabbling. Your accountant, he's not the first person to lose their life. I was lucky. You think I've been off spending the money? I've been in hiding."

A third slap. This time she tasted blood but she stayed on her feet. He should extend his repertoire.

"We saw you in the hotel, the helicopter, the clothes, the suite. And this charity? Of course you're spending the money!"

"Okay, I got some of it. But not as much as you think. Not three million. The lifestyle, it's all for appearances. To generate more." She was expecting another swipe but none came. He was rubbing his palms together. Gratifying to know that her face was hurting his hand.

"I don't believe you," he said simply.

She raised her hands. "A few hundred thousand. Any more than that is more complicated. Not impossible, but complicated. And it'll take longer."

"How much longer?"

"I can discuss that with him. Take me to him so we can talk face to face. Or you can accept the smaller amount. Is he here?"

The fourth slap had the strength of the first three put together. She fell onto her side. Her head smacked into the floor. Spots of darkness formed. Something was dripping from her chin.

Kamal, above her, was unmoved. "You're not in a position to bargain."

She tried to lift her head but felt sick. She wiped her face. Her hand came away red. "He'd approve of this, would he, your boss? See you slapping a woman around like this? That's how he wants you to behave when you're representing him?"

He kicked her. His shoe jabbed a rib, making her suck in air. "You will not see him. He doesn't want to meet you. So, you will make the arrangements and give the money directly to me."

She managed to sit up. "I will deal only with him."

Again he was swift. Before she'd even registered that he'd moved she was staring up the barrel of a gun. "He isn't here. He's not even in Italy. He's at home."

She swallowed. Her head throbbed and her face felt thick. "If you kill me, you'll get nothing."

"I think we get nothing anyway, because you're just playing games. I am authorised to kill you in that case. No money, but satisfaction. That's almost as good."

His face remained impassive. His finger tightened on the trigger.

Chapter 40

Zack knocked. "We got it. Downstairs, now."

Outside, a car was waiting. Zack and Sarah were already inside. Fairchild joined them and they set off. "Where are we going?" he asked.

"Heliport," said Zack. "Got a bird lined up already."

"Where to?"

"South of here. Quite a way."

"Only one copter?"

"That's all we've got. Anyway, the landing site's limited. It's tight, kind of on a cliff-edge."

"Everything's on a cliff-edge here."

"FBI is going in by road. But it's not quick. We'll be first. We need to make our presence felt. Nail everything down until the Feds get there. They'll call in the authorities."

At the helipad was a US military helicopter and three Special Forces soldiers already inside it. They took off, and geared up in the air. This included weaponry. It was high-calibre stuff. Fairchild was familiar with it; so was Sarah.

Zack had a detailed map on screen. "This is as close as we can get without risking being heard from the house." He pointed.

"That's too far," said Fairchild. "It'll take too long. We're playing catch-up, remember?"

"We can't get closer to the house unless we want to announce our arrival. A boat would work if it weren't for those cliffs."

"It's too slow."

"It's as quick as we can do it. Remember, this guy wants his money back. If he just wanted to take her out there'd be plenty of easier ways."

"Nice thought."

"We've got to be subtle or he'll just run and it's all for nothing. It's not a great entry point but there's not too much climbing. I've done this before, Fairchild."

Fairchild didn't reply.

Zack's voice hardened a notch. "All right. Put it this way. Get on board or sit this one out."

Fairchild relented. Zack was right – he'd already pushed as hard as he could. "Okay. I'm in. Your rules."

It wasn't a bad plan given the time Zack had to develop it. Fifteen minutes later they were rappelling down into an orchard of some kind. The copter hovered for what felt like seconds while they slid, then it moved off, its beating fading into the rustling of trees, then silence. They spread out following Zack's schema and worked their way towards the house, up through what turned out to be a lemon grove onto a layout with gravel paths, vines, steps, hedges. They were edging their way through a formal garden. Clearing a trellis, Fairchild got a first view of the house and could see the corner of the building and the access points just as Zack had surmised. But something was wrong.

The lights were on in the windows. Not just one or two, but all the windows. And then he heard something equally wrong. He was expecting a forbidding silence but the sound that drifted to him was conversation, chatter. And then a splashing sound. Like people gathered round a pool. A pool party.

"This isn't right," he murmured into his mouthpiece. "This can't be the place."

"What's the problem?" Zack was also on the ground and sounded out of breath.

"Well, put it this way. I should still be wearing my tux."

Something rustled behind him and he spun, gun at the ready. But instead of some burly security guard he saw a couple hand in hand climbing through the trellis, her in a pink dress, him in a dress shirt. The woman gasped and put her hand to her mouth. The man just stared at the gun. Fairchild stowed it and retreated. Out of earshot he got back on the radio. "This is a wedding party, for crying out loud! No way could she be here."

"A wedding party? Shit. All right, let's get away before anyone starts screaming."

They regrouped and were airborne again in minutes.

"That was from the flight plan?" Fairchild asked.

"Nope," said Zack. "The hire company said the flight plan was wrong. They gave us this place. Devious, these Tunisians. They knew we'd come looking."

"What now?"

Zack's eyes were on the coastline below, his forehead a deep frown. "We go back, we do more analysis, we work out some options."

Fairchild couldn't trust himself to say a word.

Chapter 41

The silence stretched out. Kamal's trigger finger was the only thing in the world. Then the world shattered into a thousand pieces.

All Rose could register was noise: furniture scraping, a man shouting – screaming – and rapid footsteps. Kamal backed up, as startled as she was. Rose pulled herself away. Something launched itself at Kamal. There was a struggle, but a brief one. By the time the two heavies were anywhere near, a man Rose had never seen before was kneeling, the tip of his gun pointing straight into the back of Kamal's head.

"Back off! Back off now! Hands in the air!"

Kamal was looking at her, his expression unreadable. The two guards raised their hands. The unknown man motioned to Rose. "Disarm them."

She hesitated.

"Do it!" Whoever this guy was, he sounded American.

Rose scrambled up and checked them for weapons. Only one was armed. She took the gun and backed off, aiming at them. Kamal watched, wordlessly.

"What now?" she said.

He kept his eyes on Kamal. "We're going out the front. There's a red saloon on the drive. Keys are in the ignition. When I say go, go, get in, start the engine and leave the passenger door open."

"There's no one else in the building?"

"For sure there is. Which is why we need to hurry. Go!"

She backed to the door, turned and ran. Towards the main front door she tripped over the hem of her dress and staggered. Rapid footsteps pounded down the stairs. "Stop there!" a voice shouted. She raised her gun. The guy froze, arms up. But she had to turn away from him to open the door. It wouldn't open. She fumbled with the catch.

"Hurry!" shouted the stranger, glancing back at her from the inner doorway. Footsteps hammered on the floor above – a lot of them. The catch shifted. She held it back and was pulling on the brass handle of the door when a hand grabbed her arm. The man from the staircase was dragging her back. She swung and knocked him on the side of the head with the gun. His grip weakened. She chopped his arm, twisted and kicked. He cried out and fell to his knees. She turned and prised the door open. She ran down the steps towards the car but he'd recovered and was right behind her. He threw himself forward and grabbed her round the waist. She turned as they fell and grappled. The gun flew out of her hand. He was powerful, but she was better trained. A blow to his nose, his eye, his tender area, and his grip weakened. She wrenched herself free and sprinted to the red saloon. She jumped in and started the engine. Already the guy was on his feet again and staggering towards the gun. Where was the American? She revved the engine. He appeared at the door just as the Tunisian picked up the gun and aimed it at her. She lurched the car forward. Her bare foot slipped on the pedal and the car bucked and stalled.

She turned the key. The motor whined. She heard a shot. The Tunisian was hunched over. The American was hurtling towards the car, gun in hand. The Tunisian straightened to aim. The engine finally caught. The American leaped in. Another shot. The bullet missed the car. Rose hit the accelerator and they jerked forward.

Others were running out of the house. Rose skidded, got control and straightened up. The driveway came out on a narrow, twisty road. She gunned it as much as possible but had to brake for each bend.

"Are they following us?" she said.

"Not yet. But they will."

"Who the hell are you?" She could only glance at him while keeping the car on the road. Slicked back light hair, cheap shirt, young-looking.

"FBI. Agent Holmes."

"FBI?"

"That's right. And I know you're MI6. So you can drop the accent."

Rose thought she'd already done that. "If you're FBI, where's everybody else?"

"In the wrong place. Twenty miles down the coast. We were on the way there when our car came off the road. Turned over a few times down the cliff. I got out before it went up in flames. The others didn't."

"Shit." She glanced across again.

He blinked a couple of times but that was it. "I came up looking to find a phone. Ended up in the grounds of that place. Recognised one of the goons from our surveillance on Capri and thought I'd look into it."

"I'm glad you did. That was lucky." She said it before she'd had time to think.

"You might call losing three friends on a hillside lucky, but I sure don't." His accent had a slight Southern twang.

"Sorry." They were still swinging down the hill on the switchback road. "So you've got no phone, no badge…?"

"I grabbed one thing getting out of the car." He held up the gun. "Problem with that?"

"I guess not. And everyone else has gone to the wrong place?"

"I guess so." Something grabbed his attention in the mirror. "Shit. They're on the move."

"I don't see anything."

"They're up above. But it's them. I can see their headlight beam. They're moving too fast for it to be anyone else."

"We need to hide somewhere until we can call for help."

"That's going to be difficult. They're right behind us. On these roads if you try and outrun someone you'll end up…" he glanced down at the cliff and swallowed.

"Okay, so we have to dump the car and disappear on foot."

"How far can you run barefoot?"

Damn those shoes! "Good point. Give them the slip somehow?"

"That's okay in a city, but round here? There's only one road."

"Pull in and try and shoot our way out?"

"We've only got one gun."

They drove for a while. Holmes glanced behind several times. "I think they're gaining on us."

"I'm doing the best I can."

They rounded a corner and the sea was right in front of them. Rose braked and skidded to a halt. "Coast road. Which way? North is back to Capri and Naples."

"South."

"Really?"

"South is where we were headed. That's where the extraction team is. It'll be easier to find them again that way."

Rose hesitated.

"Well, whichever way it is, hurry up!" said Holmes. "They're right behind us."

Rose turned south. This was a faster road and she pushed it as much as she could. It was busier than the switchback road but quiet given the late hour. Distant headlights appeared in the rear view mirror. "Is that them?"

Holmes turned to peer through the rear windscreen. "That's them."

"Are you sure? How did they know which way we went?"

"They must have been close enough to see. And yes, I'm sure."

She sped up. The car behind kept a steady distance. "I can stay in front of them but we need a plan."

"Yeah, I know." He kept glancing up at the mirror. Some of his confidence seemed to have ebbed away. On their left the cliffs rose up straight from the road. On the right was nothing but the sea.

"We must come to a place of some size eventually," she said.

"I guess. I've never been here before."

"Me neither."

"Should we try and stop to find a phone or something?"

"What, a payphone? They still have those?"

"I dunno. By the time we find out they'll be on us. Why aren't you wearing a tracker, anyway?"

"That bit of the plan went wrong. Hence the mistake with the extraction team. The only thing I can think is to carry on until we get to a town that's big enough to lose them. Not some crack in the cliffs with only one road."

He grimaced. "That could be some way off."

"Tell me about it. If you have any other ideas in the meantime, let's have it."

"They might get help. Get another car coming to meet us the other way. We'll be stuck in the middle on this road with nowhere to go."

"That's not an idea."

"No, but—"

"We'll just have to hope that doesn't happen."

They drove in silence for what felt like hours, though it was probably only about thirty minutes. Rose's foot throbbed. They passed through numerous places that were just a few lights, gone in a moment. Every time Rose braked Holmes glanced at the mirror. He was checking what she already knew: the headlights were still there.

They came to a place where the land on the seaward side of them expanded. Up ahead, lights in the air suggested sizeable docks. "Finally!" said Rose. The coast road merged with a bigger road coming from inland. *Salerno*, announced a sign. Entering the town they were forced to slow. Holmes was again looking in the mirror.

"We need to dump this car and get away from it as fast as we can," said Rose. They were entering a major commercial zone – shops, offices, hotels. Plenty of traffic, plenty of streets.

"You call it. Find a place, park up, we jump out and move off."

Rose glanced over. "If the idea is we blend in, you need to leave the gun."

"What?" He looked down at the weapon on his lap.

"You can't keep that hidden with no holster or jacket. You don't have any ID. Neither of us do. We do not want to get picked up. We're hiding now, not fighting, until we can get word back to the others."

He looked pained. "Just leave it in the car?"

"Yes." They were coming into a square next to a garden with trees and a fountain. "This is as good as anywhere. Plenty of streets off it, places to hide. Can you see them behind us?"

"No, but there's other traffic. They could be there but I can't pick them out."

"Well, we've got to do this." She pulled nose first into a space. Holmes slid the gun under the seat. They got out and Rose locked the car. As they walked away she dropped the keys into a litter bin.

"This way," she said. There weren't enough people to blend in – it was too late at night. They needed to disappear down a side street.

Holmes glanced behind. "Shit! They've seen us! Down here!" He grabbed Rose by the hand and pulled her into a covered walkway, a colonnaded part of the building that lined one side of the square.

"No! If we go down here we—"

"We don't have time to discuss it! They'll have a clear shot of us. Keep moving." He was muttering into her ear.

"You think they'd shoot us here, out in the open?"

"They're terrorists, aren't they? You want to risk it?"

The walkway opened out into a large space, covered and well lit, with glass doors along the front. Rose caught sight of some branding on the displays. "It's a train station. We're in the train station."

"Really?" Holmes suddenly looked energised. "Is there anything about to leave?"

"Seriously? Get on a train?"

"Why not? As long as we're quick they won't see which platform we go to." He steered her towards a departure screen. "There's one going in about four minutes. From Rome."

Rose tried to make sense of the numbers. "No, that one's gone."

"No, it's delayed, look! It's about to arrive. Come on! Before they come round the corner!" He was tugging at her hand again, casting a worried look behind.

"We've got no tickets."

"We'll think of something."

"Like what? We've got no money either."

"Do you have any better ideas?"

"Well, yes, we could have gone up into the town and lost them there, gone into a bar—"

"Too late! We're here now, if we backtrack they'll see us. And we can phone from the train. We just need to keep moving."

"Phone from the train how?"

"Leave that to me. We don't have time for this!"

Rose gave up. They ran through to the platform entrance and up the stairs. No one was checking tickets onto the platform. Too late at night, maybe. On the platform itself a fair number of tired and disgruntled passengers were waiting in silence. Rose and Holmes weaved their way through, getting as much distance between them and the platform entrance as possible.

The train pulled up within a minute. Avoiding the gaze of anyone in uniform, they boarded. They waited, hanging back from the doors. The train sat there for an agonising two or three minutes: ample time for Al-Hashemi's people to get on if they'd been spotted. There was no way of knowing if they had or not until the train was on the move.

An alarm sounded, the doors slid shut, the train moved off. A long announcement presumably included an apology for the late running. If it included any destinations Rose couldn't make them out. "Where's the train going?" she muttered to Holmes.

"No idea."

They hovered in the vestibule until the travellers who actually had tickets found their seats. Holmes peered into the compartment. "Plenty of space. If they do show up we'll be safer in a carriage, in full view."

They took a couple of seats, Rose next to the window, but as soon as they'd sat Holmes was on his feet again. "What are you doing?" she asked.

"We need a phone, right? And tickets. And money. Wait here."

"What am I supposed to do if they show up?"

"I won't be long."

"Or a ticket inspector comes along?"

"Just think of something."

"Holmes?"

He walked off and disappeared out of the compartment.

Rose shivered. The air conditioning was way too cool. She rubbed the goosebumps on her bare arms and watched Salerno slide past the window and fade into darkness.

Chapter 42

Fairchild faced Zack across the empty space of the room. Behind them the techies continued to search and screen, search and screen. Zoe was up here as well now, the party downstairs continuing for the determined few. Sarah was here too, forlorn without her subject. That didn't seem to bother the two Georgs, who were either out drinking somewhere or just asleep. It was gone one in the morning.

Zack was, Fairchild had to admit, bearing himself pretty well given the situation. How long had this huge brick wall of a man been his friend? Long enough for it to count for something, he'd always thought. Zack knew all his secrets. They had a mutually beneficial relationship, Zack getting the arms-length specialised help he needed, Fairchild being paid well for his work. But the risk was always with Fairchild. Zack could walk away any time. So could Fairchild, in theory. They even talked about that. But they both knew Fairchild couldn't do it. In the early years he needed this life, access to the clandestine world, to retain any hope of getting the answers he needed about the fate of his parents. More recently those mysteries had all been resolved. Fairchild no longer needed the inside track like he used to. And emotionally too he'd moved on. Contrary to all his expectations, the woman he'd loved since the first time he saw her had seen something in him too, and now he could wrap all the meaning in life he needed around her. How did Zack really feel about that? Was there some unacknowledged resentment that his friend no longer needed him the way he used to? And if so, how deep did it go?

A gloom had settled, everyone drawing into themselves. It was Zoe who broke the silence. "Anything from the satellites?"

Zack took a moment to respond, as though he were emerging from underwater. "They're working on it. Like I said, we weren't expecting to need it." He glanced at the tech team who tapped away, stared at images, tapped away some more.

"We know for sure she was on the helicopter?" Zoe was being thorough, thinking it through right from the start.

"Our agents have spoken with people who saw her get on. She was on it when it took off," said Zack.

"Are we looking at the sea? They could have thrown her out. I don't want to be melodramatic, but..." She glanced at Fairchild.

"If he just wanted to kill her he could have done it. They took her off for a reason."

"It definitely went south?"

Zack was patient. They'd been all over this, but Zoe wasn't to know. "They wouldn't be so blasé as to submit a flight plan that had them going south and then head north. It's got to be in that direction somewhere."

"There can't be too many places you can land a helicopter on that coast. Are we doing it that way? Checking the topography, narrowing down the options?"

"We are. But you don't need that much space to land a copter. Not a small private hire one like that. That's kind of the point of them."

Fairchild's self-control took a break. "So, are we building a list of possible places, or aren't we?"

"We're working on it." Zack was unfazed. One of the techies looked up and gave what he probably thought was a reassuring nod. Don't worry, you're *girlfriend*'s off the map with a terrorist who thinks she's a swindler he's sworn to kill and we have no idea where she is — but we're working on it. Fairchild gripped the arms of the chair and took a deep breath.

"Could they have gone to another island? Or double-backed and come back here?" Zoe again, working through all the options. She could certainly keep her head in a crisis.

Zack shook his head. "They went to the mainland."

"We think," said Fairchild. "We guess."

"It's not a guess. There's no island that way, and they didn't come back. Where else could they go? Between here and there is nothing except sea!"

"They could be on a yacht," said Fairchild. "Plenty of super-yachts out there with helipads. They could have touched down on a boat and be motoring over to Tunisia right now!"

"Al-Hashemi doesn't have a super-yacht." That was Zoe.

"You can't know that for sure. With all his shell companies and entities on entities?"

"I've studied them. I know this guy and his offshore ecosystem. He doesn't have a yacht. It's not his style, anyway."

"Well, he could have borrowed one. Called in a favour somewhere."

Zack put his head back, closed his eyes and held his breath. Then he opened his eyes and faced off his friend again. "We will find her. We're doing everything we can. And she's good, Fairchild. You know that. We haven't sent out some innocent. She'll play for time, she'll keep him hanging. My money is on her calling in before we track her down. And if you have any faith in her, yours would be too."

"That only works if he believes her story. If she can keep it up through interrogation. If it comes to that." Fairchild wished he hadn't said it out loud, the word *interrogation*. Sarah, in his peripheral vision, shifted in her seat.

"If anyone can," said Zack firmly, "she can."

"Larry." One of the techies was calling the boss over. Larry stood behind him staring at the screen. He looked up at Zack.

"Got something?" Zack went over and watched. "That a copter?"

"Looks like it to me," said Larry.

Fairchild joined them. The satellite feed was poor and it was dark, but it did look like rotary blades catching in moonlight. "When was this?"

"Two hours ago," said the techie.

"Two hours?"

"Best we could do," said Zack. "Get the coordinates. I'll pass them onto the mainland team leader."

Zack called and passed on the information to the FBI coordinator. Fairchild stared at the still, got the techie to enhance it as much as possible. Zoe and Sarah also came over. Zack, on the phone, turned to them.

"There's a car load of agents five minutes away from there."

"We should go over," said Fairchild. "We can secure it better than they can."

"Didn't you hear me? They're five minutes away. Let them check it out. It could be nothing."

"It's not nothing. It's a helicopter landing right in the middle of our time window."

Zack had turned away, phone to his ear.

"Are we not even going to scramble?"

Zack held a finger up. "They're pulling into the driveway now. No cars, a couple of lights. Probably empty."

"Well, I hope they're a bit more thorough than that," said Fairchild. Zack said nothing, intent on the call. Even Zoe was looking askance at Fairchild now. He entered the coordinates into the map on his phone.

"South of Sorrento, north of Salerno," he said. "Very close to where we were. In the air it's just a few minutes away."

"Or by water." That was Zoe. It was an interesting thought.

Zack ended the call and turned to them. "They searched the whole place. Nobody there. But – looks like there was a bust-up of some kind. A window's been smashed. Furniture knocked over. It doesn't look lived-in, so why was anyone there at all? And the front door was wide open, like they left in a hurry."

"Let's get over there," said Fairchild.

"What's the point? They've gone. If it was them at all."

"So we just sit here?"

"No, we do more deskwork and try and figure out where they might have gone."

"Figure out?" He was shouting, he knew it.

"It could just be a house that's been burgled." That was Sarah. She'd been looking at the map and rubbing her face thoughtfully.

"Then what about the copter?" Zack asked her.

"Could have been someone else. There are lots of flights, lots of boats with helipads down there."

"Look, if you won't do anything, I will." Fairchild walked out of the door.

Zack followed him out into the hallway. "Look, I know you like to be your own boss, but…"

The staff door opened. Adel stepped through it. The three of them stared at each other.

"What's he doing here?" asked Zack.

"I don't know. Ask him," said Fairchild.

Adel tried to answer. "I just—"

"Spying, are you?"

Adel tried again. "No, I was—"

"He works here, Zack! He comes and goes. He's doing a job."

Zack rounded on Fairchild. "Yeah, a job working for you! I see what you're doing, placing your minions everywhere. That won't wash with me. I won't be undermined, Fairchild. I was sent here to get something done and I'll see it through. You need to buckle down. I don't care that you own this place, this is my show and we will all – all – do it my way!"

Fairchild punched him in the face. He staggered back, into the wall. Adel's eyes were round.

"If it's your op," said Fairchild, "for God's sake, do something!"

Zack was up and going in for a punch, but Zoe stepped in front of him.

"Zack! Don't. There's no point. Let's all just calm down. This doesn't help anyone."

Fairchild was breathing deeply. His heart was hammering. Sarah was at the doorway. Behind her, Larry and the others were standing and staring.

Zack was exploring his jaw. Fairchild hoped it hurt. He turned to Adel. "What are you doing up here, anyway?"

"I just came to ask if I could do anything before I go off shift."

Fairchild sighed. "Well, I don't think so, but the big guy here is in charge. Ask him."

He retreated to the Blue Room. Nobody tried to stop him.

Chapter 43

With no watch or phone Rose was struggling to keep track of time. Holmes had been gone long enough for her to start to wonder if she needed to go and look for him. But then he appeared, carrying a drinks holder and two hot drinks, with a pleased expression on his face.

"Cappuccino," he said as he sat down. "I guessed."

"You guessed right." Rose took the cup with relief. "But how? I'm guessing you didn't try and persuade some random stranger that you're with the FBI."

"Well, you're probably not going to like this…" he rested his head on the back of the seat.

"Go on."

"I found a guard and told him that I'd been on a stag party and was a victim of a practical joke which left me miles from my hotel with no phone or wallet."

"I see. And how did you explain my role in all this?"

He went slightly pink. The silence grew.

"You told them I was an escort, did you? Or some random woman they organised for you?"

He raised a shoulder. "You are kind of dressed for it. And it worked. He took pity on me. Thought it was funny. He said we could ride blind to the next stop."

"Which is?"

"About forty-five minutes. And a guy overhearing it let me borrow his phone."

"Great! So you called in."

"I did. And they'll be waiting for us at the station. And as well as that, he bought us a couple of drinks. So – any complaints?"

She sighed. "I guess not. Any sign of trouble?"

A shadow crossed his face. "No. We'll just have to stay in plain sight and hope they don't try anything, if they're even on board. As soon as we step off the train we'll have backup. If we are being followed it may be our chance to apprehend one or two of these lowlifes."

His face settled into an expression of bland competence, but clearly he had a flair for blagging which he secretly enjoyed.

"What's your first name?" Rose asked.

He looked surprised at the question. "William."

"And what do people call you?"

He frowned. "William."

"Well, thanks, William. Not sure I'd be alive right now if it weren't for you."

He looked pleased but a little embarrassed. "Just doing my job. We'll be back at base shortly anyway. We can relax, for now."

"I guess." Rose turned back to stare out of the window but couldn't see much beyond her own reflection. The air conditioning had settled down to a more comfortable level. She sipped her cappuccino, and William Holmes next to her did the same. She thought about the evening's events and what might still come, and William Holmes, she presumed, did the same.

Chapter 44

Something was interfering with Rose's shoulder. She tried to push it off but it came back. A shape hovered in front of her. She tried to wave it away. It was saying something. "Wake up! For Christ's sake, Rose, wake up! Now!"

She opened her eyes. A face, young-looking, light hair slicked back. "Come on! We've got to get off this train. Move it, now!"

Her mouth was dry and her tongue felt huge. She was on a train? She looked around. The seating, the window, the empty coffee cup on the tray in front of her, they all looked familiar. Then it came back to her. The helicopter, the villa, the shooting, the chase, the station. This guy. What was his name? Holmes, that was it.

"What's going on?" She felt the vibrating rhythm of the train, but it was slowing down. Outside, she could see platform lights but nothing else.

Holmes put his mouth close to her ear. "I've seen them. They're coming. Al-Hashemi's people. We have to get off now!"

The train jerked to a stop and the doors opened. Holmes was trying to pull her up. "Quick! Quick!"

She got up, and almost fell again. Holmes grabbed her and propelled her in front of him down the aisle. She was still trying to make sense of things. "But where did you—"

"Just get off! I'll explain later." He turned back. "Shit." He pushed her onward. "He's there! He's right there!" he muttered in her ear.

"Where?"

"Don't turn around! Just get off, for Christ's sake! If we're quick we can beat him to it."

Rose was passing through the compartment door. She managed a quick glance back. A tall man in a checked shirt was coming towards them. The alarm sounded for the door. "Go!" Holmes barked. She threw herself out of the door onto the platform. The door started to close. Holmes' elbow stopped it. She grabbed the edge of the door with her fingers, and leaned back with all her weight. Holmes squeezed through and it slid shut.

"This way!" He made for the only structure on the platform, a waiting room. They crouched behind it, watching for any movement, listening for any sound. After a pause the train started moving. They could hear nothing else, no running, no shouting. The train gathered speed and left the station.

Rose stood.

"Careful!" said Holmes in an urgent whisper.

Rose slid along the side of the building and quickly looked out, up and down the platform. She stood straight and held her arms out. "No one here."

Holmes remained crouched. "Maybe they're out of sight."

"The guy you pointed out couldn't have got off. You think someone else did? That there was more than one on the train?"

"Yeah, there were two of them."

"You're sure? I didn't recognise that guy."

"I did. He was on Capri. For sure."

"Well, if the other one's here there's only one of him. And he's keeping a low profile."

"We'd better get out of here before there's more. Al-Hashemi has people all the way down this coast. They saw us get off. They'll send others."

Rose looked around at the single-platform station. A couple of cars had been outside meeting passengers but they'd now driven away. Beyond the lights she could see nothing. "Where the hell are we, William? What happened to the backup?"

"Backup? That's long gone. We missed our stop. Don't you know what time it is? It's four o'clock in the morning!"

"What?"

He pointed at the station clock. Four thirteen, it read. That made no sense. "How can it be four thirteen? We were meant to get off at the next stop!"

"I know. I slept like a baby. I guess you did too. Woke up a few minutes ago desperate for a – to go to the bathroom. So I did, and that's when I saw the guy, coming out of the can. And he saw me. We were slowing down so I figured we'd better get off. We'd have more options."

She still couldn't compute. "We *slept* through it? We slept through the stop? And for hours after that? I don't sleep as heavily as that. I don't believe I'd…" Then it came to her, where she recognised this feeling of grogginess, the dryness in her mouth, the pounding headache that was starting up. "William, when you got those drinks, did you actually see someone making them?"

He frowned. "No. It was a friend of the guy whose phone I borrowed. He went to get them for me from the buffet car. Come to think of it, he did take a long time. Are you thinking—?"

"Those drinks were spiked. It's the only explanation for how we were both out like a light for so long. But if that was Al-Hashemi, then how?"

Holmes rubbed his chin. "We know his men were on the train. They must have got to people, set it all up. Hell, maybe the guard was in on it! Or the guy who lent me his phone!

And there was me thinking I'd done a great blagging job."
He looked crestfallen.

"But if they managed to drug us, why did they let us get
off? They should have been right there in the carriage
keeping an eye on us."

"Maybe I woke up a lot sooner than they expected. Or
they needed to go to the john like me. That's where I saw
the guy. I guess they thought we were out for the count until
Palermo."

"Palermo? What do you mean, Palermo?"

He looked surprised. "Well, it could be Syracuse. One or
the other. If my geography is right." He stared at her
incomprehension. "Where else would a train go for hours on
end south of Naples? We must be on Sicily by now."

"Sicily? How can we possibly be in Sicily?"

"I don't see how we can be anywhere else."

"But Sicily's an island! How can we end up on a train on
Sicily?"

He looked bashful. "I read somewhere they have train
ferries to Sicily. You know, the train goes onto a boat across
the strait? Then it rolls off the other side."

Rose tried to comprehend what he was saying. "We must
have been dead to the world to sleep through all of that."

"I guess. But we got away from them. If we can escape
from this station all right."

They both listened to the silence. "If there is someone
here they're showing a lot of patience," said Rose.

"Biding their time. They know company is on the way."
Holmes sounded grim. "All we can do is make a run for it
and hope to take them by surprise."

"Okay." Rose had been studying what they could see
outside of the station, which wasn't much. "Which way? I
reckon there's only one road out there. Up or along?"

Holmes shrugged. "What do you think?"

"Up, I guess."

"All right. Ready?"

They broke cover, running straight across the tracks towards the main station building. No footsteps, no gunfire, nothing.

"Stop! Stop!" Rose pulled up as they drew alongside the building wall.

"What are you doing? We need to keep going!" Holmes' eyes darted around, wide like a hunted animal.

"Have you any idea how painful it is to run over iron rails and rocks in bare feet?" Her soles felt like they were on fire.

"Well, no, but would you prefer to get shot?"

"Try it!" She bent over, feeling sick.

"Are you asking to borrow my shoes? They'd fall straight off you. I have enormous feet." He sounded ridiculously proud of the fact.

"How about your socks? That much would help."

"Fine. But let's get further away first. I thought I heard a car just now."

They checked the coast was clear, then sprinted across the road and dived behind the next building. They paused for breath then did the same thing again and again. After that, there were no more buildings. If someone was waiting at the station, they weren't coming after them.

They followed the road upward. Rose could only manage a limping walk. Away from the station the only light was intermittent moonlight. Around them loomed hillsides of bare rock, nothing more.

Chapter 45

Erik did as he was told and returned to the staff quarters. He lay on his mattress but didn't sleep at all. Early the next morning he put the uniform back on, smartened himself up and went over to the hotel. Adel wasn't on the front desk. Off duty until noon, he was told. He didn't really know any of the others. They seemed suspicious but no one challenged him. He was working there after all, even if he didn't have paperwork.

He wandered through the lobby and garden into the ballroom. Ooff, what a mess! An army of workers were tidying up, pushing decorations into huge canvas bags, taking apart the stage and the catwalk. They had another event there that evening, they said. Erik helped for a while, collecting up stuff from the tables and carrying it out. He chatted to one or two of the staff who were on duty last night. No one mentioned a kidnapping or anything at all like that. Apart from the staff, he saw no one he recognised. Eventually the place was clear and he drifted out again. Still ages before Adel would appear. He went through to the back and revisited the doorway where he spoke to Ulia Popovic. A thrill passed through him at the memory, but then it faded. If Popovic had been kidnapped, would he get his money? Suddenly he felt tearful. He'd come all this way and felt so close to putting everything straight, but then it was all snatched away, like Popovic herself. And no one seemed to care! Where were the police? Erik had witnessed a crime. Did they not want to talk to him? But then, they might have some questions about his lack of paperwork and why he was wearing a uniform. Perhaps as well there were no police around.

Inside, Erik paused at the bottom of the staff stairs. He knew the big fancy rooms were on the top floor. He'd bet anything that was where Popovic had been staying. He could just go up and see if anything was going on. Make an excuse for being there if anyone asked. He ran lightly up the stairs right to the top and pushed the door open. Funny, these places. The staff areas were all white and grey, plain, but you stepped into a guest area and everything turned plush. Thick carpets, patterned wallpaper, brass handles everywhere. He emerged and let the door close behind him. It wasn't a big area, only a few doors off it. Outside one of the doors was an upright chair, and in the chair sat the female bodyguard of Popovic, the one he saw last night. She looked pale and distracted.

As soon as she saw him she rose and came forward. "Can I help you?"

She wasn't too friendly but Erik persisted. "You were there last night. When the car pulled up. You came through the door. You tried to stop them."

Her eyes narrowed. "That was you?"

"Yes, it was me!" He rubbed his chin where the Arab had hit him. "So what's happening? Where is she? Is she safe? No one seems to know about it!"

"She's fine." The woman spoke shortly. "She's absolutely fine. It was all a misunderstanding. She was going to meet someone, that's all. She's back in her room now."

"Really?" Erik looked eagerly at the door behind her.

"She's got a migraine. She's lying down. She needs absolute silence, no visitors at all." Her face was impassive.

"Oh, I see." But he didn't, really. "A misunderstanding, you said? Must have been a pretty serious one."

"It was."

"You came running out. I saw you. You thought someone was taking her!"

"That wasn't what it was."

"You misunderstood?"

"That's right." She seemed super-composed, but her eyes looked kind of red.

"Look. I was talking to her earlier. About the coin and the launch and so on." The woman said nothing but she was listening. Erik continued. "She promised to refund my investment to compensate me for all the delays. And the journey here. I came from Kenya, you see." Again nothing, but her eyes were on him. "Maybe you could check? That it's still okay? That she can still do that? My name's Erik. Could you ask her when she's feeling better?"

She thought about it. "How much did she say she'd give you?"

"Three thousand. Dollars. Three thousand dollars." Erik felt the heat of embarrassment. It suddenly felt like he was begging for it. "She said she'd leave it for me at the desk. For Adel. He works here, you see. He's my – he works here."

She looked puzzled but didn't comment. "I'll let her know when she wakes up. I'll pass the message on."

"You sure that's okay?"

"Yes, I'm sure. You'd better go. You're not supposed to be up here."

Erik made some effusive thanks and slipped away.

Hope, Erik, hope. Maybe it would all be okay after all. Just maybe.

Chapter 46

Rose jerked awake. She was lying on a dirt floor. It was light. Holmes was standing up in front of her, stretching. She sat up slowly. Her head thudded as it all came back to her.

They were in a tumbledown stone shed they'd spotted just off the road out of the village, sunk low so it wasn't noticeable from the potholed track the road had become. Despite the hard floor Rose was still drowsy: whatever sedative had knocked them out on the train was still circulating in her system. The last thing she'd seen before falling asleep was Holmes, sitting with his back against the wall, eyes closed, as if he were meditating.

A low rumbling sound built and then faded. They looked at each other.

"Truck going past. Just a farm vehicle," said Holmes. Rose felt stiffness in all her limbs and her mouth was dry.

"Any idea what time it is?"

"Nope."

She rubbed her face. "Shit."

"What?" He seemed quite unfazed.

"This, all of this! What do we do, stay here waiting for God knows what? No one knows we're here. We need to get a message out at the very least."

He smoothed his hair back where it had frizzed up. "You're right. I'll go back down to the village."

"Is that wise? What if Al-Hashemi's men are at the station?"

"I'll have to be careful. Check the place out before making myself visible."

"We should both go. It gives us more options."

He grimaced.

"Why not? What's the problem?"

"Because you'll stick out like a sore thumb."

"Me? What, you think you look like a local?"

"No, but at least I'm dressed ordinarily. Not like something out of a horror movie."

"Oh, thanks!" But then Rose remembered all the makeup she had on. She had no idea what she looked like. "Do I have panda eyes?"

He seemed embarrassed now. "I shouldn't have said that. But yeah, you kind of do, and then with the black dress and no shoes and all."

"Okay, I get it. But what about Al-Hashemi? They won't just give up on us, will they? If they saw us getting off they'll still be around."

"All I need to do is make a phone call, right? I can knock on a few doors. Car broke down or something."

"How's your Italian?"

He shook his head.

"Fine on the train to find English speakers," she said. "This is a small Sicilian village. You might struggle."

"I'll think of something." He probably would, as well. "And if it doesn't work out, at least I've got shoes, so I can do a reasonable job of running away. Speaking of which…" He nodded towards her stockinged feet.

"Oh, you want your socks back? Fair enough."

She had to prise them off her soles, which had bled and made a crusty mess. He took them with a look of distaste and put them on with the minimum of hand contact.

"Thanks for the loan," she said. "Just as well I'm staying here."

He got up. "Hopefully this won't take long. The next thing to happen is they'll send someone for us. A car, maybe a copter if there's some place to land. So if you hear something—"

"But how will I know it's our lot and not Al-Hashemi?"

He paused. "I don't know. All I can do is try and get back here as soon as I can."

"Unless they shoot you."

"Well, I guess. But I'm going to try real hard to avoid that. Be easier if I still had my gun."

She ignored his pointed remark. "Bring back some water."

He turned to climb out.

"And some food. If you can. Please." She suddenly didn't want to be on her own. But he was right – it made sense.

"I'll do my best." He scrambled over the fallen stones to climb through the gap in the wall they'd used to get in. Then he was gone. Silence. She lay back down again, not expecting to sleep.

She woke. It was warmer. The sun was shining directly on her through a hole which used to be a high window. Its heat was intense. She sat up and shuffled out of its way. She felt groggy. Those sedatives! But they were beginning to recede now. She had a raging thirst and felt weak with hunger.

What was the time? How long had Holmes been gone? What was happening out there? This was all getting pretty frustrating. She got to her feet using the wall to balance. She grimaced, working her ankles, feeling her feet on the dirt floor. Not too bad. Her dress was coated in a grey dust and there was a large tear below the knee which was making it difficult to walk. She knelt and ripped the material, ending up with half the skirt in her hands. She threw it in a corner and clambered through the gap to get outside.

The heat hit her. The sun was directly above. Its brightness made her blink. She took a few steps and stumbled. The ground was made up of rock and thistles. She must have come this way last night but they were hurrying, focused on finding somewhere to hide. Baked in the sun, the rock seared the soles of her feet. She made for a clump of vegetation. A thorn pierced the skin between her toes. She cried out. She limped a few more steps to see the track where they'd come last night. The way down led back to the village. In the other direction it continued up and over a featureless stony hill. No other buildings were in sight. The sun was already giving her a headache. Her mouth was sticky-dry and beads of sweat were forming on her face. She needed water. But the idea of staggering over these rocks in this heat – and where would she get some? The whole place looked as dry as a bone.

She returned inside. She could at least wait until the sun had passed overhead. Maybe Holmes would be back by then. She curled up again on the floor to wait.

Chapter 47

Erik went and lay down again until noon. Then he got up and went back to the lobby, but Adel was late on shift. Erik waited, then he saw him come down from upstairs. He didn't look very happy but he was carrying an envelope. Erik's heart raced. He wanted to dash forward but hung back anxiously. He didn't have long to wait before Adel came over.

"My friend," said Erik. He couldn't make sense of the expression on Adel's face.

"So, I have something for you. I think it's what you want. So. I guess – if you have what you need, you'll be going home, then? No need to stay here if it's all resolved."

Erik had given no thought at all to this. "Well, I guess so. Sure, yes! I mean, I've got no money to get home, so…"

"Meet me in twenty minutes," said Adel. "Change out of that uniform and get all your stuff together. I'll come with you. Okay?"

When Erik returned, Adel walked with him down the steps. They stopped at a place where the pathway widened out and made a platform. There was a little chapel there and a bench under some trees. They sat and Adel passed him the envelope. Erik opened the seal carefully. He couldn't stop himself making a little excited noise. He pulled out the notes, not all the way, only so that he could count them. Thirty crisp, clean one hundred dollar bills. That was a sight he'd never seen before. He put them back, re-sealed it and stashed it in his pocket. "What a lady she is. Amazing."

"Yes, amazing."

They carried on down the steps. "So what will you do with it?" Adel asked.

That puzzled Erik. "Give it back, of course. Back to my mother and sister. They were saving it up to spend on the farm. They want a new barn to store food. Maybe a better truck." He chatted away about the crops and the animals and how difficult it was sometimes, and what they did when they managed to make a surplus. Adel was very quiet.

"You know, man?" Erik finally said.

Adel seemed to come back from his own thoughts. "What?"

"All of this I'm talking about – do you understand what I'm saying? I mean, really?"

"Yes, I know. I grew up on an island in the Philippines, in a village. My family were farmers. Everyone was a farmer."

"You moved away for work?"

"To university. To better things. I thought."

"What did you study?"

"Economics."

"Economics? Like Popovic! That's a good thing! You can change the world like she did. Give access to everyone, opportunities to get rich. Why are you working in a hotel, then? You could do better, my man!"

Adel looked like he was thinking hard. "Yes, maybe so. Maybe I could."

They got to the harbour. Adel insisted on buying Erik's ferry ticket back to Naples. It didn't leave for another hour. "You want a drink?" said Adel.

"Oh, man, I don't drink. Bad for the health."

"Me neither." They both laughed.

They sat at a cafe on the esplanade with glasses of lemonade, and talked about the hotel and the huge event and all the guests from all over the world coming to see Popovic.

"You know, that wasn't the name of the woman you met," said Adel, a little bit cautiously. "She called herself something else."

"What? Oh, it was her. I spoke to her. It was definitely her." Erik patted the envelope in his pocket. "She's for real. Not everyone is. Some of those guests, they're just playing a big game."

Adel nodded at that. "For sure. Did you speak to the young Englishman? Raphael?"

"Oh, that boy! 'Bring me some shampers, you there!'" It was a bad impression but Adel still laughed. "But I don't think he drank champagne with his Arab friends."

Adel stopped laughing. "What do you mean?"

Erik told him what he'd realised when he saw the guy last night. It was the Englishman that he'd seen meeting one of the Arabs that time when he was waiting for ice. Adel frowned, but then changed the subject. They talked about home and family and life and friends and beliefs. Hope and the future. Erik told Adel he must come and visit him in the family village in Kenya. Adel said that he would, but he didn't offer the same in return. They exchanged numbers and shook hands like the best of brotherly friends.

They went to the jetty together. "Be careful with that," said Adel, nodding towards the envelope in Erik's pocket. "Naples is a big city. Keep it hidden away, and watch who's behind you."

"Sure, my friend." They shook hands for the last time. Erik got on the boat, and as it backed and turned, he saw that Adel was still there, standing on the jetty. He waved a goodbye and the boat motored up and sped towards Naples.

Chapter 48

It was a noise that woke her this time. Tyres on bumpy ground, an engine working as it came uphill, getting louder. Then it cut out. She lay motionless, listening for any further sound. Nothing.

It could be someone else entirely. Or, they could be out of the vehicle and surrounding the place already, creeping round the sides. Where was Holmes? Was he still alive? A picture flashed in her mind of him face up in the middle of a dusty street, his blood drying in the heat. Like the aftermath of a duel in a Spaghetti Western. Except that Holmes didn't have a gun.

She rolled and grabbed the material she'd torn from her skirt. She ripped it in half lengthways and wrapped each one around her foot, again and again, binding it as tightly as she could and tying the ends behind her ankle. She tore some more off her skirt to finish the job on her other foot. It would help with the heat if not the cuts. She climbed over the pile of stones and peered out. Nothing. But if she could see something from here it would already be too late. Maybe it was too late already, but she had to risk it. She moved into position, then dropped and ran.

She aimed straight for the brow of the hill, sprinting flat out. There was no cover. All she had was speed, a chance to get out of sight or firing range before they even caught sight of her. For the first twenty paces she thought she might have managed it.

The shouting started from two different sides, at exactly the same time. She made out no words, just an attention-grabbing baying, male voices summoning others. This was for her all right. Then came the first shot, an echo then a ding as a bullet hit rock, throwing up a shower of dust. Rose zigzagged crazily up the slope, as unpredictable as she could make it. Her thighs burned. Her lungs were on fire. More shots, raising echoes and dust all around. She was stupidly visible, a dark blob on a light hill, but she was on the crest now. She threw herself down and rolled, shielding herself below the brow. The shooting ceased. She lay wheezing in a cloud of dust. She could hear footsteps already, uneven on the rocky ground.

Whoever was shooting at her knew what they were doing. They were aiming ahead of her, anticipating her path. A few more seconds up that hill and she'd probably have been hit. She had to keep moving. Another track passed just below her and wound back and forth across the downward slope. Just the other side of the track the land dropped sharply away, and then flattened into a sloping bank covered with wiry yellow grass and studded with bushes. At the bottom of the hill was a cluster of square white buildings, flat-roofed, within a fenced rectangle of land. In this featureless landscape it might seem the obvious place to hide. Rose ran across the track to where the ground fell away, breaking up into a mess of rough boulders and dense thorny bushes. She turned and lowered herself down, tucking herself into a crevice. She found a reasonably firm foothold and froze.

The running footsteps came closer. They were on the track now, right overhead. They stopped. Had she got far enough? She held her breath. The seconds ticked past. Then the running continued, down along the track. Rose risked more movement, tucking herself in behind a large thorn bush. If someone crossed the track above her and looked straight down, they would see her. If they followed the track round and looked up when they passed below, hopefully she was nothing but a dark shape behind a bush. If she kept still.

More footsteps. Muttered voices, walking breaking into jogging. She couldn't see either up or down. Three or four men, she thought, maybe more.

All sounds faded away. Still she waited, dust in her mouth, thorns scratching her skin, her legs complaining, her feet throbbing, until she lost all track of time.

Chapter 49

When Adel got back to the hotel, he was heading straight upstairs but spotted Fairchild in the bar. Zack was there, too. In his Hawaiian shirt and shades, he was meant to be behind the scenes but now he was here at large, as himself. The show really had ended.

Zack was on a sofa tapping on a tablet. Fairchild was in an armchair reading an Italian business daily. It was as if they were both pretending the other didn't exist. Adel approached with caution and waited to be noticed.

Zack was first. He lifted his shades. His jaw was still a little swollen. "You gave him the money?"

"Yes."

"Put him on a boat?"

"Yes."

"Saw the boat leave?"

"Yes."

"With him on it?"

"Yes."

"All right, then." He replaced the shades and went back to the tablet.

Fairchild gave Adel no more than a glance, but it was enough. Adel retreated and made himself busy on the front desk. After three or four minutes Fairchild came past and left the hotel. Adel followed.

Fairchild went up the road until it rose and turned, the hotel just out of sight. He stopped by a railing. Adel caught up with him. They leaned on the railing looking out to sea.

"Well?" said Fairchild.

"Erik saw Raphael talking to those Tunisians. The ones who staked out the hotel."

Fairchild turned to examine him, then went back to gaze at the sea. "So what? He was probably trying to buy cheap cigarettes or something."

"He's not who he's claiming to be."

"Looked him up, did you?"

"I did a bit of research. No one called Frank Zella has ever stayed at the Rosaria. The guy is not some billionaire's playboy son."

"You're right." Fairchild acknowledged Adel's surprise. "Raphael is a small-time conman, talking his way into an extravagant lifestyle. He flits from hotel to hotel spending as much as possible before anyone realises he can't pay the bill. He plays people, tells them what they want to hear. Gets a kick out of it. Another ten years and he'll probably see the error of his ways, if he doesn't fall in with the wrong crowd in the meantime."

How could Fairchild be so laid back about this? He couldn't even look Adel in the eye. Adel didn't try to hide his anger. "You're going to save him, are you? Point out to him where he's going wrong? Offer him a chance to help you out in your latest crusade?"

Fairchild didn't react. "So what if I am? How does that impact on you exactly?"

"It doesn't, I suppose. But I thought you were a better judge of character."

Now he turned to look at Adel – inspect him, searching for clues. "You think Raphael is my latest project? That I've taken someone new under my wing? That I go about rescuing people and bringing them into the light? Is that it?"

Adel could summon up an icy stare when he wanted to. "I'm not sure I know you well enough to say."

"Of course you do."

Adel didn't relent. "I made mistakes in my life but I was never like that. I never scammed people just for pleasure. I did the wrong things but for the right reasons."

"Yes, you did."

Fairchild's affirmation affected him, made him feel warm, but he didn't want to care any more about the good opinion of this man. "It wasn't a random conversation about cigarettes. They'd arranged to meet. The man is racking up the mother of all hotel bills and he's lying about himself, his background, his identity. But you don't care. What is it? Does he remind you of yourself when you were that age? A privileged rich boy gone wrong?"

Fairchild wasn't looking at him any more. Adel had gone too far, yet still he carried on. "And this venture, this op. The holes in it! Why were all the tracers lost? Why no satellite coverage? And the whole idea of setting a trap like this, it's just bizarre. All the times I've worked with you, but this one…or maybe they were all like this and I've only just noticed."

"You think I'm getting sloppy? Or that I've always been sloppy?" Fairchild was quiet, contained. Adel knew what was going on inside the man, but he didn't care right then.

"You wanted me to be your eyes and ears. I'm doing that. I'm bringing you this but you don't seem interested."

"You're barking up the wrong tree. You have some issue with Raphael. You're letting it cloud your judgement. Is he even around any more? Have you seen him today?"

"No, but I only came on shift at noon. And then I was sent to escort Erik onto the ferry."

"That was Zack. And we had to pay him off, didn't we?"

"It wasn't a payoff. You see, this is what I mean! Erik is an innocent victim of some global scam, and when he tries to do the right thing you people think he just wants to extort a bit of cash. I don't want to think like that. I don't want to see people that way."

"You want to quit. Is that it?"

Adel took a sharp breath. That wasn't in his mind at all. But once Fairchild had said it, it changed things. "Maybe."

"Well, I'd appreciate it if you could hang around for a day or two. Things aren't quite over yet. At least I hope they're not."

Fairchild turned away again. He wasn't looking at the sea, Adel realised. He was scanning the coast, the mainland, where Rose had been heading when she was last seen. As if he might, impossibly, be able to divine her whereabouts.

"Of course." Adel was chastened, but not quite enough to apologise.

Fairchild took a breath and tore his eyes away from the coastline. "We should go back. Forget about Raphael. He's probably skipped town already."

And that was how they left it. Adel went back to work and kept doing what he was doing. But he wasn't surprised when, much later that evening, it turned out that Fairchild was wrong about Raphael.

Chapter 50

Nico approached Fairchild as he came back into the lobby. "I have something." A meaningful look and a mutter in his ear. Fairchild listened, and went straight back out again.

The place wasn't far: right in the centre of Capri. He turned things over in his mind as he walked. Zack didn't know what Fairchild was about to do. Would he approve? Maybe not. But Fairchild didn't care. To him this was more important than the entire operation, more important than anything.

It was about the most standard hotel there was on Capri, solid but nothing special, exactly where a Communist Party employee would choose to stay for an overseas work trip. Old habits died hard. Nico, accessing his network of hotel general managers on the assurance that this was a serious security matter that would be dealt with discreetly, had given Fairchild the room number as well. Fairchild went up and knocked on the door. Silence.

"It's John Fairchild." He spoke in Mandarin. More silence. "I know you're in there, Chu. I know what you're doing here. We need to talk."

He waited. The door opened. The face in front of him took him back, just for a moment, to a small room in a remote facility in China, where Fairchild for a while feared he might meet his end. Chu had been angry then, and she didn't look much happier now.

"Are you alone?" she asked.

"Yes. Are you?"

She let him in. It was a small room: bed, desk, two chairs, TV, obligatory sea view. Too cramped, too much sun coming through the window, too hot. The Rosaria had nothing to be jealous of here. He wondered if Chu realised there were probably a dozen FBI agents staying in the same place.

He sat. "I know what you're up to."

"So you said." She sat on the end of the bed. As ever, her make-up was immaculate. Her trademark streetwear had been given a Capri touch: white trousers, shocking pink crop top. It was like talking to a mannequin.

"I don't suppose you wanted me to spot you yesterday. It was only for a second. You were in the back of a cab. But yours is a face I could never forget."

"Likewise. You seem to have some good eyes and ears on this island, Mr Fairchild."

"And so do you."

"Really?"

"A guest at my hotel was shot at on her balcony yesterday. She's lucky to be alive. It was a long range shot from a sniper's rifle. I recall you having access to resources like that. In fact, I recall you deploying them after me at least once."

"I am no longer in the same job, Mr Fairchild."

"No, but I imagine you still have very good contacts with whoever the Chinese government might use. Even if you are contracting privately now."

Chu made no comment. Fairchild had little interest in who she was working for.

"It isn't her," he said.

Again she said nothing, but an intensity in her eyes betrayed her interest.

Fairchild continued. "The woman in question is a financier and philanthropist called Julia Michalaedes. She is not Ulia Popovic, the person I'm sure your client is keen to – neutralise."

A slight narrowing of the eyes. "We have heard otherwise."

"There have been rumours. The rumours are false."

"Why are you telling me this?"

"I'm doing you a favour. It would be embarrassing, wouldn't it, if you took your fee and then it was discovered that the person in question was still alive. That wouldn't reflect too well on yourself."

"I don't expect a favour from you."

"That's for sure. I just don't like to see innocent people being gunned down for no reason. Maybe I'm soft."

"There must be more to it than that. How are you so sure about the identity of this woman? You can't possibly vouch for all your hotel guests in this way."

"I can't tell you that. But be assured you have set your sights on the wrong person. Quite literally."

A touch of hardness around her jaw. "I cannot be assured until I understand how you know this. I will need to explain it, as I'm sure you appreciate. The person for whom I operate has already put significant resources into this target."

"Well, they should be delighted, then, that you're saving them from wasting any more of it."

A slight shake of the head. "Insufficient. Those rumours were circulating for a reason. I'm not the only person to have come here on a false pretext, if indeed it is false. I know your line of work, Mr Fairchild, and you know mine. If you expect me to pack my bags and go, I'll need more from you."

This was what Fairchild had been afraid of. Zack wouldn't approve. Fairchild was jeopardising the entire op. Well – so be it.

"I really am doing you a favour here, Comrade Chu."

"I no longer use that nomenclature."

"I'll always think of you that way. But do you accept that this information has some value to you if you can be persuaded I'm telling you the truth?"

A slight nod of the head. "I suppose it does."

"So, I can tell you how I know this. But it must remain a secret."

"How long for?"

"For ever."

"And what would happen if it doesn't?"

"Then you would be answerable to me. We have a long history, Chu. At times we've been on the same side, at other times not. I don't mean you any harm. I simply want you to move on. If I tell you this, will you undertake to pass it on to nobody, including your client, and resume your search elsewhere?"

She thought about it. "It's a reasonable request."

Not exactly a promise, but probably the best he was going to get. "Ulia Popovic is a popular woman. Or rather, a very unpopular one. A series of rumours about a possible appearance by the woman might draw an interesting crowd."

He waited. Did he need to say more? A very slight smile told him he didn't.

"You're involved in a trap? Some kind of deception to draw someone out?" Her face became about as animated as he'd ever seen it. "Who are you working for?"

"Please, Chu! Suffice it to say that none of this involves the Chinese government or any Chinese citizen. But you can understand how your involvement here might have undesirable consequences." He waited.

She was actually smiling now. Being distanced from the Communist Party might be doing her some good. "I am impressed. Whoever that lady is, she is a very brave woman. I didn't think the capitalist system nurtured such loyalty."

"It's your system now, Chu." Fairchild got up.

"Do you know where she is?" asked Chu.

"Michalaedes?"

A slight pause. "Popovic."

"I'm afraid not. I hope not to see you again."

His heart was hammering as he left the hotel. Whoever she was working for, Chu was a dangerous operator, and he was in her hands. The very fact that she was still here suggested she thought Popovic was still alive. That was good news. But that last exchange left him with an uneasy notion that Chu knew a lot more than she was saying. And in particular, that she knew where Rose was.

Chapter 51

When Rose finally dared to move, the sun had tracked round but was still high in the sky. She'd shifted position to rest, but something else was now prompting her to act: thirst. The last thing she'd had to drink was that infernal drugged coffee on the train the previous evening. In this heat, water was a must. She also needed to get to a phone. And she had to hide from people who wanted to shoot her. But out of those three needs, water had crept up the list just as the sun had edged across the sky.

She'd studied the landscape in detail over the past hours and all she could see was dust and dryness. Natural water sources would be scarce around here. What she needed was plumbing: a house or building that was actually being used. The thought of cold clean water gushing liberally out of a tap made her mouth even drier.

Following the men who were hunting her to the settlement below seemed foolish: they may still be searching for her there. Same for the village where they'd got off the train. Holmes had vanished: she was on her own. How many of these men were there? Who exactly was after her? Going into a village may be a huge risk. She needed to go where people were, but until she could summon help she needed to stay invisible.

The best option seemed to be to follow the track away from the compound below. It didn't lead back into the village: if it had, the men would have returned to their vehicle and pursued her by car. If an isolated settlement was at one end of it, it stood to reason that whatever was at the other end was less isolated. So far no traffic had come past. She set off, ready at the faintest suggestion of vehicle noise to dive off and conceal herself.

Her progress was slow. The rags around her feet were already wearing thin. Heat radiated off the track, and there was no shade. She looked around constantly for places to hide, though for stretches at a time there was nothing but rocky ground, wiry yellow grass and tiny thickets. She tried to stop thinking about her parched throat and scan the landscape below for movement.

The track curved through a long, slow corner. The land on the higher side grew and steepened. Round the corner, the track itself rose, leading to a distant cluster of walls on top of a steep hill. The track swept back and forth towards it, going higher and higher. A climb! In this heat! But as her heart sank she also realised that hills offered more places to hide than flat ground. And whatever was up there was substantial enough to have running water – and phones.

A low rumbling sound reached her – a car. She darted off to the side, where some thick bushes sat below the level of the track. The vehicle got nearer, but then its noise dwindled away before it passed. She carried on. A little further along, the track joined a surfaced road, still narrow, but a road that led somewhere, and there would be more traffic. She would have to find another way up.

That, as she spent the next half hour discovering, meant clambering up through thorny bushes over uneven ground, tearing clothes and skin, having to backtrack to find a way through the ever-thickening vegetation. The extra cover was useful, but the effects of dehydration were really hampering her now and she was stopping more and more to get her breath back. At times she felt so dizzy she had to stop and lower her head to the ground until the feeling passed. But still there was more height above her. She had to go on.

Over the top of a rocky hillock the vegetation cleared a little and she could make out a fence built from horizontal branches. The back entrance to something on the lower fringes of the town, hopefully. She approached. The gate, while it didn't look much, was sturdy and reinforced with wire mesh. That should have told her something, but her only thought was relief that it wasn't locked. She slipped through and closed it behind her. The land was flatter here – maybe she'd finally made it to the top. Across a yard featuring a collection of ancient garden equipment was a recessed doorway in a stone back wall. Rose could hear nothing. She crept over, keeping an eye out for an outside tap or hosepipe, but saw nothing. The door inside was half-open. She pushed. It led to a kitchen, rickety off-white cupboards and a terracotta floor. She went in. There was a sink, a tap, and, as if inviting her, a single long glass next to it. She wasted no time. She grabbed the glass, filled it to the top and drank it down straight away. She did the same thing again and had filled it up for a third before she heard the growling.

It was a very low rumble, like thunder. At first she couldn't see where it was coming from. But then at the far doorway she saw a snout, contorted, with teeth on full display, spittle oozing from drawn-back gums. Above the snout, fierce black eyes watched her.

The animal stepped into the room, lowering its head as if getting ready to pounce. The beast was as tall as a greyhound but a lot more substantial. Its fur stood on end right along its spine to its tail, tucked well under its hind legs. Trying to make friends seemed like a long shot. Rose turned and ran for the door.

Its claws clicked on the tile, but just for a moment. The dog was already outside and she was half way across the yard.

Now it was barking, a deep, throaty, sonorous bark that would be audible a mile away. Rose threw the glass of water down and leaped through the gate. She slammed, and it made contact with the drooling snout. The barking gave way to a brief yelp, then a wild angry growling.

The dog hurled itself against the gate. The gateposts sagged but held. Rose turned and ran.

Chapter 52

Returning from his talk with Chu, Fairchild made an appearance in the bar. Zack was still there. "Any news?" he asked the American.

"Nope."

He couldn't sit still. He set off on what he told himself was an inspection of the hotel, though it was more of an aimless wander. The Rosaria had partied hard last night and woken up with a hangover. Though it was late afternoon her head still throbbed and her temperament was fragile. Her guests were subdued and her staff bleary-eyed. The whiteness of her walls was harsh, her floral displays limp in the heat, her scent cloying, her sea view washed out. The courtyard walls were constricting and its statuary trite. Its shrubbery whispered little evils to itself in the breeze. The ballroom, configured for some run-of-the-mill reception, seemed devoid of occasion, as if the Rosaria, groaning at the excesses of last night, were saying *never again*. This was not just a hangover. Regret hung in the air. The Rosaria had partied too hard. The evening had got out of hand. Things had been broken, that couldn't necessarily be put back together again. Adel had been right, in so much of what he'd said. But they were in play now: the juggling balls had been thrown in the air and he, and Zack, Adel, maybe also Rose, were just waiting now, staring up into the sky to see where and how they would come back down.

Fairchild didn't look out of the arches; he'd spent too long gazing into the distance. He caught up with Nico. He went to his room, but couldn't settle there. Sat for a time with the tech team, still processing, processing. Then he returned downstairs and sat opposite Zack, though they had nothing to say to each other. And then he saw something that reminded him of his conversation with Adel. Adel was hot with a young man's anger, but maybe he'd feel vindicated at this sight, because the person who'd just entered the lobby, and lurked pale-faced inside the door, was Raphael.

The man looked tired. Not just morning-after tired, but beat, exhausted. Tense, as well. Nervous, even. Raffa, the suave talker who surfed on a wave of confidence, looked lost and aimless. His gaze slid over the front desk and across the lobby. When he saw Fairchild, he stared for a moment. He also looked oddly at Zack, who by this time had picked up a magazine and was flicking aggressively through the pages while dipping his hand in a bowl of salted nuts. Raffa gave a kind of shudder. Then he turned on his heel and left.

"Did you see that?" Fairchild said to Zack.

"Nope."

Fairchild stared after Raffa.

"Anything relevant?" The American reached for more nuts.

"Probably not." But Fairchild kept looking. He was on the verge of getting up when Raffa appeared again. This time the young man looked defiant, but also scared. His eyes searched out Fairchild, then shifted to Zack and then back to Fairchild again. Then he broke off and jerked into motion, heading out to the pool terrace so rapidly that the porters looked up and stared after him.

Fairchild got up.

"What?" Zack looked up himself, finally.

"Nothing."

Fairchild followed Raffa up. The man was hunched over on a chair in the far corner of the terrace, facing away from the pool, away from the hotel, away from everyone. Fairchild pulled up another chair and sat next to him.

"You know something, don't you?"

He didn't respond.

"Tell me."

Raffa glanced across. His lip trembled.

"There's something going on and it's got something to do with me," Fairchild said. "So spit it out, whatever it is."

Raffa took a breath but still said nothing.

"Let me guess. You're in debt to the wrong people."

There was no recognition, no relief in the young man's face. That wasn't it, then. Something worse.

"You want me to go away and leave you to it?"

Another long pause. It could be that he was in too deep now, or he was too proud to admit things had caught up with him and he needed help. Fairchild was leaning forward to stand up when Raffa started talking, barely audible.

"This isn't me. I talk a big talk and I get champagne and dinners and hotel rooms. That's me. I tell a few lies to live a good life. Where's the harm? These places can afford it. But this? This, oh my God, this is way outside of my league. Those guys..." He shook his head and tightened his hands into fists.

"What guys? What guys, Raphael?"

"The Tunisians!"

Fairchild stopped breathing. Raffa looked at him with pain in his face. "I know, okay? I know who the Tunisians are, their leader. I know that Michalaedes is a fake and you only want to draw him out. I know because they told me, Fairchild! They told me! I didn't want to know! I just came here to party, just come to the show, have fun, leave again, work up a massive bill, yes, I know, I put my hand up to that – but now I'm lost, I'm totally out of my depth." He rested his elbows on his knees and put his head in his hands.

Fairchild stared, then: "You already knew the Tunisians? Before all this?"

Raffa didn't lift his head. "We had some unfinished business. Some – substances. They felt I hadn't compensated them enough."

"Drugs?"

"Don't say it like that. Everyone does drugs these days. But they noticed me when they were checking out the hotel and now they've got me involved in all this and I have no choice! I hate this, Fairchild! But I've got no choice."

"No choice about what?"

Raffa looked up at the horizon and swallowed. "They've got her. They've got Rose Clarke. They've kidnapped her and they know that she's MI6. They're holding her somewhere. They want a ransom. And they sent me here to pass the message on. To that American in there. Zack. They think he's in charge. Anyway, that's my job. I've to go over there and ask him for fifty million dollars."

Fairchild thought he'd misheard. "Fifty million dollars?"

"Or they will kill her. And they want it tomorrow. What the fuck do I do, Fairchild?"

Fairchild sat back. His mind was spinning, almost out of control. "How do they know all this?" He could hear a tremor in his own voice now. "They know everything. They know her name, for fuck's sake!"

"They've been watching you."

"Of course they have, but—"

"But that was the whole idea! I know, and so do they. They thought of a way of playing you at your own game. So they snatched her and now they want money. They can't come back here themselves because it's not safe, so they sent me."

"Jesus. Fifty million dollars." Fairchild lapsed into silence, turning it all over in his head.

Raffa looked at him. Then he glanced over his shoulder back at the lounge bar. "I guess – I guess I go and tell him, right? The big American guy? He needs to know."

"Wait." Fairchild raised his hand. "Just wait a minute."

Raffa waited, his eyes returning to the bar.

Fairchild tried to get his thoughts straight. "You know, don't you, that these Tunisians you've been dealing with are terrorists?"

Raffa's eyes were wide as saucers. "Look, I just bought some stuff from them, I had no idea about that!"

"They fund radical Islamist groups. They support jihad, Raphael. Attacks on western nations. And now they expect the security forces of the USA and the UK to stump up fifty million dollars for an MI6 officer? It's not going to happen, Raffa. They won't do it."

"But what about—"

"They don't pay ransoms. Out of principle, but also because they think it would put their people more at risk."

A long silence. Then: "They'll kill her. They'll bloody well kill her, Fairchild!"

Fairchild said nothing but he let the horror of what Raffa had just said show on his face.

"Can't you persuade them?" Raffa said. "There must be some exception, something they can do? They can't just walk away!"

"They can. Believe me. I know how these people think. It's all about the greater good. They'll sacrifice any individual for that. Rose always knew what the deal was."

"You can't really mean that. You can't really be okay about this?"

"Of course I'm not! But I know what will happen when you go in there and tell Zack what's going on. I didn't say I liked it."

"Christ." Raffa sat back in the chair. "Shit, I don't know what to do."

"Where are they holding her? Is she on Capri?"

"They wouldn't tell me any of that. They just approached me."

"Where?"

"They phoned. They phoned me." He looked bashful. "I don't know anything about where she is."

"What about proof of life? How are we supposed to be sure she's not dead already? Or escaped somehow?"

"All they told me to do is make the approach. They gave me nothing. I just have to put them in touch. Then they'll talk to Zack to make the arrangements."

"Raffa, with Zack there aren't going to be any arrangements. That's what I'm telling you!"

"But I can't just go back to them with that. They'll kill me as well as her."

"Then don't." It slipped out so easily he barely realised he'd said it.

Raffa frowned. "How's that going to—"

"I'll pay it. I'll pay. Just don't go anywhere near Zack. Just let me…" He was struggling to think quickly enough. "What are they expecting? How do they want to be paid?"

Raffa seemed on the verge of panic. "I – I guess they have a bank account to pay it into. But they're expecting Zack to —"

"Listen." Fairchild leaned closer. Raffa had to focus. "Tell them they'll get their money. They'll get it, but they leave Zack out of it. Tell them to give you the details. Then you'll deal with me. Can you do that?"

Raffa blinked. "I suppose so. They'll get their money either way."

"This is the only way they'll get anything, Raffa! Zack will give them nothing. I guarantee it. You said they wanted it tomorrow. How much time do we have?"

"Fairchild, they want it tomorrow morning."

The air seemed to get sucked out of Fairchild's lungs. "Tomorrow morning? That's not even twenty-four hours! Have you any idea how much money that is, Raffa?"

He looked pale and hollow. "I'm just telling you what they said."

Fairchild closed his eyes. He had to get his head around this, but he had no time. Things were moving too fast. He opened his eyes. Raffa was watching him anxiously.

"All right," Fairchild said. "Go back to them and get the bank account number. Tell them we need to meet. They have to bring Rose. They can name the place, but I won't make any payment until I've seen her with my own eyes. Got that?"

"What if they don't want—"

"If they want the money, those are the terms. And I'm dealing directly with you. Message the details to me. No one else. You'll be there as well."

"I don't see why—"

"You'll be there, Raffa. Just you, just me. Okay? We show up. Then they bring Rose. When she appears I make the payment. Now I need to make some phone calls. A lot of phone calls."

Fairchild went through the staff quarters to get to his room. He didn't want to pass through the bar. So Zack didn't see him. But Adel did. He'd spotted Raphael in the lobby and observed the exchange on the pool terrace from a discreet distance. He was back on the front desk when

Raphael left the hotel a short while later. Adel watched him disappear out of the door, and frowned.

Chapter 53

Rose kept running, she didn't care where, carried down by the slope of the land, but its vicious thornery grabbed onto her dress and forced her to slow. Heart beating, lungs heaving, she pushed herself through until its thickness defeated her and she curled up in the middle of it and lay shaking.

Dogs. What did people see in them? She'd never had time for the creatures, but a mild dislike had over some years crystallised into a kneejerk horror. In her head she was standing in a street in Lali, Georgia, watching one of the beasts edge towards her, its chops coated with human blood. Her body convulsed. She sobbed without making a sound.

Time passed. It was getting dark. In the town above, people were just walking about with mobile phones. All she needed was one short call. Pull yourself together, Rose. She uncurled herself. Her dress was ripped anew and her skin stung in a dozen places. She moved into a crouch. The water had helped, but she was still woozy, desperate for food. She clambered up the slope and worked her way around, winding up and down to avoid impenetrable thickets. A concrete wall loomed up behind the vegetation. She crept closer, but saw no lights, heard no sound. It was a huge edifice, but only half-built, three quarters of the way up the hill. If they'd got as far as windows, it would have boasted a spectacular view. Whatever money-making idea had been behind it – a hotel, probably – all work had been abandoned long ago and nature was gradually reclaiming the immense shell. But on the other side was what she'd been seeking: an access road, no longer used, leading upwards.

She sat on a window ledge and watched the sun set over a vast landscape dotted with olive groves and a distant view of the sea. As darkness grew, a few lonely lights winked on. Occasionally some noise reached her from above – conversation, the clash of plates. An outdoor restaurant, or maybe several. She tried not to think about pizza, or those two delicious glasses of water, now some hours past. And she tried not to think about the Hotel Villa Bianca Rosaria, and what its guests would be doing right now.

When it was dark, she set off. The road took her towards a gap in the wall which seemed to encircle the town. A gate barred the road. Beyond it, a small piece of flat ground just inside held a few parked cars. Above it on the other side, mature ornamental trees rose up out of raised ground – a park or garden. The streets of the town must be beyond that. Rose was simply looking for the nearest person who might be persuaded to lend her their phone, but when she approached, she realised it wasn't going to be that simple.

Two police cars were parked in the small space. Leaning against them talking were four or five uniformed officers. Rose ducked out of sight to consider what this meant. Were they there for her? Should she give herself up to them? She had no beef with the Italian authorities and strictly speaking had done nothing illegal since arriving in the country, apart from board a train without a ticket. But she had no ID. They might, perish the thought, think that she was the internationally sought alleged fraudster Ulia Popovic. If they detained her, would they let her make a phone call? That was all she needed. But how could she be sure? The men who'd shot at her before, were they police? Steer clear, her gut was telling her. Find another way to call in. She crossed the road, intending to stay below the officers' line of sight and sneak past them round the hill. So much for intentions.

The slope under her feet turned into scree, loose dirt. A street light illuminated the car park above but Rose moved out of its range and her eyes took a moment to adjust to the moonlight. Treading blind, she missed her footing. Her feet slipped from under her. A rush of gravel and she was sliding down on her front, feet first. She rolled, grabbed handfuls of long grass, and stopped. But she'd already heard a shout from above. She looked up through a cloud of dust to see two officers coming over. She scrambled across the scree, almost losing her footing again, and dived down amongst a thicket of thorns.

Her eye exploded with pain. She clapped a hand over it. It burned like someone had stuck a red hot poker in it. She held her breath and lay as still as a statue. The officers were at the top of the scree. Their torch beams moved over the slope. A comment, a nod, and they turned and went back. They hadn't seen her, probably assumed the noise was an animal.

Rose hunched over and breathed in and out rapidly. Underneath her palm, her eye felt wet. There was a pain against the inside of her eyelid, as if her eyeball were rubbing against the edge of a knife. She took her hand away and tried to open the eye. The pain made her gasp. She saw a blur of red. She covered it with her hand again and bowed down. A wave of nausea passed over her.

She couldn't stay there. Slowly she extracted herself from the bushes. One hand stayed over her eye. Her other hand touched her stinging jaw and found blood. She limped back to the shell of a hotel, trying to get used to her throbbing eye. Every muscle was aching. It seemed to take forever to get there. When she finally arrived, she lay down. The blood in her head was rushing. She was so hungry she couldn't think. With her good eye, the moon hanging over the landscape seemed to blur and shift, then right itself again.

Why was this so difficult? Maybe it wasn't. Maybe she should just stay here and they'd find her. Surely they would. How could she go anywhere like this? She could barely walk and barely see. Just stay here and hide, Rose. Don't keep making things hard for yourself. No more dogs, no more shouts and bullets, no more rocks and thorns. She wasn't sure she could get up anyway, now.

They'd find her. They'd find her. She closed both eyes and relaxed.

Chapter 54

Adel was making a nuisance of himself. At other times in his life he would have tried not to. He would have gone with the flow, happy to be a foot soldier in a battle strategically planned by others. But not now. Not any more. Was there even a strategy? And whoever was doing the planning sucked at it. This was all such a waste of time, but not just that – a dangerous, stupid, extravagant vanity. One that could lead to people being bankrupted, or killed, or behind bars. And even though he'd specifically been told to leave it alone, to do as he was told, the ties that bound him to John Fairchild could not readily be loosened. Fairchild was the person who'd brought him into this, the one who'd persuaded him away from jihad, who'd had such a profound influence on the course of his life. Fairchild was also the one who was making him spitting mad right now, but still, he couldn't just walk away.

Last night, when he'd come up here, he'd hesitated before knocking on the door. This morning he didn't. And when last night he'd waited politely for the door to open, this morning he didn't. Zack was sitting there on the office chair, just as he had been yesterday. Maybe he'd been there all night. Adel didn't care.

"Oh, it's you again," Zack said.

"Fairchild's left." Adel wasn't in the mood for pleasantries either. "He's taken a backpack and he's heading down to the marina."

"Did you check he had a good breakfast before he went out? Took a shower? Cleaned his teeth?"

The two men stared at each other. As ever, the tech team were busy at their screens and Sarah was sitting in the corner. Had she been here all night as well?

"Where's he going?" demanded Adel.

"How should I know? The man's a free agent. He can come and go as he pleases. He's probably gone out for a walk."

"No, he hasn't. He's got a backpack with him and he's going to the marina."

"And that proves what? You need to calm down, boy. And get out of my face. We've got work to do here."

It was pretty much what Zack had said to him last night, only with a little less finesse. Adel wasn't going anywhere. "Last night, he and Raffa talked."

"You told me that already."

"For a long time. About something serious. It wasn't just chit-chat. I said that. And now Fairchild's doing something. He has some plan that you don't seem to know about. You don't think there's anything off about that?"

It was a full-on confrontation now. The techies were listening, though they hadn't turned round to look. Zack leaned forward.

"What I think is that you have a problem with that little English squirt who looks up at Fairchild like a puppy. He's just a barfly with a cut-glass accent, an English boarding school waster, spending other people's money. Forget about him! He means nothing."

He leaned back and folded his arms. Adel glanced sideways. There was a faint smile on Sarah's face. "Then where's Fairchild?" he asked.

Zack shrugged. "I don't know."

"What's he doing?"

"Adel. Seriously. This is starting to sound like an obsession. Why don't you call him and ask, if you're that bothered?"

"I did. He's not picking up."

Zack shrugged again. "Not sure I blame him."

If Adel thought he was angry before, he'd found a new level. "Do you have any idea what's going on? This is your operation! Rose is lost, after your pathetic trackers didn't even make it across the island. You've no idea if she's alive or dead. This Tunisian is running rings around you. And then some conman, who we know has connections with the Tunisians, walks in here yesterday and has a heart-to-heart with Fairchild! The next morning Fairchild is off somewhere, without talking to you, and you don't even seem to care! What kind of an operation is this? It makes no sense! What's really going on here?"

The atmosphere chilled by several degrees. Zack removed his shades and locked Adel in a stony glare. "What's going on is that people who know a lot more than you are running an op that you are barely even involved in. You do as you're told, or you leave this building and you leave this island. Right now. You got that?"

The pause was broken by a tinny rendition of *Copacabana*. Zack drew out his mobile phone and answered.

"Yes?" He jumped to his feet. "Rose! Where the hell are you?"

Chapter 55

Someone laughing. That was what had woken her. Just a laugh, an ordinary laugh. A young voice, female. But it was soon joined by more. She lay, eyes closed, floating, enjoying the sound of fun and normality. Then she remembered where she was, and tried to open her eyes. She flinched. Something sharp was surely digging into her eyeball. She put her hands up to her face. The injured eye was big and bloated. She steeled herself, took her hands away and opened her one good eye.

It was daylight, not that early. The laughter and chatting was outside, at what would probably have been the front of the hotel. She shifted to her knees and raised her head just high enough. What she saw made her hope that finally she'd been rewarded with a little bit of luck.

Sitting in a horseshoe shape looking out at the view, on a variety of rocks and makeshift chairs, was a group of young people. Teenagers, she thought. A couple had cigarettes in their hands. They were relaxed, at ease. This was their den, their hangout spot. Nice place. She hoped she wasn't going to spoil it for them.

Stepping back from the window she tried to neaten herself up, but it was hopeless. Her eye felt huge and gritty. She could feel a raised ridge along her jawline. When she moved, everything felt unreal, like a dream.

She stepped out of what might have been intended as a doorway. The sun was warm already; she blinked painfully in its glare. She was behind most of the group but a guy at one end of the horseshoe saw her. His eyes widened. The others were still talking but he held his hand out and shut them up, urgency in his voice. They jumped up. There was a sudden silence and Rose was being examined by half a dozen shocked faces.

She held her hands out high and walked towards them. "Hey." Hopefully they'd know a little English: that was her best bet. "Sorry. I don't mean to scare you. I'm lost. Could I borrow a phone?" She made the hand sign for a phone and smiled. It didn't have the calming effect she'd been hoping for. As if of one mind, they backed off, then turned and sprinted away up the track. One of them even dropped their cigarette.

"Shit." Rose watched their backs disappear up the hill. News of her presence had clearly spread far and wide, and not in a good way. She picked up the cigarette, took a drag and crushed it into the rock. Then she noticed a litre-sized bottle of water left on the ground. She grabbed it and drank half of it in one go. Finally she stopped and wiped her mouth. Then she sensed it. Someone was standing behind her.

She spun round. It was a boy, same age as the others. Dark curly hair, blue and white striped t-shirt that made her think of fancy-dress-style sailor suits. He'd come to join them, presumably. He looked warily at her.

"I'm not dangerous," she said. "I'm just lost. I need a phone. That's all." She screwed the lid onto the water bottle. "Thirsty," she said apologetically, holding it up. She put her hand on her stomach. "Hungry. Thirsty."

He looked her up and down, taking in her bandaged feet, torn dress, matted hair and lopsided scratched face. He seemed more curious than afraid. Rose took a tentative step towards him. He didn't back off. She held out a hand. "Your phone? One call. Just one." Still he stared. "Please?" He blinked, then pulled a phone out from a back pocket, activated it and passed it to her.

Rose's expression conveyed her thanks. By prior agreement, the emergency number they'd all memorised went through to Zack. He answered straight away.

"It's Rose."

"Rose! Where the hell are you?"

"I'm in Sicily."

"Sicily? What the fuck?"

"We jumped on a train. Ended up here. But I need an exit, Zack! Fast!"

"Sure. Where exactly are you?"

"Some town." Rose looked round to ask the sailor boy, but he was no longer there. Then she saw why. Coming down the track were the police officers she saw the night before, heading straight for her. "Shit. I've got to run. I don't know the name." She headed downwards, phone to her ear. "Did Holmes get out? He can tell you."

"Who?"

"Holmes, William Holmes, the FBI guy!"

"What FBI guy?"

"The one who came to the villa, who got me out! Is he there? Is he missing?"

Zack sounded perplexed. "What are you talking about?"

"Stop! Don't move!" Her pursuers were gaining ground, and they were shouting this time. Did they have guns? She wasn't planning to find out. She needed two hands. Here we go again, she thought, as she threw the phone into a bush, dived off the track and plunged into the undergrowth.

Chapter 56

Zack, Sarah and Adel were all on their feet. Zack was shouting into the handset. "Rose! Are you there? Rose!" He looked at the techies. "It's still connected. She must have dropped it. Can you trace it?"

"We can try," said Larry. Zack passed it over and he got busy on his terminal.

"She's on Sicily? Why?" said Adel. This op was getting more and more surreal.

Zack didn't turn to look at him. "No idea. She was going on about some FBI guy."

"Someone from the FBI was with her?"

"That's what she said." Deep frown marks were appearing on Zack's forehead. He turned to the tech team. "Can we access a list of FBI agents involved in this op?"

"We can ask their team leader," Larry said.

"Do it."

One of them reached for a phone.

"Is someone calling Fairchild?" asked Adel.

"I've got a location," said Larry.

"Call it in," said Zack. Larry glanced up at him and started making a call.

The other techie was talking to the FBI leader. "What was the name?" he asked Zack.

"William Holmes."

The techie repeated it. There was a pause.

Adel repeated his question: "Zack, are you calling Fairchild?"

The door of the room clicked. Adel turned. Sarah was no longer there.

"Where's she gone?" He turned to query it with Zack, but Zack was looking at him, not after her. "Don't you think that's odd, that she left just now?"

Zack was about to say something when the techie held his finger up, still on the line. "There's no William Holmes involved in the Capri operation," he said. "And – What?" the person at the other end was talking again. "Right." To Zack: "Not only that, but there's no employee of the FBI anywhere in the world with that name."

Zack took a moment to absorb that. "Okay. Interesting."

"Interesting? What does that mean? What's going on?"

"Take a seat, Adel," said Zack. "It's all under control. Least I think it is."

"Are you mad? It clearly isn't. Why aren't you calling Fairchild? And where's Sarah going? Does she know something?"

He made for the door but somehow Zack's hand got there first, his palm pressed against it hard. "I don't think so, soldier. You're staying right here."

Adel had had enough. Pure anger gave him the strength to shove Zack aside and get the door open. But he'd not got a foot outside when some force lifted him off his feet and he was sprawled on the ground in the middle of the room. Zack, standing above him, closed the door and looked down at him, arms folded. "Like I said, you're going nowhere."

Adel climbed to his feet and aimed a punch. His fist froze mid-air as a giant hand gripped his wrist and locked it into place. With his other hand he aimed for Zack's lower body, the soft parts. But he found no soft parts at all. His knees landed hard on the ground as both arms were held from behind, twisted high. Zack bent and spoke in his ear.

"You still think you can get out of that door? Sit down, shut up, don't say a word and don't move. Or I'm really going to lose it."

A spasm of pain made Adel gasp before all support was removed and he fell to the floor. His arms ached. He crawled up and sat on a sofa.

Zack resumed his seat on the office chair. He turned to Larry. "All right. Now it's just us, how are we doing?"

"They're already in place."

"Already?"

"More or less. They have their own sources, remember."

None of this made sense. Adel touched the skin of his wrist where Zack's grip had immobilised it mid-air. So fast! How could such a big lump of a man move himself so quickly? It niggled at him, and then all of a sudden revealed itself, like the sun coming out from behind a cloud.

"You let him!" It burst out of him.

Zack glanced his way but turned back to Larry. "...soon would be good. If we can avoid an international incident, so much the better."

Adel stared at nothing as his thoughts leaped from one revelation to another. The show was over, he'd thought – but maybe it wasn't. Maybe it was still going on. But why? He tried again.

"You let Fairchild hit you. In the hallway. You could have stopped him. But you didn't."

Zack turned properly this time, and contemplated him. Larry was doing the same. They looked at each other. Behind them, the techies stopped working and looked up at Larry.

"Well?" Adel demanded of a silent room.

A phone on the table rang. Larry picked up. The techies slowly went back to their work, with half an eye on their boss. Zack rested his chin on his hand and contemplated Adel again. Adel glanced at the door.

"Don't even think it," was Zack's response.

"So what do we do now? Just sit here and wait?"

Zack leaned back on the chair. "Pretty much, yeah."

Chapter 57

As Rose pushed her way into the thicket, it got denser and she was fighting the sticky, thorny branches all over again, scratches on top of scratches. The slope steepened under her feet, getting rockier as she descended. Were the uniforms following her? She could hear nothing behind. Maybe that was good. But she had the feeling it was bad.

Then it wasn't ground she was on any more, but a buttress of huge grey rocks. The mass of bushes turned into individual trees with spined branches like wire brushes. Now she was being slowed down by the rocks, having to turn to clamber down with hands as well as feet. She got to a point where there was nowhere to climb, just a ten-foot drop onto earth below. She paused. No sound from anywhere. The drop extended sideways in both directions. This infernal copse was coming to an end, but she still had to hide, though not for much longer. The team had her location and they'd come for her. She just needed to stay out of harm's way until they arrived.

She moved sideways and found a place with a relatively clear landing, lowered herself as far as she could, and dropped the remaining five feet, flexing and rolling. A tree root jarred her ribs and caught on her dress, ripping the material yet again. More of this and she'd be running about naked. A few steps forward out of the trees, and she realised her mistake.

She was no longer on rocks and earth, but tarmac. It was a road, a proper highway. It would take the police no time at all to get here. She had nowhere to hide: she couldn't turn back, and the land opened out in front of her.

Parked twenty yards away was a car with tinted windows, one she recognised. And as she emerged, shading her face in the sudden sunlight, three men – Tunisians – got out of it and encircled her.

They put her in the back, just as they had on Capri. But sitting next to her now on the back seat was Kamal himself, stony-faced. No one said anything as they set off.

Kamal looked across and she could see him take in her torn dress, her scratched face, her swollen eye. His mouth twitched.

She summoned as much of Popovic as she could muster. "You think this is funny?"

His face returned to stone.

"I would like something to eat," she declared.

"Shut up," he said.

Chapter 58

On the hydrofoil over to Naples, Fairchild had plenty of time to review the previous eighteen hours. He hadn't slept. Since leaving Raffa he'd been in the Blue Room, on the phone for much of the time. The first person he'd called was his Geneva-based accountant, Freya. She knew the nature of his business interests, and the nuts and bolts of it: his accounts, his holdings, how liquid they were – or not. For that was the issue: Fairchild didn't hold a lot of cash. The purpose of his empire was to give him eyes and ears. He would acquire control of going concerns with no intention of milking them for income. As long as they made a profit he wanted them to thrive and grow, carry on as they were but adapting to changing times. He didn't bother with complex or risky derivatives: he wasn't a speculator. He had small holdings of crypto and various commodities, mainly to understand how the markets worked and foster relationships within those worlds. But fifty million? Even if Raffa claimed to have no idea how much money that was, Freya would know. She'd know, too, that he was doing this under duress, that he'd never willingly extract this much cash this quickly.

He couldn't, in short. It simply wasn't feasible to instantly produce such an amount from his own holdings. He'd need a loan, a massive loan with significant servicing costs. A loan that would demand that he ravaged everything he owned to pay it back. No country, no operation anywhere, would escape. They'd either be sold or squeezed dry. It would mean breaking promises, selling up businesses he'd visited many times, met the employees, been out drinking with the managers. It would mean shrinking his reach, removing all interests entirely in some regions, a reduction in footprint so comprehensive it would make what remained utterly unfit for purpose. It would mean a loss of trust, of the kind that was hard-won over years and would not easily be earned again. It would mean starting over. When he began all this, he was young and hot with anger. He'd moved instinctively, only recognising a pattern to it when he looked back. Could he do it again? Did he have the energy or the motivation? If not, what would he do with himself? A great gaping void came into his head, making his palms sweat. He'd be signing away his life.

And what about where the money was going? Fairchild stood apart from any particular government or ideology. He'd worked for many different regimes over the years, systematically rejecting any claims they might make to moral superiority. But Islamic fundamentalism was another thing entirely. Would he really be prepared to effectively finance the recruitment of innocents like Adel to commit atrocities in the name of an aberrated form of a religion he didn't even believe in? Or could he persuade himself that they would somehow trace the money after the event and claw it back? But these people were adept at making money disappear; it would sink like water through sand. Even with Zoe's help, and would she still be willing to help after this? Zack certainly wouldn't. It would be the end for them and their decades of friendship. And, for that matter, any prospect of more work stateside.

What about Rose herself? If she could, she'd tell him not to pay it. Like Fairchild said to Raffa, she knew the score and would be aghast at the idea of an op being subverted like this, delivering the exact opposite of what it was supposed to achieve. He would lose her either way. Even if she lived, she'd have nothing to do with him again. Fairchild would be the most despicable kind of male patrician, going over her head to rescue her when she didn't want it – but at least she'd survive to know about it. She'd be around to hate him for it.

It was late by the time he'd called Freya. She'd known it was important by the hour. He'd told her what he needed but he didn't tell her why. There was a long, long, silence. "John," she'd said, and there was so much sadness in that single word.

The docks of Naples grew, through the spray-flecked windows of the jetfoil. He was early. On arrival he started out with a stop-double-back-start to ensure no one was following. The address was walkable, eastwards into the commercial area, a zone with grids of narrow streets, yards behind gates topped with barbed wire, poorly maintained office blocks, and flats with washing hanging on tiny balconies, windows that looked out onto the wall opposite. The sea itself was invisible beyond a strip of warehouses and delivery depots. The address was one of these, and a door which opened when he pushed led him into an empty room that had once been a shared office but was now empty except for a lone table and a few chairs. He was still early. He sat, opened up the laptop, and waited, conflicting thoughts swirling and fighting in his head like duelling dragons.

A scuffle by the door. Fairchild was on his feet. Raffa walked in. He was pale, eyes ringed with pink. He looked at the laptop. "You've got the money?"

"I have it ready." Fairchild glanced at the laptop. His phone was on the desk next to it.

Raffa was still looking at it. "Can anyone trace you with those?"

"I suppose they could. But the transfer has to be done online. No one knows I'm here. I wouldn't risk that. Not until Rose is returned. Which should be…" – he checked his watch – "twenty minutes."

"That's the deadline for paying the ransom. They need to see the money in the account by ten. Or she's killed."

"They're returning her here, aren't they? That's what your message said."

Raffa fetched a chair from the other side of the room and sat opposite the desk. "I said there was a ten o'clock deadline. And that they were bringing her here. I didn't say she'd be here before—"

"Are you crazy? You think I'm just going to press a button and transfer that kind of money without even seeing her?"

Raffa looked like he was going to cry. "Look, I'm just telling you what they're telling me, all right? They're getting her here. They're on their way. But they still expect the money by the deadline. Or – we know what will happen to her."

"They're running late? That's what you're saying?"

"Well, I guess."

"Why? Something's gone wrong?"

Raffa held his hands up. "You think they'd tell me that? They're on their way."

"How are they getting here? By boat?"

"I – I think they're bringing her in by helicopter. To the helipad in the city centre. Then a car."

It was fifteen minutes to ten. "Can you find out where they are now?"

"I just tried and they're not picking up!" Raffa's voice went high. He looked pretty scared, out of his depth. "I don't think they'll be here by ten, Fairchild."

A silence while that sank in. "They expect me to take it on trust? After what they've done? They haven't even proven she's still alive!"

"She is. They told me that much. She's on the way here. But they're calling all the shots, aren't they? I mean, if you don't pay they've still got her. They can do what they want with her!"

"If I pay without seeing her they no longer have an incentive to return her."

"I know, I know, it sucks. But listen. If you pay, there's a chance she'll make it. A good one. If you don't..." Raffa glanced at his watch. Ten minutes. "If you don't, you've lost her. And for what? It's only money, isn't it? You could build it up again, make a living some other way. All those businesses, anyway. You're not just some tycoon sitting on a yacht like those others. You'd be free to do anything, go anywhere. You and she could – you'll be a hero, won't you?"

"She'll never speak to me again."

"You don't know that. At least she'll be alive. You'll have all the time in the world to win her back again. She must see that you've sacrificed it all for her. At least you have another chance at things. She won't. Not if you don't pay."

Fairchild looked at the clock on his screen. Thoughts like those had prickled at him over the past few hours. Was his whole empire an encumbrance now? Could he settle for a simpler life? Logically, Raffa was right. He should pay to have any chance of saving her. He stared at the screen, at the button and the time on the clock, the seconds disappearing. And Raffa stared at him, hardly breathing.

There was another footstep at the door. They both turned.

Chapter 59

The ferry back to Palermo was full, so Erik had spent the night in Naples. He had walked around, happy when he felt the wad of cash in his pocket, but not wanting to spend it. He climbed streets so narrow you could almost touch both sides. Churches everywhere! And giant wooden doorways and crumbling stonework, balconies full of potted plants or hanging clothes, or old folk sitting in the heat. He walked along great wide boulevards with palm trees and so many cars and revving mopeds, and grand old palaces with white walls turned to grey. He peered into tiny shops and passed through markets selling tomatoes and cherries and loaves of bread and big slippery fish, wet cardboard and squashed fruit all over the pavements, and a sweet smell of rotting food.

He saw restaurants and hotels, and very beautiful clothes shops, their windows glowing as it started to get dark. In between he saw scrubby patches of land boarded up with planks where bits had been torn away, weeds sprouting from broken paving stones, shadowy figures moving in the dusk while police sirens went off in the distance. It was more real, this place, the good and the bad, the rich and the poor, rushing down these noisy choked up streets like blood pumping through veins. Capri was scrubbed clean and bright with its white painted walls, its washed tiles, its pretty flowers arranged nicely. It was all for show, that place.

He slept in some bushes behind a car park near the port. Next morning he found the shop that sold rice balls. He bought a couple and sat on a bench on the yellow grass looking over traffic out to the harbour. His ferry wasn't for hours. The coast road ground to a halt, cars sitting in all the lanes, engines going, while the mopeds weaved their way through. The lights went green to red, then green again but nothing moved. Drivers were getting out and trying to see what the problem was. A crash maybe, or something spilled in the road. One car, some big dark saloon, was stuck right in the middle. Someone got out of the back and jogged forward to the junction. Erik watched, and then he stopped breathing. The skin on his arms felt cold. He knew that guy! It was one of the Arabs from the hotel! He'd been in the car that Popovic got into. In fact, that was the guy who'd punched him in the face!

The Arab peered ahead and left. Erik's heart was hammering. He watched and thought back to that whole event. When the bodyguard told him Popovic was okay he'd put all of that out of his mind. Especially after he got his money. But really, something was very wrong. All a misunderstanding? How could that be? She was pushed into the car. He'd seen it. He'd tried to help and got a bloody nose for it. Just going to see someone? No. It was another thing, another part of the pretence that was Capri and that silly fancy hotel. Here in the glare and blare of the city, seeing the man again made it seem ridiculous. Erik hadn't set eyes on Popovic since that night. Someone had left money for him, but was it her? Was she back at the hotel, in her room like the woman said? Was everything okay now? Maybe not.

The Arab returned to the car and the traffic started crawling, then flowing. Erik got up and set off on a steady run, easily keeping the car in sight as it turned off and took a side road that led into the docks.

Chapter 60

The figure standing at the doorway was Sarah. Raffa frowned. He was going to say something but checked himself. She hovered at the threshold.

"What are you doing here?" said Fairchild.

"You need to leave. They're onto you." She was talking to Raffa, not him. Raffa's face showed nothing. Her eyes moved to Fairchild, down to the laptop, then back to Raffa.

"How did you find us here?" said Fairchild.

Her chin jutted out. "I followed you."

"No. Nobody followed me. You knew this was the meet point already. You've just incriminated yourself."

"Get out," said Sarah, looking straight at Raffa. But he was looking down at the floor.

"You heard her, Raffa." Fairchild spoke softly. "She's talking to you. I believe she's trying to give you some advice. She's sacrificed a lot to do so. Maybe you should listen."

"I said they're onto you." Sarah's voice trembled. "They're looking for the FBI guy. William Holmes. They'll figure it all out. You can get away clean if you go now."

Raffa slowly looked up at her. His face was different — harder, pinched. "You just told him everything."

Sarah was quick. Fairchild hardly saw her move before her gun was pointed at his face. She was breathing heavily. "I do this, we can both get away."

"Not without the money." Raffa spoke low and sure.

"You just click. We can shoot him and then do it!"

"No." Fairchild spoke up. "I don't make the transfer from here. My accountant is standing by to do that. She's in Geneva. She'll only do it when I call and tell her to. We've known each other more than twenty years. She'll know if it's me or not. You kill me, you get nothing."

"Fine," said Sarah. She didn't take her eyes off Fairchild.

"Don't do it!" said Raffa.

"It's the only way we can get out of this! So what if we don't get the money? I never cared about that anyway."

"Don't shoot him!" Raffa was hissing at her. "We can still do this."

"How, Raffa?" said Fairchild. "By giving me a deadline? Time's up, by the way. It's three minutes after ten. She's dead already, if you're to be believed. So why should I pay it now?"

"If he's not paying I may as well shoot him." Sarah spoke smoothly now.

"No!" It was almost a bark. "We can still – put the gun away. Listen to me." Raffa kept his eyes on Sarah and the gun but spoke to Fairchild. "They've still got her, Fairchild. They won't return her without the money."

"I don't think so."

This was a new voice, coming from the doorway, a voice Fairchild had been thinking about for days, was hoping to hear since he'd seen the shadow of a car outside. The owner of the voice stepped through the door. Fairchild stood. His chair fell backwards, unnoticed.

In track suit bottoms and a man's t-shirt, hands tied behind her back, a huge swollen eye and scratches all over her face, was Rose Clarke. By her side, gun in hand, was Kamal.

Rose was looking at Raffa. "Hello, William. I was wondering where you'd got to."

Chapter 61

The configuration of people in the room was not what Rose was expecting. Sarah, Fairchild and Raphael, known to her as William Holmes, were positioned in a triangle. Sarah was pointing a gun at Fairchild's head. By Rose's side, Kamal was ready. As they stepped in he raised his gun and aimed at Sarah. Sarah's face registered confusion, desperation. She glanced at Rose and Kamal and turned back to Fairchild again.

"Lower the gun." Kamal spoke with a deep growl. Sarah was breathing rapidly but she didn't reply.

"I think," said Rose, "you're pointing the gun at the wrong person."

Kamal registered this and slowly turned his arm to aim at Raphael. A few seconds, and Sarah lowered her gun. Fairchild stepped forward and took the weapon off her. Kamal didn't move. Sarah and Raphael looked at each other. What that look communicated was anyone's guess.

"Aren't you pleased to see me back?" Rose said. "I made it! With the police after me and everything."

"Of course," said Raffa. With an English accent now, but it was the same voice. He glanced at Fairchild who'd picked up his chair and was seated, arms folded. Sarah said nothing. She knew the game was up. How long had she known? Raffa was the one who was lost.

Fairchild was leaving it to Rose to enlighten them. So she did. "You see, it was never about Al-Hashemi. He was already compromised. With the help of our informant Kamal here and the support of the Tunisian government, Al-Hashemi is already under armed guard back home and will shortly be extradited to face charges. That's not common knowledge, though. So we thought we'd make use of it."

Raffa's face had flushed. "Then what was this all about?"

"You, Raphael. You were our target. Along with Sarah here." Sarah looked as though she was going to be sick. "You got yourself into some hot water over in the States. Played an elaborate con on the wrong person. Someone with the resources to get their own back, and who wasn't just going to let it slide."

"Me?" He looked utterly perplexed. Kamal smirked. Raffa turned to Fairchild.

"It's true," Fairchild said. "You were the target for this whole operation. You did exactly what we thought you'd do. Kamal here can vouch for that. It was him that you approached with the offer."

Raffa looked directly at the Tunisian for the first time. It was not a friendly look. "It was a trap? All of it?"

"Not a trap," said Rose. "We presented you with an opportunity and you took it. We knew Al-Hashemi was your cocaine supplier, so you knew the Tunisians already. We let it be believed that Al-Hashemi was looking to get back the two million dollars he lost on New World Coin. You got wise to the whole deception," Rose glanced at Sarah who was looking at the floor, "and approached Kamal with an offer to work together to increase their take by holding me for ransom. I think you suggested that with your help and information they could double their money? Is that right, Kamal?"

"Something like that." Now it was Kamal giving Raffa an unfriendly look.

"The Tunisians were expecting you to come forward and broker the deal," said Rose, "but then something unexpected happened. I was rescued. By some lone FBI agent. And I ended up in Sicily."

Fairchild stepped in. "And then you showed up to broker a deal anyway. But you were representing yourself by this time. Making out the Tunisians were behind it, but you'd cut them out of the loop. This bank account was yours only, wasn't it? You'd have kept the whole fifty million."

"Fifty?" Kamal's question exploded in the room like a gunshot. "Fifty? You greedy bastard! I should shoot you now!" His finger tightened on the trigger.

"But you won't, Kamal," said Rose. She kept her voice calm though she was as shocked as he was. "If you shoot him, the deal is off. The Americans want him alive."

His finger relaxed, though his face remained as thunderous. Raphael had reverted to an expression of cautious interest, as though he were merely observing.

Rose looked at Fairchild. "That's quite a sum. Could you even have paid that much?"

"Just about. It was well judged. Manageable, but it would have left me practically destitute. He did his research. He also gave me some pretty strong reasons to pay it."

"Apart from saving my life, you mean?"

"He wanted me to pay it before you even showed up. Presumably because he had no idea where you were and didn't much care as long as he could get away. The ultimate romantic gesture, he was suggesting."

"How sweet."

"Unfortunately for him, we knew where you were all the time. More or less."

Sarah's eyes grew wide at this. It was starting to sink in, then, how deep the deception had gone.

"That's why they wanted you, Raffa," said Fairchild. "You're good. And you got bored of scamming hotels. You were moving on to other things. That made you dangerous."

Raffa didn't look at him. And Sarah didn't look at Rose, either, though she knew now it was all as much for her as it was for him.

"The backup's in place?" Rose asked Fairchild.

"The area will be surrounded by now. Kamal's men have been taken away already. It's over, Raffa." Fairchild looked almost regretful.

Rose turned to Kamal. "In that case, any chance I could get out of these cuffs?"

Kamal looked down, putting his hand in his pocket. Only for a second – but that was all it took.

The door flew open and a tall gangly figure launched itself at him from behind. Kamal staggered and fell to his knees.

"Run! Run!" the assailant was shouting. He threw himself down onto Kamal. They twisted and struggled on the floor.

Rose could hardly believe who it was. "Erik?"

"Run, Ulia!" Erik was gamely holding on but Kamal already had the upper hand. "Go! I free you! Run, now!"

Kamal shoved him onto his back. He grabbed the skinny guy and pushed him down again, winding him. He stood and kicked him in the side. Somehow he still had the gun in his hand. He aimed.

"No!" shouted Rose. "Don't shoot him! He's fine. He's fine, Kamal."

Kamal lowered the gun. "Who is this man?"

"He doesn't mean any harm. He's just…"

Erik was lying on the floor staring up at her, this new version of Popovic. "Ulia? Is that you?"

A door banged. The three of them were alone in the room. Raffa, Sarah and Fairchild were all gone.

The Show

Chapter 62

They only needed a second. Raffa and Sarah moved exactly in tandem towards the door, on the same wavelength. But as soon as Erik erupted into the room, Fairchild's eyes were on the two of them. He was out of the door straight after them.

The street outside was empty – law enforcement was under orders to hang back, and the Kamal vehicle had been dealt with already, along with its occupants. Raffa and Sarah were sprinting side by side, west towards the ferry port. Fairchild kept them in sight and called Zack. "Our friends are trying to do a runner."

"What the hell? What's going on down there?"

"A surprise visitor distracted us. They're heading back to the terminus. You've got the place surrounded, right?"

"Sure, but no one was expecting a chase. This part was meant to be easy. Did you get what we need?"

"Not sure it's enough."

"Then get after them!"

"What do you think I'm doing? You're still tracking Sarah's phone, aren't you? They're together."

"They might split up. She could wise up and drop her phone. He could still get away. You know what he's like."

"I certainly do."

"Are you armed?"

"No." Fairchild hadn't picked the gun up off the table. "Neither's he."

"How do you know?"

"If he'd had a gun he'd have used it earlier."

Fairchild hung up and accelerated. They were still in sight but had gained some distance on the long straight street in front of him. He could out-think Raffa but wasn't sure he could outrun him. Distant sirens wailed, then cut out: the Italian police were moving in, following Sarah's position. Like Zack said, getting them should be easy but Raphael had talked himself out of worse before.

Up ahead, the street ended. The two fugitives stopped, faced with a choice of left or right. Raffa glanced back at Fairchild. Left would take them into commercial docks and nothing beyond that except the sea. Right led them into the city, and the ring of waiting law enforcement, but with more options, more places to hide or double-back. They went right. Fairchild got to the intersection ten seconds after they did. The cross streets were short, and they were all empty. He could hear nothing, see no sign.

He went right, planning to take the most obvious route. But something made him pull up. A flash of light, a reflection? There'd been movement behind him somewhere. He went with his gut and did an about-turn. He zig-zagged towards the sea and the ferry terminus, scanning that bit of his subconscious that had pointed him this way. He was also thinking about what he would do in this situation. There were ways of getting out by sea. They involved planning ahead, though. It was Raffa who'd named the location. Would he have entertained the prospect of failure and lined up an exit? Even getting away was failure if there was a chase: a good con ended with everyone walking away oblivious. Raffa wanted to remain the happy-go-lucky small-time blagger thrown in over his head, while the Tunisians got the blame.

Fairchild was running out of land. He slowed to a walk, every sense primed. A faint noise reached him, a metallic rattle. He sped up towards it and turned a corner. A rusty gate to a quay was closed and locked. The disused quay beyond stretched out into the harbour, one side lined with loading bays, warehouses and trucks, the other with just a few containers stacked apparently randomly. He put his hand on the gate. It shifted and he heard that sound again, that rattle. He climbed over and dropped down the other side.

What would he do if it were him? Trying to hide and sit it out was risky – they'd come here eventually. Best to try and get clear by whatever means. The trucks looked well secured. Fairchild carried on, right down to the bottom of the quay, the spur that stuck out into the channel. Opposite, over the water, was a concrete wall, one long arm of the harbour, beyond which was the open sea, the Mediterranean. There were no more buildings down here. A solitary stack of three containers was placed at the end, as if abandoned. Fairchild slowed and walked to the water's edge. Between the stack and the water, shadowed by the metal above him, crouched Raffa.

The man looked up as Fairchild's shadow appeared on the ground next to him. He didn't try and run. There was nowhere else to run. Fairchild folded his arms and looked down at him.

"You're not thinking of swimming it? That's a busy harbour. You'll end up feeding some huge propellor."

But that was Raffa's plan: he'd already ditched his shoes. He was hesitating, though, looking a little pale.

"What will you do when you get to the other side?" continued Fairchild. "It's only a harbour wall. You'll be visible a mile off. Nowhere to hide, nowhere to go."

Raffa's expression was closed, bleak. Maybe he'd never faced failure before. Maybe he didn't care if he survived the attempt, as long as he got away.

Fairchild squatted next to him. "They'll take your youth into account. And your talents. I shouldn't say this, but they're not stupid. You show willing, you cooperate, you tell everyone what they want to hear, it won't be so bad."

Raffa looked across at him, incredulous. Fair enough. Fairchild backed up a little.

"Okay, that was an exaggeration. You embarrassed someone. You'll have to pay for that. They'll lock you up. But they won't throw away the key. Not if you play it right. That's got to be better than fish food. I was impressed and they were too. You know how to slip from one world to another, fit in, play a role wherever you go, and make sure it's the right one. Secret intelligence services invest millions training people how to do that. To you it comes naturally. You think no one's going to see the value in that?"

Raffa looked almost amused. "They're going to recruit me? After what I've done?"

"I've heard stranger things. Believe me."

Raffa stared at him then turned an empty gaze to the water.

"Besides," said Fairchild, "governments aren't the only option. There are private operators. Could be some opportunities there, if you impress." Raffa looked curious now. "And, like I said, you have."

That got him interested. "You're offering me a job?" He searched Fairchild's face to see if it was a joke.

"Are you in the market for one?"

Raffa looked thoughtful, and, gratifyingly, quite pleased. The faint sound of a power boat reached them from inshore. Raffa looked for a clue in Fairchild's face.

"Always have a back-up plan," said Fairchild. "In case an early exit is needed."

"You're serious about this? You'd let me get away?"

"Well, you'd owe me your freedom. I reckon I could get some value out of that. I run a business, after all, despite your efforts to part me from it. I've never been too hung up on rights and wrongs. And I know the real thing when I see it. I know what it's worth."

A slow smile spread across Raffa's face. "Wow. So you double-crossed me, and now you're double-crossing them! But Rose won't be pleased."

"Why would she know? Why would any of them know? I could say that you'd already gone by the time I got here. You'll need a new identity, start again somewhere you haven't worked already. South America, maybe?"

Raffa was thinking about it. The speedboat got louder. "Out of interest," said Fairchild, "why Sicily?"

Raffa grinned, hugely proud of himself like a child who'd just won a race. "I thought of it on the fly. I knew I couldn't take an MI6 officer prisoner, not on my own. I had to persuade her to come with me then leave her stranded somewhere. I thought it would be inland, but then we ended up in a train station and it seemed perfect."

"You got there by train?"

"You didn't know?"

"We had no idea where you'd gone until Kamal's people picked up that the Sicilian police were combing the island for some fraudster. Al-Hashemi has law enforcement personnel on his payroll to facilitate his smuggling operation. But how did you keep her on the train for that whole journey? It must have been hours."

"Don't be envious, Fairchild. I had a little help from a pill." The expression on his face was almost lewd. Fairchild felt an urge to thump him. It must have shown. "Of the sleeping variety."

"You drugged her? Seriously? Oh, she won't like that. Not at all."

"She seemed happy enough to me. Slept like a baby."

"I know these things, Raffa. Actually, I did it to her myself once."

His eyes widened. "Really? Wow. I think she enjoyed the whole thing, actually. She likes an adventure. Give people what they want, that's right, isn't it? You know that."

He wanted more of this chancer's version of locker-room banter. But that was the idea. The speedboat was approaching fast. Raffa stared at it and his brow puckered. "Fairchild, that's—"

"A police boat."

His icy tone wasn't lost on the boy. Raffa scrambled to his feet. "But how did they find us?"

"They're tracking my phone."

Raffa wasn't getting it. And Fairchild wasn't finished, not by a long chalk.

"Did you really think, after you abducted my girlfriend so that you could bankrupt me, after you sold state secrets to an extremist group in order to extort money, you think after that I'd want you working for me?"

Raffa stared. It still wasn't getting through.

"You're good, Raffa. But you're nasty. You poison people's humanity and use it against them. When they do tests on you they'll probably decide that you're sociopathic."

The boy's face hardened. "I wasn't helping extremists. They'd have got nothing from it. I used them!"

"Don't hold out for a medal."

Car engines, doors slamming, footsteps running: Fairchild knew without looking round that the quay was a mass of police and FBI. Raffa took it all in, then turned, broken, to look out at the sea. There was no way out for him now. He'd really believed Fairchild, really wanted what he was offering. Was it merely the prospect of a last-minute escape, or the idea of a future working with him? Either way, it didn't matter.

"I didn't kill anyone." His defiance was unconvincing.

"You didn't seem to care much if people lived or died. That's no better. Maybe even worse."

They were closing in. A uniform called out to him to put his hands on his head. He did. But he kept looking at Fairchild.

"What was this for, anyway? You were just playing with me? You like that, do you? You're no different." His eyes flashed.

"The lawyers."

"What lawyers?" They were patting him down now, but still he stared at Fairchild.

"They needed you on tape. To establish beyond any doubt that the double-cross was your idea. So you couldn't claim entrapment, or push it all onto the Tunisians. I'm wearing a wire, Raffa." He pulled the tiny recording device out of his pocket. "I've recorded everything you've said."

They were leading him away now, pushing him into the back of a car. He broke eye contact at last.

"They probably will throw away the key." Fairchild said that to the back of his head. But he heard. The door slammed. Raffa stared straight in front as the car drove off.

Chapter 63

Rose had to argue hard and fast to persuade them to hold off. But she'd earned the right. They knew exactly where Sarah was. She'd headed into a residential area between the port and the city, and had eventually come to a halt in the courtyard of an apartment building. The police were waiting by every exit, accompanied by the FBI. Sarah was important to them only in relation to Raphael's case: her actual fate was a matter for the British authorities.

A car rushed her there and she walked in alone. The police were quietly working their way around every flat telling residents to stay inside and keep away from the windows. They were armed, though Rose said repeatedly that Sarah wasn't. The tracker had her in a garden behind the main courtyard. Rose walked through and saw a patch of grass, palm trees, plastic chairs and a hammock. All empty.

"She's not here," she said in her radio mic.

A crackling sound. "She's on the move." The voice was Larry's: they were monitoring the tracker from their ops room at the Rosaria.

"Where? The building's surrounded."

"She's not going out. She's going up."

Rose looked up and counted four or five floors above her. It was the highest building in the area. "Shit. She's going for the roof." A sense of dread formed in the pit of her stomach. She forced herself to run up the stairs though her feet screamed at her. They'd take weeks to recover. Sarah, on the other hand, would never get out of this, and she knew it. That thought spurred her on.

On the top floor, an iron security gate hung open uselessly. Another flight and Rose emerged gasping for breath. Sarah stood, far enough back from the edge not to be visible, almost nonchalant, hands in pockets. She turned. She didn't seem surprised to see Rose.

"You knew all the time." It wasn't a question.

"That's why you were put on this detail in the first place. Our target was always Raffa, or whatever he likes to call himself. You were our way to get to him. That's all. They realised he was getting help from someone with special clearance."

She was still thinking it through. "It was all designed around the two of us? The whole thing?"

"The whole thing. Raphael's last victim, over in the US, turned out to be some government agency senior executive. As well as making the guy hopping mad, it also demonstrated how dangerous Raphael is. That's why the Americans were prepared to go to so much trouble."

"You knew he'd come here?"

"We hoped he would. Once he heard that it was Al-Hashemi's crew being targeted. We knew he had a connection there and might try and worm his way in. And he did. With your help."

Sarah tipped her head back and closed her eyes. "I never thought he'd do something like this. It started off with small things. A false ID, that kind of stuff. But then once I'd done that he could hold it over me, use it to get some more." She opened her eyes and looked at Rose. "It's no excuse, but he said he was in debt. Massively so. Just one more thing and he'd have enough to clear it, give the sharks what they wanted. That's what he kept saying. But the one more thing got bigger and bigger and seemed to involve him spending as much as he was making. I said all that, but he always had an answer."

"He must have had more than answers. I hope he was worth it."

Sarah stared. "You think he was my lover? That's what you think of me? Really?" Rose shrugged. Sarah looked horrified. "I'd never do all that for some stupid love affair. Jesus." She looked away.

"What is he, then?"

"He's family."

A pause. "I thought all your family—"

"My dad had secrets. It turned out. Shacked up with some American on the side. The American then had a baby when she got back home, who was adopted. Dad never told any of us. Maybe he was going to, but…"

This was complete news to Rose. "Raphael is your half-brother?"

Sarah was suddenly fierce. "He's the only brother I've got. The only family I've got."

"He came to you with all that after the accident, did he?" Rose tried to sound gentle but Sarah got her meaning.

"He had papers. All the proof."

"You checked it out?"

"I did."

"How?"

"I called his birth mother."

"Right." Again, Rose didn't have to spell it out. Raffa could have set that up pretty easily.

"He had DNA tests done. Him and my father."

"Did you get your own test done? Did you take DNA from him and compare it to yours?"

Sarah said nothing.

"Sarah, he's a conman. He tells people whatever they want to hear. Somehow he got wind of your job role, and

278

what happened to you. Put the two together and saw an opportunity."

She raised her chin. "No. I don't think so. I know he's a liability, I know all that, but I can see myself in him. We're from the same blood. You have to help family. Don't you?" She looked directly at Rose, but it wasn't a real question.

"And William Holmes?"

"He's used the name before. That persona. When Zack said it I knew you'd connect things up faster than he was expecting." She frowned. "But that phone call. You must have known already. Both of you."

"All part of the show. It was all for you."

The penny was starting to drop. "Everything in that ops room, it was all for my benefit?"

"We needed you to be convinced, so that you'd feed all the details back to Raphael."

She blinked and looked away. Another question was forming. "Did the techies know?"

"Larry did. The others didn't."

"Linda?"

"No. She may have suspected something."

"They'll be pretty cheesed off they were out of the loop."

"It's standard in our industry. We're all about secrets. They know that."

"They do as they're told?"

"That's right."

She sighed and crossed her arms round herself as if she were cold, though the sun was high and hot, glaring off the roof.

"It took me a while to cotton on," said Rose. "He staged a dramatic rescue. He can be a very convincing FBI agent."

"He grew up in the States. He can be American as easily as he's British."

"He had me for a while. But I'd studied his file. I recognised him as soon as I got a good look at him. If it weren't for that…"

It could have been pride Rose saw on Sarah's face, but it leaked away. "I could see it all coming, them taking you like that. I tried everything to persuade him there was another way. I said it was absolutely the last time I'd help him. But…"

"If all he wanted was to clear debts, there were plenty of other ways to do that. But with him it's the thrill of the chase, the game itself that he likes. He gets people eating out of his hand. Me, Fairchild. You as well."

"No. No." She so much wanted Raphael's story to be true. But she was looking now at the ledge, thinking about the drop on the other side. Rose didn't dare move.

"It shouldn't end today," she said. "Not here. Not like this."

"It's already ended." Her voice was thick.

"You've got friends."

"Like who?"

"Like me."

"I sold you down the river! I told him everything."

"You also saved my life."

"I pointed a gun at Fairchild's head."

"You wouldn't have pulled the trigger."

"I gave it all up, your name, your role. I told him who Fairchild was. I told him where you'd be. I took a promise to protect you and I did exactly the opposite. Look at you!"

Rose's hand went up to her eye. "It looks worse than it is. You didn't want to do any of that."

"But I did. I could have walked away, fessed up. I wish I'd— I wish I'd been in that car." She was looking over the edge again.

"I've done worse. Treated people worse. For reasons I thought were valid. That's all you were doing. Raffa won't be able to claim entrapment. But you could."

She didn't look round but Rose hoped she was listening. "They'll send me down."

"Not for ever. Despite everything, I enjoyed working with you. I'm sorry that things happened this way. I will speak up for you."

Finally, Rose stood aside and let them finish it. Uniforms, clustered behind her in the stairwell, swarmed past her. Sarah didn't move as they surrounded her. She wouldn't try anything now.

"There's nothing of him in you," Rose said.

Sarah didn't look round. They were patting her down, putting her in cuffs.

Rose walked away.

Chapter 64

Zack had migrated from a hotel bar in Capri to a hotel bar in central Naples. This was another of Fairchild's estate, but of a different type entirely, a standard business hotel like any other: clean, plain, respectable, rectangular. Zack was lounging on a padded brown chair drinking what looked like whiskey.

"Bit early, isn't it?" Fairchild sat. It was still mid afternoon.

"Not today."

Fairchild ordered the same. "Is this a new look, Zack? No shades, I mean?"

"Your young man's responsible for that. They got broken when I had to restrain him."

"You had to restrain Adel? Why?"

"Because he's far too clever for his own good. Wanted to come after you and save you."

"I told you he should have been in on it. He had Raphael pegged right from the start."

"You did. And you were right. He almost ruined the gig. Twice. Next time I'll listen."

"You think there'll be a next time? You think I'll do something like this again? Ever?"

"What, you didn't enjoy it?"

"I enjoyed punching you in the face. I didn't enjoy coming within a whisker of selling up my entire livelihood."

"We agreed you had to set it up like it was real."

"Or sitting about while my girlfriend goes AWOL pursued by a hit squad."

He was getting more used to that word. Zack let it pass. "Okay, fair enough. But it worked out, didn't it? Tell Adel I want to see him after."

"I will if he's still talking to me."

"I hear you. You're not the only one with a mutinous employee on their hands."

It took Fairchild a moment. "Zoe?"

"Zoe. Well, come on, then. Bring your drink. We'll need them."

Zoe was waiting in the meeting room. So, to Fairchild's relief, was Adel. Rose joined them, coming straight from a walk-in medical centre which followed directly from a video call with Walter. She looked no better, but brought two bottles of water in with her and sat languidly back on her chair. They exchanged a brief glance. Her exhaustion came off her in waves. His heart turned over. This was too painful.

Zack took charge, or at least he tried to. "So, some of you have requested an explanation. That's fine. I get that."

Zoe came in. "Yeah, I said that if you don't tell me what the hell is going on you can kiss goodbye to me ever working for you again. So spit it out. This all began with Al-Hashemi, right?"

"No. It began with Kamal." Rose's voice was low and quiet, but steady.

"Wrong," said Zack. "It began in Miami."

"What happened in Miami?" asked Zoe.

Zack answered. "Raphael, as he's sometimes known, pulled a stunt there. He was already known to the FBI as a small-time fraudster who scammed hotels and dealed a little recreational drugs, but turns out he does way more than that. His latest scam took one of the most senior operational heads for a ride. Embarrassed him enough to commit significant budget to going after the guy."

"Hence the unlimited resources available for this job," said Fairchild.

"So I did recognise him!" said Zoe. "He hangs around the top hotels. Has a line in cheque fraud. But I didn't know about the other stuff. Fairchild, you said he was British."

Fairchild came in. "He's both. He operates on both sides of the pond. His public-school English routine was probably designed for me. I was his mark before any of us even got here."

Zoe was frowning at him. "Those photos on the boat. You didn't want me to ID him."

"The FBI field agents didn't know he was the target. They photographed him along with all the others. The need-to-know ruling came from Zack."

"Okay, okay, blame me." At least Zack was back in the conversation. "So, Miami. And a pan-Atlantic team was formed, and they gave us a blank cheque. We needed a tempting setup for this guy – fancy hotel, a load of money swimming around. We knew Al-Hashemi's lot were supplying him with cocaine. Then there was Kamal."

Rose sat up, the story giving her energy. "Kamal had secrets. The kind of secrets Islamic fundamentalists would have had a problem with. In exchange for evidence to convict Al-Hashemi, we offered him a new life in the west where he could live as he pleased."

"He's gay?" said Zoe.

Rose smiled. That was the Zoe from before, the one who didn't hold back. "Something like that. But we struck a hard bargain. To get immunity he had to take part in our scam, pretend to be going after Popovic on behalf of Al-Hashemi. He agreed, but only if Al-Hashemi and his men never found out that it was him who had turned them in. That made things a lot more difficult."

"So Al-Hashemi himself knows nothing about this?"

"Nothing at all," said Zack. "On account of he was already under house arrest in Tunisia. Raffa got to hear about our plan to tempt Al-Hashemi to Italy through his insider in Special Forces. That's because we made sure this insider was part of the team. So Raffa knew that Popovic was an MI6 decoy. He went straight to his Tunisian contacts and we set him up with Kamal. He offered Kamal the opportunity to double their money by taking Rose hostage and demanding a ransom. Kamal acted keen and shared all the information with Raffa. How they were planning to take her, the location of the villa, the timing. On his side, Raffa fed them back everything that we were feeding to him via Sarah."

"Sarah? That bodyguard? She was in on it?" Zoe looked to Rose for confirmation. Rose nodded, suddenly abject. Fairchild had watched this happen, a friendship forming that was destined to be crushed. Another piece of damage this op had caused.

"The guy even took it upon himself to give the Tunisians advice about the security arrangements at the villa," said Zack. "Of course that was to make sure he knew about it all himself. He knew they'd grab Rose after she made her speech. As soon as that was over he left the party himself and got over to the villa. Probably by boat."

"He claimed to have friends with a speedboat," said Fairchild. "He could have borrowed it on a pretext. On the mainland he must have had a car waiting. He drove straight up there and would have arrived at about the same time as Rose. Then he waited for an opportune time to jump in and stage a rescue, or so it would seem."

"It was very good," said Rose. "Kamal was doing a pretty thorough job of persuading his colleagues that it was a genuine interrogation."

"You mean he roughed you up?" Zoe, again.

"A little." Rose was talking it down, Fairchild knew that. "Then in the middle of it all, some FBI agent hurled himself through a window and got me out of there. I didn't know what to make of it and neither did Kamal. But I played along, so he did as well. His men thought it was all real, of course. Raffa got us into the car and we made off. I guess it was the same car he'd just used to get there."

"Out of interest," said Zack, "how did he explain himself?"

"He said he'd been in one of the FBI cars trying to find the villa and it had gone off the road. He was the only survivor. That also explained why he had no wallet or ID."

"Was he armed."

"Yep."

"Where'd he get the gun from?" asked Zoe.

"The Tunisians, maybe?" said Rose. "Anyway, we were well on the way down the coast road before I had it figured out. Unfortunately the Tunisians had removed all the tracers so no one would know where I was, but—"

"But you went along with him anyway." Fairchild couldn't stop himself.

Rose looked defensive. "Kamal's people were right behind us. There was every chance they'd see where we were heading. And he was on his own. I even persuaded him to leave his gun behind in Salerno. I thought I could handle him."

"But the next thing you know, you're in Sicily!" said Zack.

"He drugged her." Fairchild, again.

Rose looked at him sharply. "How did you know that?"

"Raffa told me. On the quay. He said the whole idea of getting on a train to Sicily was spur-of-the-moment. Before that he'd been planning to get you somewhere inland."

286

Rose thought it through. "That makes sense. He couldn't have planned the timing of it. He made out that Kamal's people were on the train."

"No," said Zack. "They lost you on the coast road. They were out of sight even before you got to Salerno."

"So you really had no idea where I was?"

"That's right," said Fairchild, a little grimly.

"Why did Kamal's people remove all the tracers?" said Adel.

"We were hoping they wouldn't," said Zack. "But Sarah knew Rose would be wearing them. So she'd have told Raffa, who would have told Kamal. So he had to do something about it, to keep up the pretence. His men did a more thorough job than we'd have liked. But they weren't in on it, remember. Only Kamal knew the whole picture."

"But what was the plan?" asked Zoe. "Why did Raphael do all that?"

"Greed," said Zack. "He thought of a way of double-crossing the Tunisians and keeping all the money himself. Not only that, but massively increasing the take. He must have known that the FBI wouldn't pay a ransom."

"But I would." Fairchild was looking at Rose. "Like I said, I was his mark all along. All he needed was enough time to approach me and make off with all the money. He just wanted you out of the way for long enough."

Rose replied. "So he left me cowering in a hut somewhere in rural Sicily and went off, supposedly to call in and get help. He never came back. He must have just waltzed down the road and found someone with a phone he could borrow."

"Spot on," said Zack. "And the first call he made was to tip off the Sicilian police. He told them that Ulia Popovic, the famous fraudster, was hiding out on Sicily, and that she was armed and dangerous. He figured it would put you in enough of a mess that he'd have disappeared by the time it was sorted out."

"How did Raffa get back to Capri so fast?" That was Adel.

"Copter." Zack answered promptly. "We've already checked that out. He got himself to Palermo then chartered a flight straight back to Ana Capri. He was back at the Rosaria by late afternoon."

Adel's eyes narrowed. "So, when Raffa appeared in the lobby that time…"

"You thought I wasn't interested? That was part of the show. We wanted him to think that Fairchild and I weren't getting along."

Adel thought, then nodded. He was making sense of it all.

Zoe was turning to Rose, frowning. "Couldn't you just have waited it out somewhere on Sicily? You look like you've been in a bear fight."

"You don't know the half of it. But I couldn't stay put. For one thing, Raffa left me in some barn with no food or water."

"What?" Fairchild suddenly wished he'd pushed the kid off the end of the quay.

Rose put on her Michalaedes voice. "And no shoes, darling! So it was painful. But I had to assume people might be after me, even if Al-Hashemi wasn't."

"You were right," said Fairchild. "Chu must have heard about the Popovic sighting on Sicily. They must have been listening in somehow. Or they had contacts."

"Ah." That was Rose, putting two and two together.

Fairchild didn't like the sound of it. "Meaning?"

She looked at him. "I was shot at. Not just by trigger-happy police getting over-excited. By someone who knew

288

what they were doing." It was exactly what he'd been afraid of.

"More than once?"

"No, only one time. On the first morning."

So his conversation with Chu had paid off.

Zoe was shaking her head over it all. "How did you manage to get back to the rendezvous point at the right time?" she asked Rose.

"Kamal found me. They'd picked up the Popovic-in-Sicily rumour through Al-Hashemi's network. When I finally managed to call in, they were already nearby. His people still thought I was Popovic, remember. That's why I showed up in handcuffs."

"They've all been rounded up now," said Zack. "They think Kamal has been taken in as well. Hopefully that story will stack up. He's in custody until we can spirit him away somewhere."

"And Raphael?" asked Adel.

"On the way to the US. They'll have fun with him," said Zack.

"And Sarah?" That was Zoe.

"Heading back to the UK," said Rose. That look was back again.

"So! A success all round!" said Zack. "Pretty good job, team!"

But Zoe wasn't finished. "One more question. What happened in Miami?"

Zack looked pained. "Really? You need to know that?"

"Everything, Zack."

Zack sighed. "Okay, but you didn't hear it from me. The guy is seriously embarrassed."

"Whatever. Just tell me!"

"One of the regional operational heads has a keen interest in the horses. He even owns a racehorse. Very proud of it. Had some success with it. Somehow Raffa came into his life and managed to persuade him late one evening that his horse had been stolen. Lifted out of the paddock and spirited away. A ransom was involved."

"Did he pay it?" asked Zoe.

"He's not saying. And he's not saying how much."

"So he did pay it!"

"Maybe. Anyway, he discovered shortly afterwards that the horse had been dumped in a field no more than twenty miles away. Completely unharmed. Sound familiar?"

Zoe grinned. "So he did to Rose exactly what he'd done to a horse!"

"It's a pretty valuable horse," said Zack.

"Your point being...?" said Rose.

Fairchild felt the need to come to Zack's rescue. He turned to Adel. "What about our Kenyan friend?"

"Erik's fine," said Adel with a touch of embarrassment. "His ferry is leaving tonight. He'll just hang around the port until then."

Zack stepped in. "Good to know, but what does our persistent friend make of it all? That's the key thing."

Adel frowned at Zack's tone. "He didn't mention Raphael or Sarah and he doesn't know Fairchild. I think he only saw Rose and Kamal in that room. He thinks Rose really is Popovic. And that he saved her from the kidnappers. And she intervened to save his life."

"Damn right I did," said Rose. "Kamal was about to shoot the poor guy."

"He doesn't think it strange that Popovic sounded completely different?" asked Fairchild.

"She'd been taken prisoner. Stress, fatigue, it does that to someone. No, he's persuaded. That's what he was told and that's what he wants to believe. In fact, he was thinking about reinvesting the cash you gave him in New World Coin."

"No!" Rose was horrified. "That money's for his mother! His village!"

"Well, New World is still online, isn't it? He was saying it would be a gesture of support. And now you're back it will all happen, the launch and so on."

"I hope you did your best to dissuade him."

"What could I say? I was told to make sure he really thought it was Popovic. I couldn't tell him the truth."

"So, hey!" Zack was trying again to wrap things up. "I think we deserve a night on the town! What do you say, dinner and drinks? Or drinks, dinner and drinks? My treat."

Fairchild didn't miss Rose's glance towards him. "Sorry, Zack. Tomorrow, maybe?"

Rose was also looking regretful. "It's a nice idea, but…"

"Oh, you two! All right, it'll just be us youngsters."

Adel pursed his lips. "It's not really my scene."

"Okay, fair enough. Zoe, it's you and me!"

"Sorry, Zack." Zoe stood. "There's something I need to do."

"Seriously? After I answer all your questions?"

"That was just to set things straight. You still owe me." And she was gone.

The others followed her lead and filed out, leaving Zack open-mouthed. "What's the world coming to? I can't even give drinks away!"

"Rain check, Zack," said Fairchild, who was last out. "I won't forget."

"You'd better not."

Zack would be fine. He'd gone out drinking alone in practically every city in the world. Fairchild hurried to catch up with Adel, who was already outside in the street. He called after him. "Running away already?"

Adel turned, his expression unreadable. "That's it, isn't it? It's all over."

"The show, you mean? Here in Italy? Or are you talking about you and me?"

He was silent.

"Look," said Fairchild. "First, Erik coming in at the rendezvous was a good thing in the end, because it gave me a chance to talk to Raphael on his own. He said some things that will make it a lot harder for him to wriggle out of the charges."

A slight nod of the head.

"Second, Zack has conceded that not letting you in on it was a mistake. You were observant enough to realise there was more to it right from the start."

"I tried to punch him."

"That won't put him off. He's still speaking to me."

Adel gave a small smile.

"And third…" Fairchild faltered. Adel could really leave. He'd miss the guy. And he'd spend a lot of time wondering what he'd done wrong himself. "Go if you like. Do what you think is best. But there's always a way back."

Adel nodded, keeping his thoughts to himself.

"And Zack wants to see you."

"Why?"

"He didn't say. But I think he might want to offer you a job."

Adel's eyes widened.

"You've got a great skill set. And your jihad experience makes you useful. I'd take it if I were you. But don't tell him I said so."

Chapter 65

They didn't go back to Capri. They left the Hotel Villa Bianca Rosaria in peace to lick her wounds and regain composure, return to her usual state of perfumed benevolence. It was as well to let the waters close over the numerous reports that Ulia Popovic might have materialised within her elegant walls, if only for a short time, though these rumours were not followed up by any noticeable investigation or, sadly, arrests. In short time they withered, following the same fate as the many other uncertain celebrity sightings for which Capri, particularly at night, was renowned.

Nico had finally been granted his wish and was preparing for his return to Rome. A triumphant and entirely satisfied Valentina was already back in Milan. They were still short of staff, and the front desk lacked that intelligent new arrival from the Philippines, who, it appeared, had moved on to other things. The owner likewise; the Blue Room sat empty and spotless, awaiting whoever might next have the means to be its next guest. John Fairchild had been persuaded that a boxy business hotel in central Naples was perfectly adequate for the evening. No perfume or lemon-scented towels here, but the sea view was just as blue, the espresso just as strong and smooth, and the tiny pastries they brought up with room service every bit as light and moist and sticky as one would expect in the best of places.

Fairchild's duties that evening consisted of little more than running a hot bath, receiving an abundance of room service, and the administration of eye drops. He didn't seem to mind. Julia Michalaedes lived on only in some bedraggled hair extensions, a little extra around the waist, and the best all-over tan Rose was ever likely to achieve. Wrapped in bathrobes they sat side by side looking out over the city lights while the Naples traffic grumbled below them. The island of Capri glowed far off, lopsided in the water like a discarded tiara. As ever, it took them some time to get used to each other's company again. Fairchild touched the back of her hand where it rested on the arm of the chair.

"You liked her, didn't you?"

Rose felt the same pang she'd had all day at the thought of it. "Sarah? They should have looked after her. They knew her background, what happened to her family. They should have removed her from the situation as soon as they found out about the connection with Raffa. Instead they sat back and watched as she dug herself in deeper and deeper. They used her to get to him."

"We all did. That's the kind of thing you do, isn't it?"

She gave him a sideways look. "But it sucks sometimes."

"Did you submit the DNA samples?"

"Yes. Results in a week or two."

"That might change her mind. If they show no relationship."

"Of course they'll show no relationship. He's not her brother, Fairchild. I think she knows that really. What about Adel? Are you and he all right?"

"I think so. He needs a bigger role. Something that will stretch him. Zack will think of something."

"Was he jealous of you and Raffa?"

Fairchild smiled. "Maybe. He thought I saw something of myself in him."

"And did you?"

"Not in a good way. I may have behaved no better at times, but at least I had a purpose. Raffa manipulated people just for kicks."

"What about you and Zack?"

"Oh, he enjoyed it. I think he wants to do it again."

"Seriously? Well, I suppose it's all right for you lot, swanning around the hotel the whole time. I'm the one who suffered."

His expression melted something inside her. "I'm not so sure."

She placed her hand on his. His thumb traced a scratch line on the back of it. "What about you and me?" she asked. "Do you mind that I carried on with it, even though I was completely incommunicado?"

"That's like asking if I mind that you agreed to do it in the first place."

"Well?"

"I'd prefer it if you hadn't. But I knew you would. You are who you are. We'd never have met otherwise."

"And Zoe?" She had to ask.

A miniscule hesitation. "She seems to have disappeared somewhere."

"That's not what I meant."

He sighed. "It was good to see her again. That all feels like a long time ago now. Don't you think?" He rested his chin on her arm and looked up at her.

"I suppose so." He was right: it was ancient history.

"What about you and Walter? He must be pleased." He couldn't strip the disapproval from his voice. But he'd managed to change the subject.

"Don't blame Walter, Fairchild. It was my decision to do this. But he's pleased. I asked him for a favour."

Fairchild raised his brows.

"You'll see. You spoke to Chu, didn't you?"

"I did," he admitted.

"She tried to have you killed."

"That was years ago."

"What did you tell her?"

"That she was barking up the wrong tree."

Rose sat up. "You told her I wasn't Popovic? You weren't going to do that. You said you didn't want your network to know it was all a grand deception."

"I didn't."

"Well, that was quite a risk."

"I suppose it was." His thumb was exploring her wrist now, working its way up her arm. That distance was slipping away.

"Would you really have given away fifty million dollars for me?"

He looked up again, eyes simple pools of grey. "Yes."

It was a good answer. "But I wouldn't have…"

She sensed an imbalance. There was no hesitation from him at all. Those things that were important to her, would she sacrifice them? But it was hard to focus on that and follow the track of his caress. His lips touched the pale inside skin of her elbow.

"It doesn't matter," he said. "I've got what I want."

And pretty soon, making sure they both got what they wanted became all that mattered.

Chapter 66

It had been a strange day. Earlier, Erik's head had been full of questions. Why was everyone just standing around in that room? Why didn't Popovic run when he gave her the chance? What happened to the men in the car? And why after that little scuffle, when he got up and half the people had gone, had the Arab undone the cuffs from Popovic's wrists? She'd thanked Erik nicely and all, and some folk had offered him a lift back to the centre, but they'd been very insistent that he went with them, and then they never really went away. Erik wandered about restlessly but wherever he went, that car was still there in the distance, those people still watching. It was all very weird, and he had a creeping feeling that everyone was laughing at him, that they were being kind, in the same way that you're kind to a child. He didn't understand this place. He'd be glad to get on that ferry and go home.

But then Adel showed up! Erik spotted him about to walk past and gave him a shout. It was so good to see a friendly face! He had a day off, Adel said, and had come to Naples on the ferry. How about lunch? he said, and offered to pay. They went to an all-you-can-eat buffet. And it really was all you could eat, though the staff started to watch Erik after he'd loaded his plate a few times.

Erik asked Adel about Professor Popovic. But he said he hadn't seen her since the big show. He thought she was in her room. He was surprised about what happened to Erik.

"She was all beaten up," said Erik. "Her eye, her face. But it was her. She sounded funny, but only to start with."

"And what did she say?"

"She said she'd had a bit of an adventure, but it was all okay now. She was pleased I was so concerned."

"That's good, isn't it?"

"It doesn't make any sense, my man. There's something funny going on that people aren't telling me."

Adel made a weird face and said he knew what that felt like. But then he said: "I guess she lives a complicated life. It's a big venture, this coin. Lots of people involved. Maybe sometimes it gets – well – complicated. But you tried to help her. You were there for her, and she thanked you, didn't she? What more can you do? At least you're out of it now. You can forget all about New World Coin and take your money back home."

His words had made Erik feel strangely empty. No more New World Coin? But Popovic was back now! Erik knew that – he'd seen her up close, twice. The value would go up, for sure. Like Dennis said, the launch will happen now, the exchange will open, and the coin will shoot up in value like they always said it would. Now is the worst time to take money out. Now is the time to put money in!

Adel hadn't been convinced by this argument. "She may have changed her mind about the launch. Maybe there'll be more delays."

"She didn't say that, my friend. She said wait for the launch to make the profits. And if there are more delays – hey, I can wait! After coming all this way and meeting her like this, it doesn't feel right to just take the money out and go back again. This is the future, Adel! I want to be part of it."

Well, his kind friend tried to argue but eventually had to go back to Capri. Erik still had hours before the ferry was due to leave. Tomorrow he'd take all this cash in his pocket and he'd invest it in the coin. The haters were wrong. The money was there. He'd got his back, hadn't he? You had to have faith. That's what Dennis would say. And Dennis was rich.

He walked around and around thinking about all this, and ended up back on the bench he'd sat on that morning. It was getting dark. He started thinking about rice balls. Lunch was a while back. Why not? It would be his last chance. He made his way over there, doing some criss-crossing down the side streets that he'd got to know now. His thoughts turned to his home village and what his mother and sister could buy with the fortune. He wished he could speak to them, but his phone didn't work here. He made a decision to go and see them before returning to Iten. It would be so good to bring them such great news!

He heard a noise right behind him, but before he could turn, his head exploded with pain. He stumbled and fell. Everything went dark.

Chapter 67

They told her the village was four hours from Nairobi. It wasn't. It was more like six when Zoe got to a place with no sign and a makeshift roadside shop and a cluster of huts built from wood and stone. She parked her rented four-by-four where goats nibbled at tufts of grass. The shop was a kiosk with an iron grille and a counter that some young men were sitting at. The official languages of Kenya were English and Swahili. English was in short supply here, as was Zoe's Swahili. But the name of the village got an emphatic "Yes! Yes!". Zoe also had Erik's family name. This provoked discussion and pointing, and one of the young men was despatched down the road. Zoe bought chilled fizzy orange in a glass bottle. They asked her for the bottle back when she'd drunk it. She got some stares. Nothing new there. Because she was black, people assumed she was Kenyan, and didn't know how to treat her when it became obvious she wasn't. She sat on the ground, the red earth, and listened to goats bleating and snatches of conversations. It was a strong, dry heat. Zoe basked: she'd always liked the sun.

The mutter of kiosk conversation became a buzz. She looked up. The guy was walking back next to a woman with braided hair who wore the loose-fitting brightly-coloured prints she'd seen everywhere. But this was not Erik's mother: she was far too young. She gave Zoe a brief smile. "You have news of my brother?"

"You're Erik's sister?"

"Yes. I am Esther." She kept her eyes down, but her English was good. "He is coming here?"

"Yes. In a few days, maybe."

"He is where now?"

"In hospital."

Her eyes widened.

"But he's okay. A small accident. He'll be fine." Zoe had gone to check on Erik's progress herself. It seemed the least she could do given that she'd put him there in the first place, having struck him on the back of the head in a dark Naples side street. She hadn't meant him any harm, at least nothing that would last.

"I'm Ariana," she said. "A friend. He asked me to come here to give you something. You and your mother." Zoe had lied to this woman four or five times already, and hadn't even got started yet. The woman looked suspicious. Fair enough.

The young men had clustered round them to watch and listen. "Can I speak to you and your mother?" asked Zoe. "Is that possible?" This was a conversation which didn't need an audience.

Esther shrugged. "It's far. Other side of village."

"That's okay." Zoe wasn't in the mood for more driving. "Let's walk."

They set off down a dusty red track. A couple of the guys started following but Esther spoke to them sharply and they dropped back.

"What's that?" Zoe pointed to a large stone building with small high windows.

"That? Ah....store. For – I don't know the name."

Wheat or grain, they eventually worked out. Esther had more to say as they walked. She pointed out the different crops: maize, cassava, potatoes. Sugar cane, banana and coconut trees, stalls and troughs for the cows.

"You have cows?" Zoe asked.

She looked sad. "Just one."

They walked past a sign. Through a gate, a corrugated metal shed sat at the end of a dirt drive.

"This is a school?" asked Zoe.

"Yes."

"What age children?"

"From five to maybe ten, eleven."

"Girls and boys?"

"Girls and boys, yes. You want to see?"

Zoe slowed. "Can we?"

Esther led her in. Through the windows Zoe could see heads lined up behind worn wooden benches. Suddenly, chairs were scraped back and they were swamped in a sea of red jumpers, wide smiles and curious outstretched hands. A teacher emerged, smiling. She and Esther exchanged words. Zoe peered into the classroom. Bare cracked walls, a blackboard, a handful of books. Into her head came the words from a speech: *We're the ones who've had a chance to shape our lives. For many across the world it's not like that. Purely because of where they were born...*

"Come," said Esther. The red jumpers receded like a retreating wave and flooded back into the classroom. They continued on their way.

Zoe found that she had many questions. Where did the water come from? How much of these crops were for the villagers and how much was surplus? When they had surplus, where did they sell it? How did they get to market? Was there a doctor in the village? A pharmacy? Electricity? The red-brown dust covered her shoes and ankles. Beyond the green of the crops rose steep, dark mountains, their tips frosted with mist.

The Erik family residence was a wooden house with an open porch, in the shade of which sat Erik's mother, introduced as Grace. Grace spoke no English and had very few teeth, though she smiled warmly. Esther said something to her and the smile faded a little. Grace pointed at an old plastic chair and they both waited as Zoe sat and began.

"Erik went to Italy. You know that?"

Esther's eye-roll suggested that she did.

"He went to talk to the head of New World Coin. Ulia Popovic. You know?"

Esther said something very brief to her mother. "Yes, we know." She sounded weary.

"Well, he met with her." Zoe saw cautious surprise in the young woman's face. "He explained the situation. And Ulia Popovic told him that it would be a long time before the big profits were coming." Esther's face fell again. "But she was impressed that Erik had come such a long way. So, she made some special arrangements to withdraw Erik's money from the scheme. And she refunded him the money. Erik was delayed coming home because of his – accident. So I'm bringing it to you."

Esther translated. Two suspicious faces. Again, she couldn't blame them. She pulled the envelope out of her bag. It was Erik's cash she'd taken from his pocket as he lay on the ground in the alley. After everything that had happened, the idea that the man would throw it all away again was more than she could bear. She'd exchanged it in Nairobi for Kenyan dollars. She'd got a lousy exchange rate and figured these people were probably due some interest as well, so she'd topped it up with her own money. Not very much – less than it cost to rent the four-by-four. She put it on the table in front of them.

"It's yours. Please."

Esther slowly picked it up and looked inside. A glance of disbelief with her mother. She pulled out the notes. A gasp of wonder. They muttered to each other as Esther quickly counted it and confirmed the amount with Grace. The old lady's expression was pure joy, though tears escaped her eyes as she clasped hands with her daughter.

Esther turned to Zoe. "We are very grateful. Thank you so much."

"It's only your own money back again."

Esther gave a short laugh. "Yes, but we think we never see it again. We think it's lost."

"You have plans for the money?"

"Plans? Yes! We will buy another cow." Esther checked this with Grace, who nodded. "And we will build a store building. Like the one you saw. So we can keep the surplus longer and sell it for a better price."

Grace was saying something.

"We would like you to stay for dinner," Esther said. "You came a long way. Please, stay to eat."

Zoe stayed, and ate ugali and stew, rice, beans, ground nuts and bananas, and drank fresh mango juice, watching a fiery red sun setting into the mountains. She heard more about their plans. If you had a little more money, she asked, what would you do with it? And as they told her, another village grew around them. This one would only exist if they had the means, if someone would only back them like they did the big farmers, the men. They didn't want charity. A loan would be fine. With a loan they could install more efficient irrigation. They could buy better seeds and get higher yields. They would make more money and could buy trucks to take their produce to market. They could bring back nurses and medicines when folk needed them. They could buy books for the school.

As darkness fell Zoe thought about her fortune, stolen from thieves, amassed in order to finance a lifestyle of luxury from others' misery, a fortune now in her hands, one that weighed heavily.

Zack kept messaging but she hadn't replied. *Where are you?* he was saying. *When are you coming back?*

I'm in Kenya, she texted eventually. *I think I might stay a while.*

Chapter 68

Rose told Walter it would take four months. It didn't. It was more like six before she even got to Istanbul. She had high hopes. After all, she'd already tried Stuttgart and Bangkok. Rumours, as they'd just proved, often turned out to have some truth in them.

She'd persuaded Walter it was worth the time, and did some juggling, back and forth to Budapest. It was hectic but if it came off the reward would be well worth the effort. Rarely would anyone feel as much at home in someone else's head.

Remembering Linda's words she started with the nail bars, the beauty salons, the tanning stations. She began at the top end – in the hotels – and worked her way down. Then, purely because it felt right, she did the same thing with the hammams. She got a bit of local help, when they could spare a pair of eyes. In due course she found herself in the outskirts, a long way in all senses from the cosmopolitan city centre.

The woman she was watching had no tattooed beefcake bodyguards: she went about alone. She made short journeys and hurried, meeting no one's eye. She was slim – slimmer than Rose these days. She dressed elegantly but not in black. Her hair was mid-length, brown, straight but glossy. She had pale brown eyes. On paper it couldn't be her. But she had a particular look, a way of holding herself. Her lips were different but her facial mannerisms – there was something there. Rose bided her time. Then, one day, she stepped up as the woman came out of the hammam.

"Good afternoon. It's nice to see you after such a long time. Don't be afraid."

It wasn't the words so much as the language that caused the woman to start: Rose was talking Serbian. Eyes wide, she glanced behind, all around, up to the rooflines. Rose switched to English.

"You've been running a long time, I can see. I'm not going to harm you. I only want to talk. There's nobody else here, only me. Let's walk."

Reluctantly she fell into step. They walked slowly, just two women in an ordinary suburban street, unnoticed by anyone.

"What do you call yourself these days?" asked Rose.

"If you're asking my name, it's Sophia."

"A nice name."

Sophia's eyes tracked the high windows, jumped from car to car as they passed.

"There's no one else here, Sophia. I've checked. I know how. I'm MI6, British. We're one of the few countries that isn't seeking to put you on trial. A lot of people are still looking for you. Dangerous people. Are you getting tired of hiding?"

She glanced across. She did look tired. Too tired, it seemed, to keep denying it all. Or else there was something about Rose she inherently trusted.

"You have no idea."

That voice! It thrilled Rose, so low and sonorous. Really, she'd got it spot-on. "Oh, I have some idea."

A hint of a frown. "That thing in Italy? I heard about that. It was my foundation, they said. Raising money for charity." *Cha*rity. Not *sha*rity.

"You don't go in for that?"

"I have no money."

It was Rose's turn to frown. "So where is it all?"

"They took it."

"Who?"

"Those who kept it all going, made it so big. The money went to them as soon as it came in. And when it became a flood, they just wanted more and more. It spread like a cancer, growing everywhere. I wanted to stop, but they would never agree. So I ran. I've been running ever since. I know they're after me."

"They're not the only ones, I'm afraid."

"You think I don't know? Everyone's after me! All the investors, they think I have it! No point trying to persuade them otherwise. I know why they're angry. It all exploded like a bomb, a great dirty bomb with a huge mushroom cloud, and all the dirt and dust gets everywhere and never stops falling. I wish I—"

She stopped herself.

"You wish you could escape?"

She shook her head. "I can't."

"You wish there were something you could do?"

"There isn't." It was in her voice how much she despised herself.

"You know who these people are? Where they are? How the whole thing worked?"

She sighed. "Yes, I know that."

"Then there is something you can do."

They looked at each other, two women who had both been Popovic, but were both now something else.

"Let's talk," said Rose.

The Clarke and Fairchild series

Thank you for reading *The Show*! If you want to stay in touch and hear about new releases in the series before anyone else, please join my mailing list. Members of the Clarke and Fairchild Readers' Club receive exclusive offers and updates. Claim a free copy of *Trade Winds*, a short story set in Manila which relates how John Fairchild met Adel, featured in *The Show*. It takes place before the series starts, and before Fairchild and Clarke meet. Another short story, *Crusaders*, is set in Croatia and features Rose Clarke's fall from grace from the British intelligence service. This prequel is also free to anyone joining the Reader Club! Visit www.tmparris.com to sign up.

Other books in the Clarke and Fairchild series are *Reborn* (Book 1, set in China, Tibet and Nepal), *Moscow Honey* (Book 2, set in Russia and Georgia), *The Colours* (Book 3, set in Monaco and the French Riviera), *The Secret Meaning of Blossom* (Book 4, set in Japan), and *Spies Without Borders*, (Book 5, set in Hungary). All are available on Amazon, and each book can be read as a stand-alone novel, though there is a back story that links the first five books in the series.

Reviews are very important to independent authors, and I'd really appreciate it if you could leave a review of this book on Amazon. It doesn't have to be very long – just a sentence or two would be fine – but if you could, it would provide valuable feedback to me to and to potential readers. So please, if you have a moment, do leave a brief – and of course honest – review.

Author Notes

Usually I do a lot of reading to research a Clarke and Fairchild book and find inspiration for the story, but this time my ideas came from other media. Key podcasts were the BBC's *The Missing Cryptoqueen* and *Fake Heiress*, and also the series *Sport's Strangest Crimes* dedicated to the kidnapping of the racehorse Shergar. The film *Catch Me If You Can* and the 1987 David Mamet film *House of Games* were also influential, as was the Michael Douglas film from 1997, *The Game*, and, of course, *The Sting*. *The Show* is intended as an amalgam of the most fascinating and glamorous elements of all of these stories or events, set in Italy's bewitching Amalfi coast which I visited in a very hot June of 2022. The Hotel Villa Bianca Rosaria is a fictional combination of a number of hotels and villas in the general area, and its imagined back office and staffing areas may owe something to the year and a half I was an employee of Hilton International, during which time I ate the worst food I have ever tasted in the staff canteen of the Gatwick Hilton.

Kenya is a country I have not visited. The source for Erik's home and background is in fact a book, *Running with the Kenyans*, by Adharanand Finn, a British journalist and runner who moved with his family to Kenya for six months to train in Iten with the fastest runners in the world. His descriptions of the place would make anyone want to go. This was supplemented by research into the country's rural economy and the role of microfinancing. I also conducted online research into many other areas, in particular crypto currencies and the notorious OneCoin scam. One of my biggest challenges was trying to invent the name of a crypto currency that didn't already exist. At the time of writing my first draft, there was no "New World Coin". If there is now, this is purely coincidental.

The Clarke and Fairchild world is very similar to our own, but with differences here and there at the author's discretion. It's generally set "a few years ago" and therefore the series so far has contained no mention of the COVID-19 pandemic. Maybe it never will: we'll see.

I'd like to thank Ryan O'Hara for the cover design which is probably my favourite so far, and also my team of beta readers and reviewers for their comments and support over the entire series. I really do appreciate it.

About the author

T.M. Parris is the fiction pen name of Tracey Hill. After graduating from Oxford with a history degree, Hill taught English as a foreign language, first in Budapest then in Tokyo. Her first career was in market research, during which she travelled extensively to numerous countries and had a longer stay in Hong Kong which involved visiting many of the surrounding countries. She has also taken sabbaticals for a long road trip in the USA and to travel by train from the UK through Russia and Mongolia to Beijing and around China to Tibet and Nepal.

More recently she has played a role in politics, serving as a city councillor in Brighton and Hove on the south coast of the UK. She currently lives in Belper, a lively market town near the Peak District National Park in the centre of England.

She started writing seriously in 2011. She published her first novel, *Reborn*, in 2020, the first in a series of international spy thrillers. Her first non fiction book, *We're Not All the Same*, was published in 2022. The common themes of her writing are people, place and politics, and her work explores how these elements interact.

Crime and action thrillers are her favourite book, film and TV choices. She occasionally plays the trumpet or the Irish flute. She enjoys walking, running, cycling and generally being outdoors in beautiful countryside, as well as cooking and baking and, of course, travelling.

Website: www.tmparris.com
Email: hello@tmparris.com
Facebook: @tmparrisauthor

Printed in Great Britain
by Amazon